I0685189

Iron Universe Series

Iron Heart

MC D'Alton and Melanie Page

Published by Vulpine Press in the United Kingdom in 2020

ISBN: 978-1-83919-303-3

Cover by Claire Wood

www.vulpine-press.com

To my collaborator, partner in crime, fellow writer and friend, Melanie Page. Without you this book would still be stuck inside my head! Not only did you take my thoughts—sculpted them, added to them, and moulded them into the awesomeness that is now *Iron Heart*—but you gave our characters, and our world of steampunk, life. I learn so much from collaborating with you and I cannot wait to do it all over again—domestics and all.

As always, to my men—love you.

MC D'Alton

To my amazing co-conspirator, MC D'Alton. You are the one with the all the crazy, zany ideas, and you are endlessly tolerant of my persistent, pernickety predilection for detail. It has been one wild ride, and more fun than I can say.

All the love in the world to my babies: Elijah, Hailey and Liana.

And to Craig. X

Melanie Page

Acknowledgements

We would like to thank our editor, Libby M Iriks, who liked what she saw, and Vulpine Press, who took a chance on us. You guys are awesome!

Chapter 1

Galena Tindale was about to make medical history. Not only would she be one of the first female students to graduate from Edinburgh Medical College, but she was minutes away from proving that Bachvarov, whose work on the human heart had languished for nearly fifty years, had been a genius.

She placed her black calfskin bag on the floor beside the podium and lifted out the thin glass slides, each six inches square with a narrow wooden border. She slid the first into the metal frame at the rear of the vitriscope, a device that would project the slide's image onto the white silk screen behind her. She placed the other slides in a small stack before checking the tiny lantern was connected to the main dynamo. The thrum of the machine reassured her—there would be no hiccups today.

Galena put her notes on the lectern, confident she wouldn't need them. This was her crowning achievement. She had been willing to do what none of the male students dared attempt, what most of her peers called blasphemous necromancy. Her work was going to save lives, she was sure.

Dean Hopwood had been cautious when she told him she

wanted to present her research. He had simply raised his ancient white brows before listening to her arguments with the utmost patience. Despite his obvious reticence, he had helped her acquire the parts her presentation would necessitate.

At last, she came to the focus of her demonstration. Carefully, she unclasped the locks on the smooth, cedar-lined box that had been brought up from the mortuary's ice room. The lid lifted easily, and she stared down in triumph.

Inside the crate, a human heart rested on a bed of ice chips.

It was different from the heart that, even now, beat like a bodhran behind her best black silk corset. Having worked with the utmost care, she had replaced the mitral valve of the human heart with one harvested from a pig. Then, in order to show her peers her achievement, she had employed a piece of the pericardium to provide a window on the future. She took a few moments to check the sutures; the tissue had held up well.

Beside the heart sat the machine she had made—a rhythm pump that kept the heart functioning. Though she had operated this machine a score of times, nerves caused her mouth to dry, and a whispered plea to Asclepius crossed her lips.

She attached the main conduit to the central steam room valve, letting the steam power the turbines in the core of the machine. Copper pipes fed in and out of the aorta and pulmonary vein, in and out of the valves of the machine that she had tentatively named a pulmonator. She also had with her a large glass jar of saline, dyed blue with a teaspoon of ink—it would stand in for blood.

To persuade the heart to beat again, Galena moved the tiny clamps, smaller than a fingernail, to the sinoatrial and atrioventricular nodes, located in the right atrium of the heart. These were the heart's own power source. She bent to tighten the flat copper rings holding the muscle in place around the pipes. The last coil went into the saline.

Her own heart in her mouth, she flicked the switch on the Leyden jar. The heart contracted, then wobbled like jelly breaking free of its mould. Quickly, she adjusted the dial to regulate the power and gave a relieved sigh. The heart beat steadily, as though a brain commanded it to pump once more.

She watched the rhythmic swish of the liquid through the valves with pride as her audience trickled into the auditorium. Most ignored her presence, though one or two glowered at her.

Only one hurried down the aisle.

'Don't be nervous, Galena! You will be wonderful.'

Of the other six female students in Galena's class, Olive had always been her greatest ally.

'I'm not nervous.'

Galena carefully brushed her palms over her striped walking gown, glad that the dampness wouldn't show on the black and bronze material. As she looked up, she caught sight of Merrick Forsythe and a few of his friends taking their seats halfway towards the back of the auditorium. A chill ran down her back, though she was glad he chose not to sit in the front row. She didn't need to see the derision written on his face, today of all days.

'You are going to make history!' Olive took her hand and squeezed it gently, her excitement evident.

'I would be satisfied with making sick people well.'

'That too.' Olive gestured to the side of the front row, beyond those reserved for the faculty. 'I will be sitting just over there.'

No more than two minutes passed before the dean came to the platform and introduced her to the room. Galena felt nerves clench in her stomach as he nodded to her and descended the three steps to take his place in the front row beside Professor Birdlaw. She laid one hand on the podium to stop it trembling.

'Dean Hopwood, professors, fellow students.'

She took a deep breath and pushed the words out.

'Every day the frontiers of medicine advance, but sometimes we move forward by looking to the past, to old ideas that had a wonderful basis in theory but were not possible to turn into reality when they were first conceived. You are all aware of Bachvarov's theory of using tissue from cadavers to replace damaged tissue in patients—some have dismissed it as fantasy, some have called it the work of the Devil—but saving lives is our calling, even if the methods are unorthodox.'

Galena explained how she had harvested the suinae tissue and used it to replace the damaged human atria. Her colleagues' expressions were a mixture of wonder and revulsion. The painted slides shining on the screen behind her brought a hush to the room as the medical fraternity considered the implications.

'And now, I would like to show you the proof of my theory and the future of medicine.'

She looked around the auditorium as she lifted the lid from her chilled crate. Directly in her view, Merrick Forsythe grinned. She had expected an outburst of disdain, but instead, he leaned forward in his seat.

Reaching into the crate, she lifted the tray on which the heart rested, sweeping it free of ice chips. She set it in the curved glass cradle on the table in front of the podium, the swish of blue liquid audible in the sudden hush.

Then, studying the heart, she frowned. It was swollen—the suinae tissue bulged—and a tremor travelled down the copper pipes.

Horrified, she bent and peered into the box. The steam release valve had twisted off and the organ shuddered abnormally. It burst, splattering the dean and the professors in the front row with blue liquid and shreds of tissue, human and porcine.

The hall erupted into cacophony—feminine squeals, a barrage of angry shouts and, over it all, a peal of horrible raucous laughter.

Galena backed away from the front of the platform, her legs trembling, one hand moving to cover her mouth.

A score of students rose and, as the first two reached the foot of the platform stairs, Galena fled towards the back door. Her hope of medical breakthrough was dripping off her audience, her dream of becoming the first female doctor in Edinburgh shattered.

'Unnatural harpy!'

'Bluestocking bitch!'

Insults flew thick and fast, the air in the corridor behind her turning blue.

Two years of writing letters and no small amount of financial encouragement had gone into achieving grudging permission to attend medical lectures. Always, the female students had been viewed askance—first when they presumed to learn as men did, and later when they proved they could. She had hoped the previous two years would have convinced her fellow students to see her as a doctor-in-training first, a woman second. It made her humiliation particularly galling.

She would not run, would not weep here. Later, she could pause and regret her flight, but now she had to show no emotion, no fear. They would smell it and their ridicule would be even more vexing.

She laid a gloved hand on the balustrade and hurried on, her ruffled skirts sweeping the dead leaves from the path. Catching the copper talisman that hung at her belt, she gripped it tightly for comfort. A Rod of Asclepius, it was the tangible symbol of the impetus that drove her to study medicine.

Behind her, the riotous laughter of her peers echoed in the forecourt.

Galena's stomach churned. This had been her moment; the moment where she had expected her research—research any man would be proud of—would be recognised for the breakthrough that it was. Instead, there was nothing here for her, nothing except shame and ignominy.

As she reached the foot of the steps, a voice rang out behind her. Merrick Forsythe stood there, Douglas Warwick behind him as always. Forsythe grinned and took a step forward, but Warwick laid a hand on his arm, speaking softly. Merrick threw off his friend's hand and spat a final dismissal at her. Every head turned at his words.

'Run and never return, you charlatan! We men of science have seen through your unnatural ideas. Perhaps now you will learn your rightful place.'

Galena picked up her striped skirts and fled, pushing through the heavy oak doors that separated the enclave from the rest of Edinburgh society. The cobbles were slick and putrid, and the tears swimming in her eyes made it hard for her to discern where she was going.

A party of women walked in front of her, twirling parasols and picking their way gingerly around puddles. In a ferment of impatience, Galena ducked around them, straight into the path of a unicarriage. She stared, horrified, at the steam pouring from the brazen nostrils and heard the shout from the driver.

Screaming, she drew herself into a ball as she fell, trying to avoid the whirling hooves on the single wheel in the centre of the vehicle. She felt a tug on her skirts and heard footsteps, plus splashes of ordure nearby.

She peeked up between her arms, still crossed over her head. The tip of the metal nose gleamed copper above her, steam drifting idly from the nostrils. One of the women who witnessed her fall screeched like a banshee while the other lay in a dead faint on the path.

A hand reached out for Galena, a white-gloved male hand. She wanted to shove it away, to close her eyes and find herself alone in her cold bed. Instead, she regretfully clasped the hand. But despite her efforts, and the gentleman's assistance, it was futile.

'I regret, sir, that I cannot get up. My skirts are caught, I think.'

The owner of the unicarriage bent forward and assessed the situation, then called over his shoulder. 'Jimmy, two feet back, there's a good fellow.'

Galena pulled her skirts free—they did not appear to be damaged by the iron hooves. The unicarriage was one of the newer models, with each of the twelve hooves on the central wheel shod with rubberised hessian. She shuddered. The design was kinder to fabric, but a blow to a limb would splinter bone.

Now, she rose awkwardly—one hand in his, the other at her ribs—and bowed her head as she drew breath back into her lungs.

She let go of his hand, perhaps unwisely for she swayed like a willow in a gale.

He tucked his walking stick, embellished with a silver horse's head, under his arm and offered her his left hand. His right arm snaked around her waist and steadied her.

She looked up at her rescuer, prepared to dislike him on sight—just at the moment, she was not in charity with men— but there was nothing to dislike. He wore leather-rimmed glasses with strange tinted lenses of a brownish hue. His curls were a titian that any woman would envy, and he was much her own age. He was pale, but there was something about his skin ...

He bowed. 'Pardon my forwardness, but you must permit me to see you home. Or can I take you to a doctor?'

She laughed at that; a ragged sound, half misery, half chagrin. 'I do not need a doctor, sir. I am a medical student.'

'I see. Can you stand unaided?'

Now that she had air in her lungs, Galena stifled a wince. With something like a pang of regret, she slid out of his respectful embrace. His eyes had not left her face, and now he pointedly offered an arm. She was no fool. She took it.

'My unicarriage is at your disposal. It would be my pleasure to take you to your destination.'

'It is not necessary, sir. I thank you. But I will be quite well.'

With unwonted forwardness, he put one finger under her chin. Though she could not see his eyes, she could feel his cool assessment. His gloved hand held her firmly at the elbow. She must look ... she shuddered to think.

'Miss, I must insist. You are in shock, or you should be. I shall take you to my father's clinic. He is a doctor.'

She looked up into his face, wanting to be angry at his presumption, but from the kindness of his expression, she could tell that he was not like the others.

He was tall and slender, but not merely lean—he was thin to the point of gauntness. However, he was extremely well turned out. His collar and the lace at his cuffs gleamed white, and his wine-dark morning coat was of well-cut velvet. As he moved, a glint of the gold embroidery on his cream waistcoat showed. His cravat was of burgundy silk, and a gold pin winked in its glossy folds.

Galena flushed to appear at a disadvantage before such a gentleman, and she gestured with one dismissive hand.

'Sir ...'

'Ah, I beg your pardon. Where are my manners? Beauden Somerton, at your service, Miss ...?'

Galena felt compelled to stretch out her hand, and he took it. Shook it lightly. Retained it.

'Miss Tindale.'

He smiled, and Galena's mind whirled. Though he wore a coat of greasepaint, when he spoke, she could see his lips were duck-egg blue. How curious!

Her arm resting on his, Galena allowed Mr Somerton to escort her to the door of the coach. The driver handed her rescuer his black silk top hat and stepped back.

'Thank you, Jimmy.'

As soon as they were aboard, the man put up the steps and took his seat in the narrow column of the equine neck. A hiss sounded as he dialled up the steam valve and the vehicle moved smoothly forward.

At second glance, Galena could see that Mr Somerton was not so young as he appeared. His thinness made his frame seem younger, but something about his posture, his demeanour, spoke of a man no longer in his prime, or of one who had to husband his energies carefully.

As Galena bent her head to fiddle with her gloves, she noticed him tap the head of his ebony cane. A tiny white pill popped from the horse's mouth; he took it and slipped it between his lips in one smooth movement. If she had not seen the pill, Galena would have assumed he was stifling a yawn.

The unicarriage increased in speed and her companion sat forward with renewed vigour.

'It seems, Miss Tindale, that we were destined to meet. Although I had not intended for us to do so in such a memorable way.'

She hoped she had not stepped into the carriage of a villain. Perhaps it was to be expected—after all, she had been chased out of medical school and run down by a carriage. Now it seemed she would be murdered by a casually met stranger.

'Indeed, sir?' Her voice was coolly crisp. 'How so?'

He laughed, slipped two gloved fingers into his jacket and removed an envelope. 'I was asked to deliver an invitation to Miss Galena Tindale.'

He passed her the envelope. There, in ebony ink, swirled in elegant copperplate on a thick cream sheet, was her name. She turned the missive over to find it embossed with a seal of blood-red wax, the device an *A* embellished with a heart.

She looked up, shocked. 'But who would want to meet me?'

'Perhaps you should open it?'

She snapped the wax and unfurled the page. Her eyes popped open as she glimpsed the signature. She ate up the words that bade her dine with the sender and his son at her convenience.

'Dr Augustus Somerton is your father? He wishes to meet me?'

'Very much so.'

She bent her head to the note again. The last sentence made her gasp.

'Your father wishes to discuss my research?' She found that idea, frankly, incredible. 'Well, he will undoubtedly change his mind after news of this morning's events reaches his ears. He will be glad he did not ruin his reputation by being seen with me.'

'I cannot imagine why. He has many friends and former colleagues at the university who have spoken of your research.'

'And he wishes to join in the general mockery? He should have been present this morning—he would have had a front row seat.'

She winced at the memory of the aftermath; her professor and the dean of the college both in the front row, spattered in flesh and artificial blood.

'Miss Tindale.'

He reached forward, but she batted his hand away. He drew back, shaking his head.

'My father heard about your work more than a month ago and requested a copy of your report. He did not want to disturb you when you were preparing for your presentation, but he is extremely enthusiastic about your ideas.'

'I am afraid that all my research is back at the university. It ...'

A lump the size of Castle Rock rose in her throat.

He only smiled. 'I'm sure I can arrange something.'

Seeking distraction, Galena studied the letter again. She had heard of Augustus Somerton, had seen his name on the university honour board. He had been a legend, one of the brightest stars in the faculty's firmament—and he wanted to meet her?

Perhaps she still lay in the road unconscious, for this could only be a dream.

Chapter 2

Beauden Somerton leaned back in his seat. His medication had eased the sharp breathless pain a trifle, but he had overexerted himself as he leapt from the unicarriage and he would suffer for it. He could feel the inexorable progress of his condition, although his father demurred. There might not be reliable medical proof, but he knew what he knew—his time grew shorter.

Still, he had refused to sit idly by when a lovely lady was in distress. Jimmy had braked sharply, sending him cannoning into the seat opposite. When he'd stepped down, had seen her lying there, it felt as though his heart had been wrenched from his chest—and that was a feeling he knew intimately.

Though he had met few women—and even fewer young ladies of repute—he thought her quite striking and studied her as unobtrusively as possible. She had some indefinable air that drew him like a lodestone. It wasn't simply the raven hair, neatly coiled on the crown of her head, tendrils shaken loose in her fall. It wasn't even her brilliant eyes—if eyes were the windows of the soul, she was both an angel and a genius.

Most young ladies would have been wearing a bonnet. Perhaps she had left hers behind when she fled the scene of whatever disaster had beset her before falling under the wheels of his carriage.

The way her eyes played over his face and dwelt upon his lips, it didn't take much intellect to realise that she read him as easily as any medical tome. He only hoped that she was as brilliant as his father believed her to be.

She drew her lower lip between her teeth and twisted her hands in her lap. A part of him wanted to reach out and comfort her, but the memory of her slapping away his earlier attempts prevented him from doing so again. This lady was anything except fragile.

They sat silently as the carriage passed the fruit market and crossed Princes Street for Leith Place.

The urge to make conversation stuck in his throat like a peppermint humbug. What should he say? The tension hovered between them like a burgeoning thunderstorm.

She lifted her head, her dark gaze piercing his very innards.

'I have heard of your father, of course, every student has, but I did not realise that he still actively engaged in medicine. It has been …'

'It has been more than fifteen years, yes. My father is interested in a particular area of research, which, for the most part, he engages in privately. He does sometimes take an interest in patients at Gillespie's Hospital. He also runs a small charity clinic in the Cowgate.'

She gazed at him as though trying to read his mind.

'I presume that your father's research is in a similar field to mine. Yet I thought I had acquired every scientific paper on the topic. Surely if he had published his work …'

'Perhaps that is something you would care to discuss with him. His research is not complete, and he is waiting for his final experiment to come to fruition.'

'I wish him every success.'

'So do I, Miss Tindale, most fervently.'

The unicarriage passed through a broad gate in a grey stone wall and into the courtyard of the Somerton family home before gently hissing to a halt. Jimmy, his goggles now pushed up on top of his head, opened the door and let down the steps.

Beauden smiled and gestured to the door.

'Miss Tindale, shall we?'

She permitted Jimmy to help her down and, as she passed beyond his ambit to look around, Beauden leaned towards Jimmy.

'Go back, Jimmy, if you please, and bring back Miss Tindale's work.'

Jimmy nodded and Beauden turned towards his guest.

***

Galena took Mr Somerton's proffered arm and accepted his escort across the forecourt. Both the paving and the wall behind her were grey. A Palladian townhouse rose up, three storeys or more, all grey stone and pierced at intervals with narrow panes of glass. Additional small windows were set a few inches above ground level. The walls were lined with planter boxes, but the few plants they contained were untended, little more than weeds. Surely a prison or workhouse would be more welcoming, despite the stateliness of the old house.

The front door was enormous, covered in pressed metal—bronze perhaps—but so thick with verdigris that the majority of its surface appeared green. The reliefs, six in all, were exquisite and captured examples of the healing arts in the Greek style. In the centre, as tall as a man, was a representation of the Rod of Asclepius—the symbol of healing. In spite of the trauma of the day, the sight of it gave Galena a sense of hope. Her hand moved again to the same symbol hanging from her waist and, with a whispered prayer, she hoped that here at least she might be among friends.

The door opened and a solid middle-aged man bowed to Galena and Mr Somerton. His shirt was plain, his cutaway jacket embellished with a double row of brass buttons.

'Master Beauden, miss. The doctor is in the conservatory.'

'Thank you, Perkins. We have a guest for lunch.'

Galena heard Mr Somerton's reply, but the vibrant, lofty entrance hall clamoured for her attention. The parquetry gleamed golden and large paintings framed in silver gilt covered vivid turquoise walls. To her right, a curved stair wound upwards to a small balcony landing. The railing, made of intricately wrought silver lace, reflected coloured light from the stained-glass window over the door. The window featured a woman in a long gold gown, and she cradled a baby, also wearing a long gown, in one arm. Her other hand, upraised, held a heart.

'My late mother.' Mr Somerton looked up at the image, a warm smile playing across his pale lips.

'Oh, I beg your pardon.'

Mr Somerton smiled. 'Please don't apologise, Miss Tindale. My father commissioned it in her memory. He would be glad you admire it.'

Galena looked up at the stunning artwork. 'Are you the child she is holding?'

'No. That is my sister.' He removed his hat but not his tinted glasses. 'Shall we go in? My father is waiting to meet you.'

They passed down a short hallway with doors to the left and right. The flames in the candelabra lining the walls did not flicker.

'Your gaslights are unusual.'

'Dynamic lights,' he said, gesturing, 'a by-product of the steam-generated heat that Father uses to supply the kitchen and bathing rooms with hot water.'

They passed into a vaulted room and Galena gasped in pleasure. It was easily the most beautifully appointed room she had ever seen. Although shallow, it ran the full width of the house. Facing her was a double-height extension, a conservatory constructed of arched windows, each with a dozen panes of glass at least. The curved roof was made of smaller panes of irregular shapes, enmeshed in a steel web. To her right, a painted cupola hung from the ceiling on a steel cable as thick as her wrist, suspended over a pair of chesterfields in rich brown leather. On the other side of the room, bookcases stood perpendicular to the walls, and a stair led to more books with a reading nook above. In the alcove immediately beneath the reading nook, an enormous desk—fashioned from huge metal gears, oak and black leather—bore a welter of books, pens and paraphernalia. The walls were a brilliant scarlet, like the inside of a heart.

Before she could get her bearings, a man came to stand before her. He was not as tall nor as slender as Mr Somerton, but there was no mistaking this was Mr Somerton's father—Dr Augustus Somerton. The other difference was the impact of age. This man wore the silver threads in his beard and in the wings of hair at his temples proudly.

'Miss Tindale, I presume? It is an honour to meet you.' His bass voice held a hint of kindly amusement and his soft hazel eyes twinkled.

Mr Somerton stepped forward. 'Miss Tindale, may I introduce to you, my father, Dr Augustus Somerton.'

Galena offered her hand and the older man took it, shaking it lightly.

She made a small curtsey, feeling as if she were meeting medical royalty—no demonstration of respect could seem excessive.

'Thank you, Doctor. The honour is mine.'

Dr Somerton offered her a long smile before he glanced at his son. 'Have you informed Mrs Perkins, Beauden, that there will be three to lunch?'

'I sent a message when we arrived, sir.'

19

The doctor turned from Galena, his assessing glance lingering on his son before he pulled him into an affectionate embrace. Galena had rarely seen this kind of affection publicly displayed, not least between father and son.

'You look ...'

Dr Somerton glanced towards Galena and then back towards his son. His words made Galena miserably aware of the deficiencies in her appearance. She had been almost trampled under mechanical hooves. She must look a fright.

The doctor smiled warmly. 'Would either of you care to freshen up before lunch?'

'I am perfectly all right, sir, but Miss Tindale might care for a few moments. I'm afraid we met rather abruptly.'

'I see.'

The doctor trained the full power of his medical expertise on her.

'I am uninjured, sir.' Galena hastened to reassure him—and herself. 'Mr Somerton halted his vehicle before I was harmed.'

'Hmm.' He reached out a hand. 'May I?'

'Of course.' Standing still under the revered doctor's scrutiny, she felt like a bug under a glass.

Dr Somerton took her chin in one firm hand and turned her head. He touched a finger to her brow and she stifled a wince.

'A slight mark but no abrasion. Do you have any dizziness? Nausea?'

'No, sir. Nothing of that nature.'

He nodded and withdrew his hand. 'I don't believe any damage has been done, although once you've had a chance to freshen up, I might prescribe a small sherry.'

She stepped back. 'Thank you again, sir.'

Dr Somerton lifted a brass horn the length of a man's outstretched hand and, flicking a tiny switch protruding from the wall, spoke into it.

Galena exchanged platitudes with her hosts until a matronly woman in a buckled navy gown came and escorted her to a bathing room.

***

Beauden felt his father's fingers on his wrist.

'You seem somewhat on edge, my son.'

With an unaccountable spurt of anger, Beauden pulled away. 'Not at all, sir. I am quite well.'

He took a seat on one of the chesterfields.

His father raised an eyebrow and took the one opposite. 'If I might trouble you for an explanation?'

'I mentioned earlier that I met Miss Tindale in rather exciting circumstances—it asked a little more of me than I am accustomed to, I admit. But sir,' he leaned forward, 'there is no need to coddle me. I know my boundaries and respect them.'

Beauden immediately regretted the harsh tone of his words. He had not meant to speak so to his father who adored him, who would lay down his own life for him without hesitation—indeed, who had already done so. But in the short ride home from the college, something about Miss Tindale had affected him more than he cared to admit. He knew that his father saw her as the key to his survival. Nonetheless, having such a beautiful woman see him only as a specimen in a jar was rather abhorrent. And if she saw him as only a pitiable invalid ... that would be unbearable.

His father looked him over coolly and poured small measures of fine dry sherry into three tiny crystal flutes.

'I sometimes forget, Beauden, just how limited your exposure has been to young, respectable ladies. Save for the lasses you see at the clinic and those you employ in the workshop, you have no female acquaintance. And you rarely have the opportunity to engage in social intercourse with women of your own station. So a pretty young bluestocking ...'

'I do not fully grasp her research. I leave that to you, sir.' He gave a courteous nod of thanks and accepted the glass his father handed him. 'But Miss Tindale has demonstrated great independence and a degree of self-confidence. She is deceptively fragile, yet she has a spine of steel.'

'Why do you say so?'

Beauden frowned. 'I think something happened to upset her before I made her acquaintance. Jimmy said she dashed right into the path of our carriage and she has seemed ... on edge.'

'Do you have any specific knowledge?'

'No, not exactly sir, though she spoke of mockery. I assume she has been the victim of some discourtesy.'

He remembered her pale face and the tremor in her voice and an unfamiliar fury licked through him.

'She was angry. And frightened, too, I think. Most women would have wept, but not she. She is, or at least she seems ... valiant. With such a heart and mind, she can set the world on fire.'

His father considered his words. 'If she is as you say, then she is an answer to our prayers.'

'So her research ...?'

'Meshes perfectly with my own. It is better than I could have hoped, my son.'

Beauden sat back with a sigh and sipped his sherry contemplatively under his father's appraising eye. In a way, it was both their lives at stake—his father's and his own. His father's research had been so long devoted to giving Beauden another chance at life that it would kill the old man to fail. But even though Beauden had made peace with the spectre of death, he could not help but grasp the thin thread of hope being offered.

Hope, though, was not responsible for the electrifying, unfamiliar sensations that flickered through his body and weighed heavily on the lump of metal in his chest. He closed his eyes and tried to calm his mind—but it was no use. A lithe form enticed, a pair of rich brown eyes pleaded with him to hope.

***

23

Galena followed the housekeeper down the hallway and up the teak stair, one hand on the silver balustrade. She could see another floor above and, looking down, a heavy-banded door set discreetly into the wall near the front door. She wondered what lay beyond.

Galena was relieved to be shown into an elegant powder room, beautifully appointed, with black wallpaper embossed with copper foil suns. Copper pipe, exposed and polished to a high sheen, ran across the wall to a marble washstand that housed a beaten copper bowl.

The woman twisted a bright copper sun on a small cupboard, unlocking it to reveal lovely rose soaps, talcum and lotions.

'If you would like to call me when you are ready, I will help you tidy your hair, miss.'

Galena picked up the soft cloth and wiped away the marks from her forehead that she noticed in the mirror. As she washed the stains from her hands, she struggled to come to terms with the events of the day. If it had all gone to plan, she would have vindicated the work of Yevgeni Bachvarov and cemented her place in the medical pantheon. But it had not. And now her slides, her research and all her young life's work were gone.

Yet here she was, a guest of one of the most famous medical men of the century—and he wanted to discuss her work!

She stared at herself in the mirror, incredulous at the twists fate had taken. A laugh escaped her. What more could today bring?

'If there is nothing more, miss, I'll take you down to the doctor.'

Galena murmured her thanks. She had a host of questions about Dr Somerton's concern for his son—and about the younger man's bluish lips. That he wore what appeared to be theatrical greasepaint suggested he felt compelled to adopt a disguise. Perhaps the two things were linked. She recalled again the tablet Beauden Somerton had slipped between his lips and how his expression had eased. Was he ill?

'I hope Mr Somerton is well.' That was a suitable opening gambit, Galena hoped.

'I hope so too, miss,' was the housekeeper's serene reply.

Galena felt a sting in the glance that followed and reluctantly curbed her curiosity.

The housekeeper led Galena to the conservatory door and set her hand to the knob. As she turned it, Mr Somerton's words floated into the air before her.

'Are you sure she is the one?'

The housekeeper's lips pursed slightly, but Galena kept her face impassive before entering with a smile.

Dr Somerton turned as she entered and shot his son a look. 'Ah, Miss Tindale! Some sherry?'

She accepted the bronze liquid in a delicate crystal glass.

'Thank you, Doctor.'

'My son tells me that you left your presentation rather abruptly. I take it that my esteemed colleagues did not take kindly to having such a lovely young woman as yourself come up with a brilliant medical advance?'

She swallowed uncomfortably. 'You could say that, sir.'

'Well, when it is convenient, I should like to be an appreciative audience of one. Still,' he gestured to the inner room where she saw a table laid for three, 'let's have luncheon first. Shall we?'

Beauden Somerton offered his arm. 'Miss Tindale.'

Galena wasn't hungry. The trauma of the morning still affected her, playing in her mind like an echo. And now, being a simple student who found herself the guest of a famous and respected physician, she felt out of her depth.

The maid put a tureen of soup down.

'Thank you, Alice. We will serve ourselves.'

Dr Somerton ladled a portion of soup into a bowl and set it in front of Galena before serving his son and himself.

Not wanting to appear rude, Galena dipped her spoon and sipped slowly. The broth, a rich Scottish oxtail, stroked her taste buds and reminded her just how insubstantial her breakfast had been.

'So, Miss Tindale. Is the soup to your liking?'

Galena swallowed a sputter and dabbed her lips with her napkin. She needed time to form a reply. 'Sir, I would be honoured if you would call me Galena.'

'I would be delighted. Were you named after the father of medicine?'

'I was. My father was a doctor in York and had read everything he could on Galen's work. He was determined to honour him, although he would have preferred a son, I think, to carry on his work.'

'No doubt you will make him proud yet. So, are you finding your studies agreeable?'

She laid the napkin down and fought to keep her voice steady. 'They are … daunting.'

'Ah.' He nodded and paused for a second, staring down at his plate. 'Yes, I can imagine. There are few men in this day and age who are sufficiently enlightened to realise that women are as capable as they of making use of a robust education.'

Dr Somerton's tone was overlaid with compassion. She set the spoon down, suddenly unable to swallow.

'I am sorry, Galena. You have suffered at their hands. Did they harm you?'

She shook her head. 'No, sir. But they have crushed my dream.'

He paused. 'The day is not yet done, Galena. We will see what can be achieved later.'

She took a sip of the claret in her wine glass, a hearty accompaniment to the rich soup, and strove to change the subject. Mr Somerton had been quiet, though she was exceedingly aware of his presence. She turned to him and attempted a smile.

'I wonder, sir, that you did not come into the presentation. Members of the public are not excluded.'

'I do not go out much in public, Miss Tindale.' He looked

27

down and she cursed her unruly tongue.

Dr Somerton stepped in. 'I am glad you could join us for lunch, my dear. My cook has prepared salmon for us, and she does a fine berry trifle.'

'Thank you for inviting me, sir.'

Galena was confident that the good doctor did not make a habit of entertaining medical students. Why was she there?

Chapter 3

As he set down his wine glass, Beauden's eyes glanced over Miss Tindale's face. Father believed that she would put aside the preconceptions and shibboleths they faced. He hoped it was true, for his father was about to open their closest secret to another soul. For so long, it had been only his father and their trusted staff who knew of his condition and the means by which he'd been kept alive. What if his father had misjudged her?

Perhaps his father's instincts were well-founded, for her countenance shone angelically bright. Either way, his days were numbered as the sharp stutter in his chest reminded him. Would Galena Tindale alerting the authorities to his father's unnatural procedures result in his death, or would the failure of those unnatural procedures themselves be the cause?

Beauden wiped his mouth then set his napkin beside his plate. He rose, one hand on the back of his chair to steady himself, endeavouring not to let his weariness show.

'Pardon me, sir, Miss Tindale. I know there are things my father wishes to discuss with you, but I believe it would be better for you to talk freely without me. Father, I will see you in the basement shortly.'

Beauden wanted desperately to witness her reaction to the story his father was about to tell, yet he also did not want to see disgust or—God forbid—terror on her face. In any case, it was far more urgent that he make his way downstairs for his afternoon's rest.

With a courteous nod, he made his way towards the exit, but, as he slipped through the narrow door into the hall, he glanced back. Despite his heart's inability to throb, this petite genius kindled a heat in his blood that he could not ignore. He wanted to hope but was too wary of allowing himself any prospect of a life beyond tomorrow.

***

Dr Somerton set the fine china cups aside and took a long breath.

Galena waited. This was the moment of truth; this was why she had been asked to come here.

Dr Somerton steepled his hands in front of him and studied his fingertips before speaking. 'You will have noticed my son suffers from ill health.'

'Yes, sir. Is it of recent date?'

'Not at all. Beauden was a twin, but he and his sister were born several weeks premature and very small. Augusta, my daughter'— he smiled, yet Galena saw the ghost of pain—'lived only for an hour. Beauden survived, but he was always weak and sickly.

'My medical skill was enough to keep him alive, though it grew more and more difficult as he got older. His heart had a defect, you see, that grew worse as his body grew larger, made more demands on it.'

She clenched her hands in her lap. 'What did you do, sir?'

Her father had had one such patient—an infant. Galena knew that most babies born with a defective heart would not see their fifth birthday. That Beauden Somerton had made it to adulthood was not to be believed.

'I withdrew from the faculty of the university and dramatically reduced my practice. I have a small estate in England, so I am not dependent on the income from my practice to keep a roof over our heads. I had the ability to devote most of my time to finding a solution to my problem.'

She nodded, knowing how her father had wrestled to save his patients. Dr Somerton would have moved heaven and earth to save his son.

'Though I grieved my daughter and had no illusions about my son's prognosis, I did not give up hope. You see, I had read the work of a Bulgarian doctor—'

'Bachvarov!' Her heart bucked in her chest.

He smiled like a professor who had a particularly clever pupil.

'Indeed, Galena. I read the works of Yevgeni Bachvarov and his theories about building a heart from flesh and metal. In the meantime, I learned as much as I could by helping patients in the infirmary, and at my own clinic, who had damage to the heart. I discovered a great deal, but it took me years of reading, years of planning and experimentation, and months to build a prototype. It seemed to work well, but before I could refine the design and begin work on a more efficient model, Beauden contracted scarlet fever.'

He shook his head and his voice became harsh; grief bowed his shoulders.

'I thought he would die. There were a dozen different times when I was certain that his young body could take no more punishment. To my astonishment, he pulled through. But he was weak—impossibly so—and failing. I could wait no longer.'

Galena froze as she took in the full import of the doctor's words. 'Do you mean to say …?'

He stood. 'Come downstairs, Galena. It is best that I show you.'

Galena picked up her skirts and followed Dr Somerton down the steep steps to the banded oak door she had noticed earlier. With a flick of his wrists, he turned the gears and the massive latches slid back. He pushed the door open.

Galena's blood froze in her veins.

The basement laboratory was unlike anything she had seen before, and mostly below ground level. Galena saw the two windows, set high in the wall, and realised they were those she had seen from outside at ground height. The room itself was huge, perhaps as wide as the house and half as deep. Copper panels covered the walls, and each panel bore a lamp of the same design as those she had seen upstairs—neither candle, nor gas, but powered by the spinning turbines in the house's steam boiler. High shelving sat to her left, filled with boxes and loose papers. A massive desk ran along the wall, covered in tan leather, and featured a long workbench. Set apart at the front of the room, between the two high windows, stood a strange iron orb.

The globe rose to almost the full height of the room, its shape more a suggestion than an actual sphere, for it was constructed of iron circles crossing over one another. But it was the object standing in the centre that was the source of Galena's fear—a large padded table, furnished with leather straps.

A shadow fell over her shoulder, causing her to gasp.

Mr Somerton shook his head. 'Don't be afraid, Miss Tindale. It's not an instrument of torture. It's my bed.'

Her heart still hammering in her throat, she turned to see Dr Somerton standing at the wide bench along the left-hand wall. With a gesture, he bade her come to him and turned again to the dozen sheets of paper on the bench, filled with diagrams.

Galena gasped. 'Is this …?'

'Yes, my dear.' He gave a beaming smile. 'These are the plans for the original iron heart.'

Galena was briefly distracted by the sight of Beauden Somerton, standing by the torturous bed, slowly removing his frock coat and cravat. But despite the strangeness of his action, the sheaf of papers clamoured for her attention.

With her finger, she traced the intricate lines connecting the four chambers of the heart, the two atria and two ventricles. The fine design of small metal valves between each space reminded her of the blades of a ceiling fan, like those which hummed around the edges of the laboratory now. The only difference being, these blades did not spin. Instead, they were designed to open and close, allowing blood to pass through, to and from each chamber of the heart.

It was daring—more daring than anything she had believed possible.

'This is what you made? You were able to use metal in tandem with human tissue?'

Dr Somerton nodded. 'To attach the tissue of the aorta and pulmonary vessels to the corresponding metal openings of the heart? Yes.'

Her hands fell to her sides and she slumped against the desk. 'How did you power it? Maintain function?'

'Ah! Straight to the heart of the matter, I see.' His eyes lit up as he pointed and leaned closer. 'You see here? This is the pinnacle of the design—it's quite ingenious. The power of the diaphragm causes this pendulum to swing. Its momentum converts to an impulse to supply power to the organ. It is essentially self-powering. Rather neat, don't you think?'

Galena shook her head and bent again to the diagram.

'It's impossible!' Her words were a mere breath. This was more than she had dared dream.

'It's perfectly logical, Galena. Consider the laws of momentum and kinetic energy. Elastic collisions, ones in which objects rebound at the same speed as they were previously moving, generate a great deal of force. What is force but another name for power?'

Galena straightened, as still as a marble statue. She looked up, her eyes scarcely taking him in, her brain trying to process one revelation after another.

'This is ... utterly inspired. Why have you never presented it to the world?'

This was far beyond what she had attempted.

'Do you need my help to build this, or to transplant it into your son's body?'

She felt a kind of horrid pride at the prospect and, when he shook his head, a tinge of disappointment. But how indeed could it be that? The thing was still a mere design.

'No, Miss Tindale.' His voice was oddly formal. 'I need your assistance in designing a more proficient heart to replace the one I have already implanted.'

Galena's world went black.

***

Beauden moved automatically, in time to stop her head from hitting the stone floor. She was only unconscious for a matter of seconds, but it was long enough for him to feel the iron heart in his chest fall to the pit of his stomach.

Together, he and his father eased her into the high-backed leather armchair beside the oak table. Her eyelashes flickered. She looked so delicate, a water sprite transplanted into the human world. She was lovely, too—her hair a midnight black, her eyes as bright as Venus in the evening sky. Yet despite her ethereal air and apparent fragility, she had a powerful understanding and a steely core of courage.

His father poured a tot of brandy into one of the port glasses from the sideboard and held it to her lips.

'I'm sorry, Galena. I did not consider what a shock this must be.'

'Sir, permit me.' His father's enthusiasm could easily overwhelm her again and she would run screaming from the house.

Beauden pulled a second hard wooden chair over to her side, held the little crystal goblet and waited until the haze vanished from her eyes. He offered her the glass and she sipped from it.

'Brandy?'

He smiled softly. 'You've had rather a shock.'

She laughed. 'Mr Somerton, after the day I've had, I'm only surprised I'm not curled up under the table, hugging a bottle of gin.'

He sat back a little. 'You are a remarkable woman, Miss Tindale.'

She could still blush.

'Under the circumstances, could I request that you call me Galena?'

He picked up her hand and kissed it. It seemed the thing to do. 'Galena, I am Beauden Somerton. I am delighted to meet you.'

His father cleared his throat. 'I daresay you must have a thousand questions, Galena.'

36

'Not even close, sir.'

He nodded. 'I can appreciate that, my dear. Beauden must rest after lunch—one of the symptoms of his affliction is terrible fatigue—so I had hoped to show you a little of what we have achieved and then answer your queries as best I can.'

Beauden reached out a hand and laid it over hers. 'Galena, you are under no compulsion. Not to be down here, to listen to my father's requests, or to do anything that makes you uncomfortable. It is something I insisted upon when my father first mentioned bringing you here.'

Her eyes skimmed over his face.

'Your eyes.'

She reached out the tip of her finger and then drew back. Her voice was filled with awe and confusion, and Beauden couldn't decide whether she saw him as a curiosity or a medical marvel.

'They're so unlike anything I've ever seen, almost unnatural in their shade.' She blinked and slowly withdrew her hand. 'I'm sorry, I should not stare.'

'Galena, the reason why you might be able to help us is because of your passion for medical knowledge. Of course you have questions. Ask anything you wish.'

He sat forward in his chair and looked into her chocolate fudge eyes. He was determined to stay still, though her scrutiny made him uncomfortable in a way he had not expected. She drank in his appearance with every evidence of rapture—and yet she was not looking at him. She merely studied the faulty shell that housed him. Oh, that she would look into his soul with a tenth of that passionate intensity!

She gave him a look of gratitude before turning her attention back to his eyes. Her hand rose at her side, almost of its own accord, and flitted lightly at the skin beside his eye like a butterfly wishing to land. She shifted closer, leaving mere inches between their faces. Her eyes grew wide, drinking his in. Wretched pain dragged at him, to have so beautiful a woman look so deeply into his eyes and see only his condition, not who he was as a man. He admitted the rueful truth. He wanted more.

'The pupils and lenses are as dark as any I've seen'—her focus was intense—'but your iris is a palette of copper, bronze and hazel, which I suspect is your true colour.'

Only his lips moved. 'My mother's eyes were hazel.'

Her brow wrinkled. 'But, are those faint lines of iron in the sclera of both eyes?'

She turned and looked at his father, who nodded.

'Beauden is suffering from a toxic accumulation of iron in his system. That is what is causing the discolouration to his eyes and skin, the fatigue and—'

'Father!' There were some humiliating aspects of his condition that he would prefer a lovely woman not to know.

His father nodded. 'Indeed. In addition, the heart is failing. It is suffering from oxidisation caused by the blood passing through it. That is the reason for the cyanosis—the traces of blue in his lips and fingertips. That is why I must remove the iron heart that has been keeping him alive these fifteen years, and I cannot do that until I can replace it with another, one that he can keep for the rest of his days.'

Beauden watched as Galena considered, processed the information, and seemed to come to a decision.

'May I see it?'

She would think him a freak, that much was certain. Whether she felt repelled by what had been done to his body in order to give him life, or whether she found him an intellectual curiosity, there was no doubt about it, she would think him a freak—because he was. Beauden was under no illusions about that.

He had already removed his collar and cravat, and now, he pulled the drawstring of his shirt loose and, closing his eyes, lifted the garment over his head. Beneath it, he wore a muslin under-shirt—much like a lady's chemise—and over it a boned corset, high in front. When he first wore it after the operation, it had pleased him to think of himself as a knight of old. But he had been only a child then; it was a long time ago. He pulled the straps loose and set the stiff linen aside. This was the moment of truth. He exhaled and pulled the muslin over his head, holding the garment to the centre of his chest.

It was surprisingly painful to be exposed before her. He was an unappealing specimen of manhood, he knew, cadaverously thin, but … well, there was no point in delaying the inevitable. He reached out and drew a stool towards him, perched on it and deliberately set the undershirt aside.

Galena gasped and her eyes widened.

As she bent closer, Beauden struggled to keep his breathing even. It had been drummed into him since his childhood ended at age twelve—excitement was his enemy. Steady breaths ensured a steady heartbeat. And yet, the way she responded to him, the amazement in her gentle inquisitive touches, the hint of lavender in her hair, so very close to him, beguiled him.

He knew what she saw, he had looked in his mirror often enough. Pale, thin skin that stretched across where his ribs ought to be, and the dark grey shadow in the centre of his chest—all that could be seen of the iron heart his father had built and his mother had helped implant into the chest of her twelve-year-old son.

She pulled back a little and met his eyes calmly. Her voice was as soft as butter. 'Does it hurt?'

'No.'

She nodded. 'So the medication you took in the carriage is not for pain.'

'How did you …?'

She made a vague, dismissive gesture. 'I saw you pop a small pill from your stick. Your colour improved markedly afterwards.'

Beauden felt a smile curl around the corners of his mouth. This girl was everything his father had expected, perhaps more.

Bending from the waist, she inspected him closely once more. He looked down, entranced. Unlike his own, the musculature of her chest was extremely pleasing.

She glanced over her shoulder. 'This is remarkable, sir. How do you keep it in place?'

His father stepped closer. 'It was quite a feat, and I made adjustments several times as Beauden grew, but fortunately, that phase is behind us.'

She rested her hand, oh, so lightly, over the thrumming engine in the centre of his chest before tracing the long pale scar up and along a rib. Her fingers were as soft as butterfly wings and Beauden twisted away.

She snatched her hand back as though scalded.

He kept his smile steady, hoping the disappointment he felt at the loss of her touch didn't show on his face.

'Shall we go upstairs while my son rests, Galena?'

'Oh, of course.' She stepped back.

'Perhaps, in an hour or so, we could take a walk?' Beauden did not want to appear overeager.

She flushed slightly. 'Thank you. I will look forward to that.'

He, too, would look forward to it. Perhaps, if luck were on his side, she would come to see him as more than just a fascinating specimen.

Chapter 4

Galena waited at the foot of the stair while Dr Somerton assisted Beauden to replace the muslin undershirt and buckle on the reinforced corset.

Beauden lay on the bed and drew a light silk cover over his body. Dr Somerton adjusted the angle of the bed so that it was no longer flat, but sat at about sixty degrees, then he threw a small lever on the side.

Galena heard a whirr, and the pipes that presumably ran through the walls to power the bed shuddered audibly.

Slowly, the bed began to rotate clockwise, speeding up until it reached a steady pace, and the arms of the skeleton orb surrounding it rotated counterclockwise.

Dr Somerton crossed the room to Galena and offered his arm.

'What is the purpose of such a bed, sir?' She turned, taking a final glance.

'It eases the strain of the iron heart. As you know, the heart is powered by a pendulum. The spinning creates a small magnetic current, so while Beauden is still, this does some of the work that would otherwise be accomplished by his movement.'

She nodded, no longer certain of anything she previously accepted as gospel, and accompanied him upstairs.

In the sumptuous scarlet conservatory, Dr Somerton led her to his desk and unrolled a series of dusty plans. He used them to explain how he had constructed a cage in his son's chest, wrought of bone, copper and gold, to support the weight of the iron heart. While the doctor's diagrams of the heart had stretched the bounds of possibility, this was straight out of a book by the Brothers Grimm.

After the first hundred or so of her questions, Dr Somerton laughed and called a stop.

'First, a cup of tea. And then, my dear, I want you to explain your research to me.'

Galena swallowed. 'Sir, I had barely begun to present my research to the university. I was shouted from the stage after less than five minutes, and all my work'—she drew a deep breath, remembering the horrid moment of the explosion—'is still there.'

He leaned forward and patted her hand. 'Of course it isn't. Beauden sent Jimmy to retrieve it as soon as he brought you here. Ever resourceful and devoted to Beauden is Jimmy.'

She stood quickly, overturning her chair. 'And the heart, sir? It was destroyed and the machine damaged.'

He looked at her pointedly. 'Do you have the skill to rebuild it, or was your success a mere accident?'

She stared at him, speechless.

'I thought not. Do not be troubled, Galena.' He shook his grizzled head. 'You will build something even finer this time. And you will help save my son.'

***

With a hiss of steam, the unicarriage came to a halt. Galena felt the vehicle rock as Jimmy jumped down and the door opened onto the stone-pillared entrance to Victoria Park.

Jimmy let down the steps and Beauden descended before turning and holding out a hand to Galena. She took it gladly and stepped down, blinking as she emerged from the dim carriage into the afternoon sunlight.

The park was full of children and young people. Babies kicked on rugs, watched over by their nursemaids; a small group of lads played a game of cricket; and several girls, in long curls and pinafores, fed the numerous ducks. Galena's spirits lifted, and the weighty events of the morning suddenly became less important than spending this perfect moment with a kind and dashing gentleman.

Galena opened the parasol she had borrowed from Mrs Perkins. Made from black lace and, with the small addition of a knot of bronze ribbons tied to the point, it complemented her black and bronze walking dress to perfection.

She slipped her arm through Beauden's as Jimmy folded the step and dusted off his hands.

'Right then, sir. I'll be back in forty-five minutes and I'll be waitin' by them trees. Now, you have your writin' mirror in case of need?'

'Go away, Jimmy.' Beauden spoke entirely without heat. 'If I needed a nursemaid, I'd choose one with a prettier countenance than you.'

Galena laughed for the first time that day. 'Thank you, Mr Ayre. I can work his device if we need you.'

Beauden turned to her. 'Please, for pity's sake, don't encourage him.'

Jimmy tipped his cap to her, studiously ignoring his master, and swung himself up into the cab. The unicarriage clip-clopped away until the sound was lost in the hubbub of city traffic.

Galena strolled across the grass on Beauden's arm. She had met him only that morning and yet she was entirely comfortable with him. He didn't browbeat her or talk down to her as dozens of her so-called peers at the medical school had done. The best had wished her well but treated her as though she were out of her depth. The worst … well, several had made it clear they thought her attendance was some elaborate husband hunt. And then there was Merrick Forsythe, in a class of his own.

'Perhaps I can offer you an ice?' Beauden gestured to the small cart with a candy-striped awning sitting off the adjacent path.

'Why, thank you. I haven't had one since I left York.'

Galena hadn't been to this park, either. She had, since coming to Edinburgh, lived her life within the clammy stone walls of the university—for all the good it had done her.

'Two of your lemon ices, please.'

Galena watched the vendor's face as Beauden leaned closer to take the scooped ices. People seemed to notice Beauden's differences in spite of the carefully applied greasepaint and the impeccable attention to his appearance.

'Thank you.' Beauden handed one ice to Galena and dropped a shilling into the vendor's hand, a generous bonus.

He got a dour, 'Thank ye, sir,' in response.

'So, why medicine?'

They turned along the path, the lake glistening at their right, and shady copse enveloped them.

Galena shrugged, at a loss to put her compulsion into words. Her hand moved of its own volition to grasp the tiny copper Rod of Asclepius that hung at her side.

'Ever since I can remember, I've been intrigued by science, especially that of the human body. I used to slip blades and bottles from my father's surgery to catch insects and small creatures—I'd pretend they were my patients and nurse them. Mother's plants never lived very long as I had a penchant for dissecting and sewing their parts back together. As I got older and could understand the Latin, I spent hours secretly reading Father's medical journals in my bed when the house had gone to sleep.'

'So it is a calling for you?'

'Oh yes. My father had an extensive practice in York. Not among the gentry, but more the middle sort, and he spent some time in the charity hospital. His passion was contagious. It kindled in me a desire to solve the puzzles that medicine posed. However,

46

as I began to assist him, I saw not diagnoses or problems to be solved, but people to be healed.'

She glanced at him ruefully. 'I'm sorry. I run on like fiddlesticks when I get excited.'

His smile was as radiant as the sunrise after a stormy night—bright, bold and clear. 'I like it, the fact that you care so very deeply. Isn't that what a medical calling should be?'

'Thank you.'

'Where did you acquire your Rod of Asclepius?'

'It was my father's. Mama gave it to him when he first opened his practice. When he passed away, and I chose medicine, she gave it to me. I wear it often.'

She held the ancient symbol and, sighing, traced her finger over the single snake that twisted around the ancient staff.

'You miss them.'

'I do. But I have a wonderful opportunity here.' She armed herself with a smile. 'Will you tell me about yourself?'

He looked away and a little of his warmth dissipated. 'There is little to tell.'

He gestured at their surroundings, encompassing the children at play around them. 'This was not my childhood. I seldom came to the park, and running was impossible. By the time I was ten, a gentle walk exhausted me. My parents made the house a haven and I spent my time with them. I was forever in Father's workshop.'

'Did you assist him with the heart?'

He laughed. 'Oh no, Galena. I was still a child, though I do make things now and again to assist those who need it.'

'Such as?'

He cast a glance in her direction. 'Did you hear, last year, of an artificial leg discovered at Capua? Some believe it was made around the time of Alexander the Great.'

'Yes, of course. It was much discussed at the university.'

'There have been such devices made for centuries. I remember reading Pliny's account of such a one, but of late, science has been improving, perfecting ...'

'You are referring to the work of Ambroise?'

'And others like him. There is a fellow in London called Bly—

'

She caught up his hand, stopped still. 'Is that what you do? Help those who have lost limbs to amputation?'

He nodded. 'Where I can. I understand, you see. Although my prosthesis is internal, invisible to most, the similarity is very real.'

'You make devices, but you are not medically trained?'

'For what I do, I do not need to be. I work on the engineering aspect, trying to balance flexibility and function. Happily, I've a sponsor, a Viennese merchant whose son lost his left arm when the bones were crushed. He considers himself a patron of sorts and sends funds as well as such materials as I request.'

He stopped and held his hand out in front of him. 'There are twenty-seven bones in this hand, Galena, and muscles, tendons, nerves. With our poor science, we cannot hope to emulate the design of such a masterpiece, but there is a vast difference between the rudimentary hook of the past and what we can yet achieve. I am looking at creating gears and miniature pulleys to replicate some of the functions.'

She took the hand he held out and wrapped her fingers around it. They continued walking, hand in hand. She felt a kinship with him, a shared wish to make others' lives better, happier; to do what lay in their power to banish the misery that follows after illness as night follows day.

'It is a calling for you too?'

He nodded. 'There is so much I cannot do, you see. I've never been to school or travelled beyond Edinburgh.'

He gestured again at the children. 'I've never played cricket like those lads or danced with a lady. But I've been given a precious gift, and that is to know that life is fragile. If I can make a difference, then the debt of love and care my parents left me will be discharged.'

He lifted a brow. 'Would you care to see some of my work?'

'May I? That would be wonderful.' She may have seen his body, but his willingness to share his work with her was a truer communion.

A shout and a shrill ringing sounded behind her.

Beauden glanced over his shoulder and clasped her to him, swinging her round against his chest as a cycle whizzed past in a cloud of steam. It careened around a bend in the path where more shouts could be heard from the walkers ahead of them.

Galena, however, was quite disinterested in the antics of a daredevil cyclist on account of experiencing mild fascination at being caught up in a pair of strong, gentle arms. She had misunderstood his thinness when she had seen his naked chest and had assumed that he would be relatively weak. Instead, his sinews were made of whipcord, his muscles banded steel wire.

She gazed up at his face, her view suddenly arrested by the tinted glasses. She wished for an instant that she could see those marvellous, expressive eyes.

He contrived to put a little distance between them while keeping her in his arms. 'You are unhurt?'

'Completely, thank you.'

'Well, well.'

The despised, pretentious tone lanced through Galena, and she turned, Beauden's arm still around her, to face her enemy.

**

Galena had been tense in Beauden's arms—hardly an improbable consequence of almost being run down by a steam cycle—but when the tall, pleasant-faced and fashionably dressed gentleman drawled out his greeting, she stiffened like a starched collar.

Sensing danger and feeling the effects of his recent physical exertion, Beauden quickly swallowed a pill. In less than a second, he felt the increase of oxygen in his veins, the surge in alertness and vigour. His blood fizzed like champagne.

Galena looked through the man in front of them and did not acknowledge his presence. She was formal and stiff. The bright and confident woman who had shared her dreams with him vanished like steam.

'Shall we go, Mr Somerton? The afternoon grows ... unpleasant.'

The man moved directly into her path. 'Won't you bid me farewell, Miss Tindale? After all, we are unlikely to meet again.'

'On the contrary, Mr Forsythe'—her words snapped like dry twigs—'I shall be there bright and early tomorrow morning to continue my studies. Nothing will keep me from it.'

'Oh, come now. We both know you will never graduate. What would be the point? You will simply waste any knowledge you might gain on raising children and taking tea with real doctors' wives.'

Beauden gently slid his arm from Galena and stepped in front of her, standing with feet apart, both hands resting on the head of his cane. He addressed the fellow quietly, his voice low and only marginally courteous.

'I am afraid, sir, that I do not have the pleasure of your acquaintance.'

He heard Galena draw breath at his back.

'Merrick Forsythe.' The fellow put out a hand.

Beauden ignored it. 'I understand you were present when Miss Tindale gave her presentation this morning?'

Forsythe smirked. 'I was indeed.'

Beauden smiled grimly. 'You are very fortunate then. One day, you will tell your grandchildren that you were present at the birth of a remarkable medical breakthrough.'

Forsythe guffawed. 'Never happen, old man.'

Beauden tapped his fingers on the head of his walking stick. 'Yes, quite right. For it presupposes you are able to find a woman willing to take on an ass like you—and that you have the manhood to beget children.'

'You basta—'

Forsythe froze at the sight of the naked sword in Beauden's right hand, the walking stick sheath in his left.

'I suggest that you apologise to Miss Tindale, sincerely and in some haste, and then leave.' He raised the tip of the sword higher.

Forsythe took a single step backwards, chin high, fists clenched. 'I apologise, Miss Tindale.'

'You were discourteous.'

'I was discourteous.' The words were bitten off.

'It won't happen again.'

Forsythe's lips pressed together. He looked at Galena, then at Beauden as if daring him to strike.

'I bid you good day.' Forsythe turned and walked away.

Beauden drove the sword into its sheath, wishing it were lodged somewhere else.

Galena put a hand to her head. 'Oh, my word! I can't believe you threatened him with a sword.'

'You would prefer I permit him to insult you?' He was stiff with anger that a man would speak so to a lady, much less this lady.

She shook her head. 'He is arrogant and pompous, but he is clever. And he thinks he is God's gift to the medical fraternity.'

Beauden took Galena's arm. He would have preferred to hold her to his chest, but it was a public park and she had known him for only six hours, or thereabouts. Still …

'Shall we find Jimmy and return home? Don't concern yourself about that fool. We will see that he doesn't trouble you anymore.'

She looked at him in wonder. 'Can you do that?'

'Oh yes, Galena. We can do that.' It would be a pleasure, Beauden reflected. An absolute pleasure.

***

The gentleman sat in his well-appointed rooms, mirror messenger in hand.

Drumming thick shapely fingers on the arm of his chair, he swore. He had received several messages tonight—good information was worth every penny—and each one had chilled him to the bone, none more so than the last. Few people knew that Beauden lived, fewer still knew of his infirmity, and a mere handful knew how close he stood to the grave.

He went to the side table where he poured whisky into a glass and then swirled it endlessly.

One might be justified in thinking a mere zephyr could topple

Beauden over the brink, but no! It seemed that Augustus Somerton's one wish might finally come true. And from such a quarter! A medical student, a female one at that, tinkering with a long-outdated, discredited joke of medical research from the turn of the century. Bachvarov!

He swallowed the dram in one gulp and hurled the glass into the heart of the fireplace. It shattered like his expectations.

The messages were startling—Augustus intended to make one last attempt to preserve the existence of his walking experiment. Not to save his son's life, for it had been fifteen years since there had been a beating heart within Beauden Somerton's chest. His father had cut it out with his own hands and put a monstrosity in its place. Beauden had been dead for fifteen years.

What to do?

The gentleman grabbed the poker and shoved at the shards of glass in the dead hearth. Perhaps justice would prevail and Beauden would go to his rest unassisted.

But Augustus had acquired a new ally, and now called on his brother's aid.

A cold hand clutched at his vitals. What if Augustus succeeded? It did not bear contemplating.

Alone with his fears, the gentleman poured another glass of whisky and sipped it, tracing the rim with one finger, contemplatively. He would do what he must.

Chapter 5

Galena slowly climbed the stairs to her small flat. It was not in the most salubrious part of town, but at least she didn't fear for her life or virtue if she went out after dusk.

As she was not hungry, she contented herself with setting her small kettle on the hob and toasting the end crust of a loaf in front of the grill.

The events of the day washed over her—her body exhausted but her mind travelling at the speed of a double furnace steam engine. Fear, anger and a sense of relief ricocheted through her. Was it luck or fate that had pushed her away from the cruel taunts of her classmates and in front of Beauden Somerton's carriage?

Bright copper-coloured eyes flitted through her memory.

Dr Somerton was a genius, and the prospect of working with him in any capacity made her tremble, but he was not the one she thought of most. She had met a man who ought not exist. And her ideas—the ones she had imagined and tested and written up here in this room—would be instrumental in saving him. Her goal was no longer simply to graduate as a doctor, or even to prove that a woman could be as fine a physician as any man—her intent was to keep Beauden Somerton alive.

She found herself in a unique position. When she began her research, it was the mental challenge that enthralled her most—the logic of Bachvarov's research. But after meeting Beauden—walking with him, talking with him—she was faced with more than an academic challenge. She had a role to play, and the stakes were high.

She contemplated all that Dr Somerton had related—the plans, the dull shadow of the metal heart in Beauden's chest, the evidence of deterioration in his body. With the doctor, she had felt confident, but now, alone in her room, doubts and fears assailed her.

She had been invited to return to the Somertons' tomorrow afternoon and had intended to spend this evening going over her researches. But right now, her head spun.

The sweet smell of the tea in her cup was a potent lure, but even that could not calm her, and she found herself mindlessly pacing the floor. Stopping at her window, she clenched her fingers tightly around the sill and stared out at nothing. The day had contained all manner of strong emotion, but the reaction uppermost in her mind was a kind of giddy hope. She could not settle to any task, not writing notes of the day or reading *The Mysteries of Udolpho*, which until now had commanded her attention.

Finally, as the sun sank below the chimney pots of the row opposite, she rinsed out her stockings, hung them over the basin, washed and went to bed. She had expected to lay awake, fretting and tossing like a ship at anchor, but surprisingly, between one thought and the next, she fell asleep.

She tossed and turned. A hundred ideas flooded her synapses

and whirled gaily around her brain. Then she was falling. A hundred jeering students around her, their black academic robes flapping like the wings of vampire bats. Copper suns morphed into copper eyes, cogs large and small pumped ink through a golden heart, and then—with a boom so loud it woke her from her fraught sleep—the heart exploded in a gory, golden mess.

She jerked awake, an iron vice clamped around her lungs.

From between the dingy curtains, she could see the sky was grey, so close to midsummer that it could be four o'clock or even earlier. She lay down again and shut her eyes, but sleep would not come. Instead, the golden heart from her dream crept into her semiconscious mind, her vision slipping through the latticework and into the structure itself. The chest cavity was gold, gleaming as though polished. Among the whirring cogs, tissue samples from her failed experiment were threaded and bound by golden rings. Blood, clear as glass, pumped smoothly through the four chambers.

Hand shaking, Galena swung out of bed and flipped open her favourite notebook. She picked up her steel-nibbed pen and dipped it into the ink reservoir, pressing the filler valve. And then she began to sketch. Under her hand, a typical diagram of a four-chambered heart emerged but with subtle additions.

After an hour, Galena straightened her back and gazed out the window. The sky was light now, but the only sounds were the rumblings of carter's wagons.

Once Galena's concept was safely on the page, she coloured the parts of the assembled heart that were not gold, but instead, were tissue from a swine's heart, like the organ she had attempted to present to her peers.

When Galena wiped the pen nib for the last time and packed the coloured inks away, the streets had begun to bustle. She left the book open at the window to allow the ink to dry and went to dress.

She chose her prettiest walking dress, frothy frills of pink lace peeking out from beneath the coffee-brown ruffles of the linen gown. Vanity did not influence her. No. Nor did she feel the need to look well in front of a handsome young man. She simply needed to feel confident and assured, and the gown would help. As she hooked her copper Rod of Asclepius to her corset and checked her appearance in the mirror, a smile flickered over her lips.

Finally, she put up her hair and pinned her confection of a hat in place. She was tired of dressing plainly. Perhaps subconsciously she had believed that doing so would make her presence somehow acceptable to her peers. Well, no more! She would dress as she liked.

Slipping her notebook into her bag alongside her study notes, she picked up her door key, but as she stepped through her door onto the small landing beyond, her foot trod in a slick wet patch. A small puddle of dark red blood congealed on the landing.

Looking up, she clapped a hand to her mouth as her stomach turned over. A pig's heart, still dripping gore, had been pinned to her door, a scalpel rammed through it.

It took all her strength to pull the scalpel from the door. At first, she considered leaving it there and showing her landlady, but she couldn't bear the thought of explaining. Instead, she wrapped the heart, found a basin and half a bottle of vinegar, methodically poured it onto the stain, and then sponged.

Her stomach churned, the horror combined with the sickly smell threatening to overcome her. But she gritted her teeth and called up the image of a grinning Forsythe. That was enough to spur her on.

It took almost half an hour to sop up the blood, and a good deal longer for her own heart to stop pounding, her hands to stop shaking. An icy rage filled her. If Merrick Forsythe thought he could frighten her away, then he was much mistaken.

Not surprisingly, Galena was late arriving at the medical school. Olive stood waiting for her, her face lighting up despite the teeth pressed into her lower lip.

'Galena, I'm so pleased!' She slipped a hand through Galena's arm, speeding up to keep pace with her. 'I wondered ...'

'If I were coming back?'

'Yesterday was so terrible. No one would be surprised if you didn't make it.'

'Yesterday was the best day of my life.'

They slipped into the back of the lecture theatre to sit with the other girls. Old Birdlaw gave them a withering look, but then ig-nored them—at least until the end of the lecture. He stopped her as she made her way to the door.

'Miss Tindale, the dean has asked that you attend him in his office.'

Olive gave her a terrified look.

Galena screwed her courage to the sticking place. 'I will see you tomorrow, Olive.'

'Will you be all right?'

'Yes, of course.' Galena squeezed her friend's hand and hurried away, heart in mouth.

It was a long, gloomy, walk to the dean's office. His study, like her headmistress' parlour at boarding school, was not a place that Galena aspired to visit. She knocked and slipped in.

'You sent for me, sir?'

'Yes, Miss Tindale. Please take a seat.'

She perched on the edge of the chair and glanced around. Gleaming walnut furniture and more books than she could count in a lifetime lined the walls. An old-fashioned globe and a perpetual motion machine, bright with brass cogs, sat side by side in the corner. The Reverend Dr Hopwood was at least as old as Moses with long silver hair hanging over his robe like thin silk ribbons. She wished the elegant frippery on her head was a dowdy black bonnet—he would never take her seriously.

He looked at her over horn-rimmed spectacles. 'I assume that your presentation yesterday did not turn out the way you had hoped.'

'No, sir.'

'Nothing in your thorough notes suggested we might expect your exhibit to explode.'

'I was as surprised as anyone, sir.'

He picked up an automatic quill and tapped it lightly. 'Oh, I very much doubt that.'

'Sir?' Her voice rose half an octave. Surely he did not think ...

'Someone, Miss Tindale, was not at all surprised to see your specimen destroyed.' He waited patiently for her to catch his meaning.

'I suppose not, sir.'

'No indeed. There have been rumours. Someone went to a great deal of trouble to bring your work to naught.' The dean put the pen down and shook his head. 'I am deeply saddened to see such prejudice among my students, unwilling to accept excellent research because of misguided ideas about the researcher. Folly!'

She breathed a huge sigh. 'Thank you, sir.'

The dean looked at her directly. 'I will admit, Miss Tindale, to my great shame, that I was not in favour of accepting ladies as students. But I have been extremely impressed with the abilities of each of our female pupils and the way in which you have conducted yourselves. I think that when the time comes you and the other young ladies will be admirable doctors.

'Now, someone is trying to put your future—and potentially the future of the other female students—in jeopardy. I have my suspicions about who that might be, but tell me, Miss Tindale, can you think of anyone whose behaviour has caused you concern?'

Galena twisted her hands in her lap. Really, what choice did she have? She still felt sick from the discovery this morning. And who could say if Forsythe was done with his malevolent pranks?

'There is one, sir. Mr Forsythe has been quite uncivil. Even threatening. And this morning, I heard a thud on my door, very early. I thought it had been part of my dream, but when I left my flat, I found a fresh pig's heart pinned to my door, sir. They'd used a scalpel.'

'Good gracious me! That is quite appalling.' He leaned towards her. 'Was there anything that would enable you to put a name to the miscreant?'

'No, sir. I'm afraid not.'

'Well. That cannot be allowed to happen again. I will speak with the faculty. And the police.'

The dean drew a letter from under his blotter.

'On a more pleasant note, I received this last night from an old friend, Dr Augustus Somerton. I understand you have made his acquaintance. He has expressed an interest in your work and has offered to act as a mentor given that you are interested in many of the same fields. After what transpired this morning, I should like to reply to Dr Somerton and suggest he invite you to visit while you are his pupil. What do you say?'

'Oh, sir, I could not put the doctor to so much trouble or intrude on his family.'

'On the contrary, Miss Tindale, Augustus would be delighted to have you. It would make it so much more convenient for you both and it would relieve my mind as to your safety.'

Her heart raced. 'Sir, what is there to say? It would be an honour to work with Dr Somerton.'

'Then, may I suggest that you take two or three days leave from the university. Please send a message to Dr Somerton at this address when you are ready to leave today. He has placed his carriage at your disposal and asks that you call on him at your leisure.'

He handed her a folded slip of paper and stood. 'Let those who are against you believe they have won. I will deal with them in time.'

Galena rose, but then paused. 'Sir, if I may?'

'Yes?'

'The other girls. Will something be done to assure their safety?'

The dean looked at her benevolently. 'Your thoughts do you credit. Most of the female students are living with family members. Only one is not—Miss Mansell. I will have my wife invite her to stay with us for a short while. Then we can both rest easily.'

Leaving the office, Galena strode briskly to the forecourt, where unicarriages set down and retrieved their passengers, and took out her palm-sized writing mirror. She inscribed her message in black wax on the silvered glass surface, closed the lid and pressed the lever. Bluish-silver light flashed from the rim of the device. Galena gave it two firm taps with her fingers, and the burnt residue of the flash paper fell free and blew away.

It seemed only minutes until a familiar unicarriage pulled up in front of her and the driver jumped down.

'Thank you, Jimmy.'

'Nah trouble, Miss Galena. Are ye going back to the house? Only, the doctor has been called down to the clinic.'

She considered. Dr Somerton had yet to invite her stay; it

would be presumptuous to go home and pack.

'I don't know what I should do.'

Jimmy rubbed his nose. 'Master Beauden said he would be at his workshop. He asked to know if ye were wishful of goin' there for a spell.'

She smiled. 'Oh. That would be wonderful. By all means, I would love to see Mr Somerton's workshop.'

A huge grin split Jimmy's freckled face and he nodded. 'It's reely summat.'

He assisted her into the unicarriage and put up the step, shutting the door after her. Within seconds they were off, trotting along narrow lanes and up Leith Walk.

Alone and with time to think for the first time that morning, Galena felt curiously ambivalent. The dean was inclined to favour her view of things. With him guarding her back, as it were, it would be difficult for those against her to act. But not impossible.

There mere possibility of staying with Dr Somerton and his intriguing son was almost enough to push the horrors of this morning from her conscious mind. It really was the most stunning opportunity. True, it was not exactly learning, but she could assist him and still prepare for her examinations. What troubled her was that it was necessary. Wanting to heal the sick was not a crime, no matter her sex. It was the nineteenth century for heaven's sake, and the greatest nation on earth was ruled over by a woman. When would her sex be free from the oppressive control of men and their petty tyrannies?

They drove past the street where the Somerton residence sat

behind its grey wall and continued on towards the docks. When Jimmy brought the unicarriage to a hissing, juddering halt, she pulled back the red velvet curtain and saw they were in a warehouse area in the street behind the main dockside. Many of the buildings were of wooden construction with massive doors for loading goods. The one Jimmy led her to was smaller than the others and made mostly of stone.

He pulled back the oak door, banded and studded with so much copper that it looked like solid metal. Inside, the single room was no more than fifteen feet wide, but was at least three times as long and divided into work areas. Against the right wall, a staircase rose to the upper level. The first storey was as wide as the ground floor but not as deep. At the far end of the long room, a forge glowed white-hot. The floor was old stone, pitted and gouged, as were the walls. Galena would have imagined that a room made of bare stone would be chilly, but between the heat from the forge and the steam turbine chugging away under the stair, the room was pleasantly warm.

Beauden sat at a broad desk, butted against the left wall. Another table sat beside him and one behind, all covered in paper and pieces of metal paraphernalia. Beyond him, a tall man with black curly hair, wearing a simple loose shirt with a drawstring neck and a large leather apron, made minute adjustments to a gleaming copper cylinder. It was not until Galena looked closer that she realised the contraption was a leg and foot, hinged and jointed like medieval armour.

'Goodness me!'

This was not a workshop—it was a cave of wonders!

Chapter 6

Beauden turned at the sound of Galena's voice. She stood in a patch of bright sunlight pouring through the upper window and stared towards the beams that ran through the double height space. He had been looking forward to this moment since he first mentioned this place to her. Was it truly only yesterday? When she had spoken of the false limb recovered in Capua, he had known even then that she would be as excited as he, that she would drink up the sights, the sounds, the opportunity and hope that his workshop represented.

The wonder on her face was all he might have hoped to see. In a way, he felt more exposed here than he had when he'd bared his body for her examination. Now, he bared his soul, his *raison d'etre*.

Quickly, he put down the diagram he held, set a large cog on it as a paperweight and made his way over to her. Galena looked at him with bright eyes.

'Back in an hour, sir?'

'No, Jimmy. We will be having a guest for lunch, so once I have shown Miss Tindale over the workshop, you can take us home.'

He tipped his hat. 'Verra good. I'll go fill up the reservoir then.'

Beauden offered Galena his arm. She looked radiant, her walking dress made from crisp linen, the colour of ground coffee, and in the ruffles and flounces of the skirt were miles of rose-pink lace, the colour of which matched her cheeks. Yesterday she had been sharp and cool; today she was as sweet as chocolate ice cream, and when she spoke, her voice held a thrum of excitement.

'So this is your domain?'

'It is indeed. I took over the lease three years ago. Before that, I had used part of Father's workshop, but I needed the forge and more space than he could afford me.'

'I didn't realise that it would be so comprehensive.' She nodded and looked around. 'I never imagined you would have people working for you.'

'Oh yes. I started with Will Ayre, he is Jimmy's brother, and then Cain came to work the forge. Now, we have clients come from all over the British Isles and the Low Countries.'

'It is quite small for so complex an endeavour.'

'It is indeed. Most warehouses in the area were designed with storage in mind, but while we keep materials onsite, each piece we make is either unique or adapted to its wearer, so we do not need to store finished products.'

'Will you introduce me to your employees?'

'Of course. Although, I think of them more as family. Will, is my chief engineer. He started out doing the smithing, but he has considerable mechanical skill. And his sister, and Jimmy's, keeps the files and orders organised. This is her now. Judith, this is Miss Tindale, a medical student at the university.'

Judith bobbed her head. 'Pleased to meet you, miss.'

Galena smiled and shook the young woman's outstretched hand.

Leaving Judith behind, they walked towards the stone forge at the rear of the workshop where a man clad in little more than a leather vest worked a glowing piece of metal.

'This is Cain. His father was a blacksmith, but his elder brother inherited the family forge. Cain isn't much of a conversationalist.'

As Beauden made the introductions, Galena held out her hand. Cain put down his heavy tongs and took her hand gingerly, though only for a second.

'Ma'am.'

They turned away from the forge. 'And I also employ Mr Samuels and Marian, his apprentice.'

Galena's eyes lit up. 'You employ a woman to make prosthetics?'

'Is that so surprising? Marian has been here for over a year. Samuels asked me to give her the opportunity when her mother passed away—it was that or the workhouse. As there is a great deal of fine work for a cogsmith, it would have been wrong of me not to take her on. Plus, Samuels pointed out that he isn't getting any younger, and the sort of work we do takes time to learn.'

She glanced poignantly at the little redhead. 'I'm just so pleased that you are willing to employ a girl in such a significant role.'

He could see the cogs in her mind spinning.

'But, surely there is not sufficient work for five people. Is there such a demand for prosthetic limbs?'

He frowned, nodding. 'Many people, for one reason or another, are deprived of a limb. Quite apart from simple accidents, we've been fully occupied in the last few years, trying to help men who suffered from the medical butchers in the Crimea.'

'Of course. But surely the army takes care of them?'

'I wish they did. Take Will as an example.'

Beauden gestured as Will, seated at the bench, set down the copper limb on a padded surface and walked across the room. Galena's eyes grew wide when she noticed the wood-and-steel prosthesis on the lower part of Will's left leg.

'He lost that at Balaclava and was lucky to come home at all. Even then, he had nothing.' He beckoned and raised his voice. 'Will, come and meet Miss Tindale.'

Will crossed the floor with the merest hint of a limp and held out a hand to Galena. 'Miss Tindale.'

'It's a pleasure to meet you.' Galena smiled at Will.

'I was just telling Miss Tindale about how we met.'

Will scratched the back of his head. 'When I came back from the war, I was no good for any work, so I came to stay with Jimmy. He went to Dr Somerton to see if he could help, but it was Beauden who managed to put a workable leg together, one that could move. And after that, I just stayed.'

'Would you say it was destiny, Will?' Beauden gave him a genial grin.

'Aye, that's what it was. Destiny knew you needed the help, so she pointed a ruddy great cannon at me. Pardon the language, miss.'

'Will's prosthesis is one of my earliest attempts. We've made a thousand since that are far better, but Will refuses to part with it.'

Will turned lambent brown eyes on Galena and gave her a wide smile. 'I'm well enough, miss. But before the war, I was a white-smith, you see, making railings and balustrades for houses, so I know my way around metal.'

'How is the new mechanism coming, Will?'

'It works pretty smoothly. I want to tighten up some of the gears in the ankle assembly.'

'Good man. I won't be in for the rest of the day, so once you're happy with that piece, have Judith send a mirror message to the client. He needs to come in for the final fitting.'

Will nodded and, with a courteous dip of the head to Galena, went back to his desk.

'The new leg gave Will his purpose back. And it worked quite well for such an early attempt, so we made others for returned soldiers who couldn't afford any better. Over time, we refined our designs and polished our skills. We've become quite good at what we do.'

Galena smiled up at him. 'It's given you just as much. Everyone needs to make a contribution to his fellow man. So, the work evolved naturally? You didn't set out to make prostheses?'

'Never. But you are right. It's been a blessing for us all.'

'I'm glad.' She reached over and squeezed his hand.

As Beauden had suspected, Galena prowled the length of the workshop, enquiring into everything. She spent several minutes in conversation with Marian, black head bent close to copper curls, over the work she had at hand.

As they returned to the front of the workshop, Beauden stood, feeling awkward, beside the chaos that was his desk. 'May I show you something?'

'What is it?'

'This is my bold new experiment.' He tried to keep the excitement from his voice, but it was a hopeless task.

Galena leaned forward and inspected the gleaming hand he had been tinkering with.

He had hung it from thin strands of sheep gut that he'd connected to a frame, giving the impression that it floated in mid-air. The fingers were minutely jointed, though the cog mechanisms standing in place of a knuckle or phalange were visible in places. It was essentially an empty gauntlet. From where the wrist should be, copper wires as thin as silk ran to copper dots that covered the surface of a black leather glove laying on a leather pad a foot away.

Galena's eyes stroked the gilded digits in a way that left Beauden drowning in a pool of envy.

'It is beautiful, but you wouldn't have gone to all this trouble to make something impractical. What does it do?'

Beauden grinned wider. 'I hope to one day employ some of Father's knowledge and connect these copper fibres to human nerves.'

'No!'

'Absolutely. It would be an amazing achievement, to integrate human and metal so completely. It is a dream, but not an impossible one.'

He slipped his fingers into the glove and gave an experimental wiggle. Suspended in its frame, the hand danced.

'Do that again!'

Again, Beauden opened and closed his hand, wiggled each finger individually and then at the same time, then clenched his fist.

'May I try?'

It was a pleasure to watch her. She was astonished, of course, but she quickly grasped the principle of the copper threads. With every appearance of regret, she slipped off the glove.

'It is a technological wonder. What makes it work?'

Beauden picked up the hand and tapped the dorsal area. A small square of copper popped open, exposing the intricate marvel of tight cogs and miniscule pulleys.

'It's truly breathtaking.'

She spoke in hushed tones, as though she considered herself to be in the presence of some miracle. That she valued his work so highly was like ambrosia to his soul.

Beauden felt the faint whisperings of dizziness and steadied himself against the desk. Galena's presence took his breath away. His physical responses to her proximity—his shorter breaths, the clenching of his diaphragm, not to mention the rush of blood to somewhere other than his brain—took their toll. A sharp jolt in his chest warned him that a spasm was imminent.

He slipped one of his pills under his tongue surreptitiously, waited a few seconds for it to work, and looked down at his watch. The medication was becoming less effective, the spasms taking longer to subside, and only delayed the inevitable. Why now? Why in Hell's name now, when paradise was almost in his grasp?

'I promise to explain it as we go'—he offered his arm and turned away from the hand—'but my uncle is coming for lunch and we should not be late.'

Galena took one last lingering look at the artificial hand and then took his arm. 'I suppose we must go.'

'You know, you can come back at any time. We can always find work for you to do.'

'Thank you. I might take you at your word.' She studied him closely and frowned. 'Are you quite well?'

Her fingers slipped to his wrist, and although their lightness on his skin was delightful, he pulled away.

'Yes indeed.'

'Your pulse is erratic, and your eyes—'

'Truly, Galena, I'm quite well. We should go.'

He hadn't meant to sound so abrupt, but his spirit was staging an insurrection. He didn't need a medical degree to understand what his own body was telling him—his time was getting short. The decay of the iron heart progressed more each day. The iron leaching into his blood was his enemy and the final battle would soon be won. In the meantime, he didn't want Galena studying the progression of his disease, or to have her fingers flitting over his pulse, treating him like a patient when he wanted to be so much more.

Beauden put on his glasses and pulled the brim of his hat low.

Jimmy opened the door of the unicarriage and looked hard at Beauden. His lips parted as if to speak, but Beauden countered his look, and Jimmy turned away silently, grim-faced.

'How was your lecture today?'

Galena shrugged. 'It was interesting enough. But I didn't pay complete attention.'

'Daydreaming in class, Miss Tindale?'

'I wish I had been. Afterwards, the dean requested a meeting.'

The unicarriage yawed into a corner and Beauden found himself pressed more sharply against her.

'Why? Not bad news, I hope?'

'No.' She turned her face to his, lit by the bright gleam of a smile. 'He believes someone sabotaged my presentation. And he intends to write to your father.'

'He often does. They are old friends. Is it about your work?'

Nibbling at her lip, she looked pensive. 'Yes. Your father has offered to mentor me. And Dean Hopwood plans to ask if I might stay under your roof for a while.'

'My father will welcome you with open arms. Does it have anything to do with the damage done to your presentation?'

'Yes. And there was an … incident this morning. Someone left a warning on the front door of my flat.'

His stomach lurched. 'That bastard—I beg your pardon—in

the park yesterday? Or another?'

She closed her eyes and shook her head. 'I cannot say.'

Beauden gripped her hand, its warmth reaching him despite their gloves. 'I formally extend an invitation to our home, Galena.'

Her eyes leapt up to meet his. 'Thank you. I accept gratefully. You are very kind.'

'Excellent.'

The pang had left his chest now and the rush of oxygen was singing in his blood. His spirits soared.

'Then perhaps, after lunch, you can take Jimmy and a maid and gather your things. I will doubtless be resting, and whenever Uncle Jacob visits, he and Father disappear into the library to sip port and trade stories.'

'Do you see much of your uncle?'

He shook his head and shrugged. 'He comes up at Christmas, of course, and in the hunting season we often see him. But Uncle loves London and thinks that Edinburgh is full of border raiders and shaggy savages in kilts.'

Galena laughed. 'I look forward to meeting him.'

Beauden glanced out the window and grinned. 'I don't think you will be waiting long.'

He gestured above to where a maroon-and-gold-striped dirigible slowly lost altitude directly in their path. 'I'll lay you any money this is him now.'

Chapter 7

Jimmy did not drive into the courtyard but stopped outside the gate. The dirigible was perhaps eighty feet overhead, far above the local rooftops. As Galena allowed Beauden to usher her through the broad gate, a guide rope dropped into the yard.

Perkins took up the thin cord and hauled down the steel-and-rubber cable, firmly anchoring the end hook to the massive iron ring in the corner of the courtyard. He gave a broad wave and stepped back.

The visitor, a mere shape in dark colours, hurtled down the anchor chain. Galena clapped a hand to her mouth, horrified. Ten feet from the end of the line, the man abruptly ceased his fall from the heavens. The rope tensed and he lowered himself the last few feet, landing softly in the yard and raising a tiny cloud of dust.

'Uncle Jacob!' Beauden took several brisk steps forward and laid a hand on his uncle's shoulder.

Mr Jacob Somerton was shorter than Beauden, with close-cropped, jet-black hair, and a strong nose and brow. His jawline held a hint of softness and humour, and he had a dimple in the centre of his clean-shaven chin.

'Beauden!' Mr Somerton looked Beauden up and down and slapped a hearty hand on his shoulder. 'Heavens, my boy, you've gotten taller! Reach up a hand would you and grab my trunk.'

Beauden threw a humorous glance up at the dirigible. 'Your jokes haven't gotten any better, Uncle.'

He held out a hand to Galena. 'I'd like to present Miss Tindale, who will be staying with us for the near future. Galena, my uncle, Jacob Somerton.'

Galena reached out a hand and Mr Somerton enveloped it in a warm, strong grip. She met his welcoming expression. He was younger, perhaps stronger, and certainly livelier than Dr Somerton and Beauden, and there seemed much to like about him.

His slate-grey eyes twinkled. 'But how charming!'

'Brother!'

Dr Somerton appeared as they entered the front hall, and he wrapped the newcomer in his arms. He was dressed informally in breeches and shirtsleeves, and, in the less structured garments, Galena noticed at once the sparseness of his frame. It should not have surprised her. He was a man approaching sixty who, no doubt, had too little exercise to maintain his muscle. She had also noted a thickening of the knuckles and a slight hesitation in using his hands. Was that the reason he needed her assistance?

'You are looking well, Augustus.' Mr Somerton looked up at the stained-glass window, a flicker of emotion crossing his face as he did so. 'Ah, that image never fails to delight me. Myra is still watching over you, Augustus. And over Beauden. He looks more like her every day.'

'He does, indeed. Come in, Jacob.'

Dr Somerton smiled at Galena. 'Miss Tindale, welcome back. I have received a message from the dean and I would be delighted to invite you to stay. Please treat our home as your own.'

'You are too kind, Doctor.'

'Not at all.' He offered her his arm and the other men fell in behind. 'I am planning to exploit your presence in the house for my own gain, work your fingers to the bone and abuse your intelligence most shamefully.'

'Disgraceful, brother,' Mr Somerton chided. 'You may call on me at any time, Miss Tindale. I will rescue you from his despicable clutches.'

Galena's heart lifted at their banter. She had not seen this side of the doctor.

'You are all too good, gentlemen.'

Dr Somerton and Beauden were warmth and graciousness personified. Mr Jacob Somerton had all their charisma and more, in his brilliant smile, his laughing eyes, and the smooth, urbane magnetism of his persona.

Galena fixed a gay smile to her lips. She was safe here, and warmly welcomed, with a chance to learn and develop her skills. It seemed as if all her problems were over.

***

As they entered the conservatory, Beauden's father escorted Galena to the chesterfields and sat opposite her. Uncle Jacob stood before Galena, indicating the empty place at her side.

'May I?'

She smiled. 'Of course, Mr Somerton.'

She took the tiny crystal glass of dry sherry from the tray Perkins placed at her elbow and took a taste. 'Do you come to Edinburgh often?'

Beauden sat beside his father. 'Not as often as we would like, Galena.'

He couldn't resist the opportunity to call her by her Christian name in his uncle's presence, stake the claim of intimacy. Beauden knew a positively shameful jealousy.

Uncle smiled at him, a glint in his eye. 'I take it, Miss Tindale, that your … friendship … with my nephew is of some duration.'

Galena kept her cool. 'We find we have much in common, sir.'

'Well, that is wonderful.'

He turned to address Beauden's father. 'Your mirror message came yesterday, Augustus, and I set a few enquiries in train before I took off from Hampstead. Of course I will help. Just say the word.'

'Can you acquire the gold mixture I need?'

Uncle Jacob flipped open a leather-bound notebook with a brass cog set in the front and read from it. '"Fifty-eight percent pure gold with silver, copper and zinc admixtures in specified proportions." I take it you are trying to strengthen the gold.'

'I must. I might as well make the new heart out of silk as out of pure gold—it is just as pliable. Will you encounter any problems?'

Beauden's uncle took another sip of sherry and crossed one leg over the other. 'I have found only one fellow who has the skill to work in the silver. Copper and zinc, yes, but silver is less common. It is quite a unique blend, in fact. He will take a week or two, and then I shall have it flown up.'

Galena leaned forward, her brows drawn. 'Doctor, will a mixture containing copper and zinc be safe? The current heart ...'

Beauden's father nodded. 'In a gold mixture, the other elements will not be free to migrate into the blood stream.'

Uncle Jacob threw Galena a quizzical glance. 'Well, well. It seems that there are no secrets here. As for the other thing'—he paused and looked at Beauden's father, who nodded—'I have sent a mirror message to a mechanical engineer in Belgium who has been working on larger scale steam engines. The size you want will take some time to acquire. I shall go and see him when I leave here.'

Beauden followed the conversation like he was a mere spectator at a tennis match. But he had no interest in the words passing between the two men who loved him so dearly and were smashing down every tenet of medical and scientific thought simply to keep him alive.

He glimpsed Galena's brilliant eyes. Her face was alive, alight as he had scarcely seen. Beauden realised he had fallen in love with this girl, and a single glance was all it took to draw his attention away from his family. Had it been only yesterday when he had looked down at the hissing kitten pinned beneath the iron hooves of his unicarriage and lost his heart?

Galena watched his father, but Beauden seemed to be having trouble focusing on her. Blinking didn't help. He felt light-headed and his fingers grew numb, so he tightened his grip on his glass. He would be better for some food, he thought, as he took another sip of his sherry, his thumb brushing against his lips as he drank. His thumb was chilly, and his lips tingled.

He felt a brush of cloth against his arm. Perkins stood beside him.

'Sirs, luncheon is served.'

Beauden rose to his feet, planning to offer his arm to Galena. But his arm would not obey him, and neither would hi—

***

Time slowed. The second hand on the grandfather clock took an eternity to tick over. The cloud passing over the sun, high in the wrought arches of the enormous conservatory windows, stood still.

Galena gasped, filled with icy shards of panic at the sight of Beauden's alabaster face and indigo lips. Even as she rose, half out of her chair, his eyes rolled back in his skull and he tumbled towards the ground.

Mr Somerton cast aside his glass of sherry and lunged forward, catching Beauden before his head could strike the granite table between them. They sank to the floor, uncle borne down by the weight of his nephew's lanky frame.

Dr Somerton dropped to the floor beside his son, taking his slack wrist between thumb and forefinger as he looked at his watch. Only in the tension of his shoulders could Galena see anything amiss.

Time returned to normal with a rush. She knelt at the doctor's side.

'What would you have me do, sir?'

'Do we need to call someone, Augustus?' Mr Somerton looked up, his face emotionless, blank. His arms still supported his nephew's limp form. 'I have my mirror messenger in my pocket.'

Dr Somerton's grave look made Galena's heart plummet, even as he shook his head.

'No, I have all I need downstairs. Perkins, get the stretcher and have Mrs Perkins prepare my instruments.'

The man disappeared, returning less than a minute later with a long leather-and-canvas stretcher. Dr Somerton and his butler moved Beauden onto it gently, and Mr Somerton secured him to it with the leather straps.

Beauden's chest barely moved and his colour grew steadily worse. Even with the greasepaint, his skin looked as grey as a gravestone.

With Mr Somerton at the foot of the stretcher and Perkins at the head, they quickly bore Beauden down to the basement. Dr

Somerton pulled a pile of white cloths from a cupboard and handed one to Galena.

'Galena, I need you to assist me. Jacob has no medical training, and we don't have much time—Beauden's pulse is extremely erratic.'

Putting out her hands, she took the coverall in a daze. She had never participated in an operation before, the little work she had done on cadavers notwithstanding. All her knowledge was theoretical, gained from books and—

'Galena! Can you assist me?'

'Yes, sir!'

The doctor's panicked words galvanised her limbs into action. Beauden might die if she did not, and the thought tormented her. That he might die no matter what she did was something she would not contemplate.

Mrs Perkins helped Galena on with the voluminous apron and assisted her to tie it, then repeated the procedure with the doctor and Perkins. After they had all washed their hands with carbolic soap and donned their sterile white gloves, Mrs Perkins took a tray of instruments from the auto-steri machine, releasing a cloud of steam.

As he reached for the tray, Dr Somerton caught Galena's eye. 'Help me save my son.'

Her heart almost broke at the tremor in his voice. 'I will, sir.'

Beauden lay on his bed on sterile linen. Mr Somerton had cut away his clothing and draped the lower half of his form with a sheet.

'Is there anything more I can do, brother?'

'Pray, Jacob. Just pray.'

Mr Somerton looked back from the doorway. 'You can count on it.'

Perkins wheeled the breathing apparatus to the head of the bed.

Dr Somerton pointed to it. 'Press that mask to his nose and mouth, Galena. It will feed him oxygen and a monitored dose of chloroform.'

She picked up the mask made from bronze and leather, and strapped it to Beauden's face while avoiding contact with a black pipe as thick as her wrist. The pipe connected the mask to a large square case, inside of which was a black balloon that expanded and contracted, so slightly, each time Beauden breathed. From the back of the case, twin pipes were connected to a polished silver canister.

Perkins appeared at Galena's elbow. 'Excuse me, miss.'

He wrapped a bladder cuff of supple leather around Beauden's upper arm.

'Watch his blood pressure, Galena, while I administer the anaesthetic.'

Galena kept her eyes fixed on the small gauge connected by a thin tube to the bladder cuff. The monitor was pure genius, a clear advancement on anything she had seen in use before. Operated by a small valve plugged into the house's steam system, it pumped the cuff and released the pressure, indicating first systolic and then diastolic pressure.

'It is one-forty over ninety, Doctor.'

Dr Somerton's lips pulled tighter as he fiddled with the valve on the mask. Beauden's blood pressure was rising and, if she'd understood the doctor's diagrams correctly, the blood vessels that surrounded the iron heart were not as resistant as those of a healthy man.

'We must hurry. Too much pressure and the arteries could tear and Beauden will bleed out.'

'How do you know how much chloroform to add to the oxygen?' Her desire for knowledge overwhelmed courtesy.

Dr Somerton looked up at her, her question giving him a change of focus.

'In the beginning, it was all experimental, my dear, but I have since developed an equation that takes into account the patient's weight, age, respiration and pulse. It's not an exact science as yet, but it is by far the best method to date.'

After a few seconds, the pallor in Beauden's cheeks lessened as oxygen flooded his system. Dr Somerton's shoulders straightened as the tension he held there seemed to ease.

'Right, now for the muscle relaxant.'

'I beg your pardon, sir?'

'You heard correctly, my dear. I heard about it from some anthropologists. Apparently, the indigenous peoples of South America have used it for years. It's a deadly poison, of course, but then, so is atropine. In the tiniest dose, however, it is a brilliant medicine.'

He looked up and smiled ruefully. 'I'm afraid I haven't yet shared my discovery. I'm convinced my colleagues would react as yours did to your exceptional research. I think they would frown upon using a chemical that blocks the transmission of signals between nerve and muscle.'

Perkins handed Dr Somerton a glass syringe with a brass cap and fine bore needle. The substance within roiled and gleamed, dark brown in colour. The doctor slid the needle into a vein near Beauden's wrist and gently depressed the plunger. Galena watched the balloon expand and shrink and then turned to the monitor. Beauden's blood pressure began to decrease.

'Blood pressure one-thirty over eighty-five, sir. Respiration even.'

The doctor gave a sigh of relief. 'Excellent. Now for the hard part.'

Perkins draped another linen cloth over Beauden's naked torso. This one had a square hole cut in it over the centre of Beauden's chest.

As Perkins tied a mask over the doctor's nose and mouth and moved behind her to do the same, Galena regarded her mentor with awe. 'You are years ahead of your field, sir.'

Dr Somerton did not respond. Instead, he stood with a gold-handled scalpel in hand and placed its razor-sharp tip on the lateral left side of Beauden's sternum.

Galena held her breath. Then, unbelievably, Dr Somerton gave a deep, heartfelt sigh and paused, scalpel still poised over Beauden's chest.

'What is wrong, sir?'

He had his eyes fixed on the blade, which shuddered slightly. 'Look at my hand, Galena. This procedure is delicate, and my arthritic joints and trembling hands have betrayed me. I can't operate like this. I need you to be my hands.'

Her ears buzzed, and for a second, she feared she would faint. 'Surely you don't mean for me to perform such delicate surgery?'

'I have the utmost confidence in you, my dear. You have the skill to perform the procedure, and with my knowledge guiding you, we can succeed. Now'—he stepped back—'come and take my position.'

She switched places with the doctor, and he moved at once to monitor Beauden's blood pressure and the flow of anaesthetic.

'Blood pressure still one-thirty over eighty-five, pulse is a little calmer but still erratic. Now, my dear, Perkins will assist.'

Galena swallowed the lump in her throat and bade the butterflies in her stomach to cease their infernal dancing. She had waited half her life, certainly as long as she could remember, to practise medicine. But never in her wildest imaginings had she suspected that her first surgery would be on someone she knew. And Beauden Somerton was a man she had come to admire in a very short time.

With a blessedly steady hand, she held the scalpel over Beauden's chest. She supported the skin with her free hand and made sure not to exert too much pressure. Unlike other areas of the body, this part of Beauden's torso was simply a thin area of skin with no underlying muscle.

The room was not hot, but tiny beads of sweat prickled on her forehead. Perkins reached over and blotted the perspiration away as she completed the incision. She peeled back the delicate layer of skin and translucent membrane stretching across Beauden's chest cavity and revealed his heart—his iron heart.

For a bare second, she forgot the urgency of the procedure and stared at the mechanical marvel keeping him alive. She recognised the genius of the design—just as she had yesterday when she had seen the blueprints—and the telltale signs of oxidisation. No wonder Beauden was sickening.

She glanced up at Dr Somerton who met her nervous gaze with his steady one.

'You are doing very well, Galena. Blood pressure and respiration are steady. Now, do you see that cog, there, beside the pendulum? Lift it with the forceps and set it down here.'

Slowly, he guided her through the procedure to place the piece of the heart back into its correct position, one painstaking movement at a time. With luck, it would keep Beauden alive a little longer.

After an eternity, Galena used the sterilised fish gut to set the final stitch on Beauden's chest and then stepped back. Perkins set about cleaning and dressing the wound, while Dr Somerton turned off the chloroform canister and came to stand beside her. She shook like a leaf. Ripping the bloody gloves from her hands, she dropped them onto the used instruments and pressed her trembling fingers to her face.

Dr Somerton pulled off his own mask and gloves and untied

his voluminous apron.

He put his hand on her arm. 'I will leave Beauden's mask in place. He will be better for the oxygen and we need to monitor his heart for a while longer.'

His fingers tugged at the knot at her waist where her gown was tied. 'Come and sit down, Galena. You are exhausted.'

She sat for a moment, eyes closed, taking slow breaths to calm the tremors that racked her body. When she looked up, she saw a tear on the doctor's cheek before he brushed it away.

'Sir?'

'I am perfectly well.' He shook his head and put an unsteady hand over hers. 'No, I am not. I must thank you, Galena, for being an angel sent by heaven in my moment of greatest need. I would have lost him today were it not for you.'

'Sir, I am grateful to have had the chance to help you. And him.'

He tossed aside his surgical garb and scrubbed his hands, and Galena followed suit. But instead of taking the comfortable chair beside the desk, she dragged one of the high metal chairs from the corner and placed it by Beauden's bed.

Dr Somerton set the bed to rotate, the thick rings spinning within one another. The oxygen bottle, now magnetised, clung to the base of the bed while Beauden slept the sleep of the just.

Watching him, Galena let the reaction hit her. This was not only her first ever procedure—and one that only a single surgeon had ever performed previously—but she had saved a life today. And it hadn't simply been the life of a nameless stranger, but of a man who was at least a friend and possibly ... well, he was a good man, with his bright copper eyes and magical smile.

She recalled the words of Donne's meditation: *No man is an island*. How true she now knew that to be! If she had lost Beauden Somerton today, though she knew him but little, her life would have been inexorably diminished. But another, less welcome thought bubbled in her brain. Where was the line that divided medicine from necromancy? How would she know? It took a special kind of courage to save a life as she had just done. And the experiments she had been conducting, that Dr Somerton had been conducting ...

Where, she wondered, did the quest to save lives end, and the hubris of playing God begin?

The thoughts swam lethargically in her brain as she fixed her gaze on Beauden's pale face, pink with health due to the rich, oxygenated blood flowing through his veins. Surely it could not be wrong to save the life of someone so kind and gentle. Let him only wake, and then she could sleep.

Chapter 8

The gentleman dashed a sprinkling of rain from his sleek leather coat and flicked a coin to the scrofulous driver. Pushing through the emerald doors, he stooped as he entered the warm, malty bar of The Hart. The sign above the doors had proudly announced the place had been built in the reign of King David. Now, the university crowd, past and present, were the chief patrons of the iron-plated counter.

'Alexander.'

It had been a while, but the place had changed little.

'Good evening, sir.' The barkeep's respectful nod showed he remembered the gentleman from his infrequent visits. 'A Belhaven, sir?'

The gentleman nodded, picked up his glass and placed a shilling on the bar before turning away. He noticed the serving girl, balancing a tray of drinks on one skilful wrist, but he had no appetite for female flesh tonight. In any case, the chit was fully occupied, fending off a university lad two tables away. Efforts to pinch her rump beneath her kilted skirts did not meet any measure of success. The boy's technique was poor, even for a man only half in his cups. The girl slapped his roving hands away and moved on.

As the gentleman watched, sipping his whisky slowly, he caught a known name in a half-heard shard of conversation. He focused and pricked up his ears, eager to hear more.

'She is by far the most intelligent, I agree.' A sandy-haired young gentleman had spoken, freckle-faced and neat, his voice calm.

'But surely there is a place for women in the medical profession.' The ginger lad, half-sprung and struggling to maintain his argument, spoke up.

'As nurses! But the medical officers who worked with Miss Nightingale in the Crimea said that she would argue with them about the care given to the men under their supervision.'

A third member of the party gave a snort and made a savage gesture. He was a broad young man, appearing morose and belligerent. 'A nurse, Warwick, for pity's sake. Arguing with doctors. Scandalous nonsense.'

'Perhaps. But she did much good, Forsythe. Saved any number of lives.' Ginger peered owlishly at his peers.

'Miss Nightingale is not here in Edinburgh. Though Galena Tindale and the other female students are. And the university supports them. No doubt they see merit in them.'

This Warwick was clearly the voice of reason tonight, but his friend was having none of it.

'It is our responsibility to do something about these bluestocking bitches who think they are our equals.'

'Why, Merrick?' Warwick appeared by no means convinced,

perhaps even challenging.

The man named Merrick leaned forward. 'Because it's obscene blasphemy to use tissue from a swine's heart and put it into a human chest.'

'You have no difficulty about putting swine flesh into a human mouth.'

'That is hardly the point. Still, if the dean won't caution her, and she has no parents or a husband to control her, what can you expect?'

'Are you volunteering, Merrick?'

'I'd give something to tame her, right enough.'

Warwick, who appeared to be the only sober one, dragged the waitress-pestering sot to his feet.

He ran a hand through his sandy hair, his voice flat with irritation. 'I won't have any part in the vendetta you are planning, Merrick. We've petitioned the dean, but he and his antiquated following will have none of it. I won't harm a woman, no matter how wrong I think she is.'

'They need to be driven out. Good God, man—'

Warwick slapped a palm on the table. 'Damn it, no! I'll play no part in it. You say you've left a message that will have her fleeing, well, that is already more than I am willing to do.'

He tossed a coin on the table, collected his inebriated friend, touched his hat politely and left.

The braggart, Merrick, swirled his glass, an ugly frown distorting his handsome face.

The gentleman hid his own smile in the collar of his jacket. God was clearly smiling down on him, to put such a useful tool into his hand like this. Something had to be done about the abomination that was Beauden Somerton. With this man as an ally, his own part could be hidden. He could be the hand, and this Merrick the glove. Or he could be lauded as a hero. Either way, he couldn't lose.

He picked up his glass and crossed to the abandoned chair, dropping into it in front of a startled Merrick. The fellow was young, but even so, the gentleman could see the bitterness twisting his tortured soul.

'For every problem, there is a solution.'

Forsythe opened his mouth to reply, or perhaps to tell him to get the hell out, but before he could, the gentleman extended a hand.

'I believe we share a mutual problem. Would you care to discuss ways in which we could find a mutually beneficial so-lution?'

'Who the hell are you?'

When the gentleman offered his name, recognition dawned in Merrick Forsythe's eyes. That was good.

He watched as Merrick considered him carefully, watched as his semi-sodden brain evaluated his goals. He even saw the point when the lad decided to accept. The fool had as much subtlety as a child's primer, but all the better for what the gentleman had in store for him.

'Indeed, sir.' Forsythe took the gentleman's proffered hand and shook it firmly. 'I'm interested.'

Chapter 9

The world was cold and dark, the air thick and oily. Beauden, eyes closed, stretched out his arms. He felt nothing. His chest ached and his lungs were starving. He wanted nothing so much as a breath of sweet fresh air.

Beauden turned his head this way and that, but for all his effort, the movement was slight. He tried to call out, but his lips ignored his brain, the plea for a sip of water staying glued to his throat.

The darkness was winning, nothing he did could pierce it. The strength he did have ebbed from his limbs, his mind.

'Beauden? Beauden, can you hear me?'

The voice was sweet and spoke to his soul. It might have been an angel, calling him from the murky depths.

'I need you to wake up. Breathe in, Beauden, please.'

He took a breath, unpleasant as it felt, and the darkness receded. Where it had been a starless night, now a golden glow shimmered on the horizon, calling his name.

It became easier to breathe—a reflex, rather than an effort. The air grew warmer, as did his body, but the throbbing in his chest had not subsided. With his new-found strength, Beauden forced open one eyelid and then the other. Dim light glimmered like a nimbus around the female form beside him. Her fingers circled his wrist.

'That's it. Breathe in.'

He felt something on his face and he moved to claw it away.

She hovered, shushing him, restraining him. 'No, you can't remove the mask. You need the oxygen.'

He recognised her now. 'Galena?'

'You passed out. But we have mended the heart and you will be all right.'

'Father operated?' His words were a mere thread and he sought to summon more strength.

'He and I worked together. I'm going to wake him now.'

'No, wait.'

With a Herculean effort, Beauden turned his head an inch. His father sat slumped in the high-backed leather chair set at right angles to the desk.

'Can I have a drink please?'

'Of course.' She poured water into a spouted cup and, moving the mask, held it to his lips. She tipped it until he had swallowed a few mouthfuls. 'Not too much.'

He managed to meet her eyes and could see she was weary as she took the cup from his lips.

Could he trust her to tell him the truth? His father lied to him, he suspected—or perhaps he simply refused to put the horrid possibility into words. But Galena would tell him the truth.

'What happened?'

The light in her eyes dimmed, and she frowned. 'What do you remember?'

'Very little. Jacob arrived. We came inside.'

'That's right. We had a glass of sherry.'

He concentrated for a few moments. 'Perkins announced that luncheon was served.'

'That's right. You stood and collapsed. Perkins and your uncle brought you down here and we operated. There was a problem with the workings of the heart near the pendulum.'

Now the savage ache in his chest made sense. He lifted his hand, but Galena intercepted it.

'Don't touch your chest. We must keep the wound from becoming infected.'

'So, it's fixed now?' He watched her intently.

'Yes. We replaced a pin that had become dislodged due to deterioration and put back the functioning parts.'

'And there are no more problems?'

She hesitated for so long that he knew what her silence portended.

'Don't be afraid to tell me. I'm quite familiar with my malady.'

She shrugged slightly, not quite able to meet his eyes. 'There is some corrosion. It looks quite severe. Which is why your father is so intent on replacing the heart.'

'And?'

Her eyes met his, and there was such sorrow in them that his heart would have missed a beat had it been capable of such a thing.

'The corrosion is so severe that your other organs are being affected by the iron entering your bloodstream. As yet, it is still reversible. If the heart is replaced, your body will repair most of the damage. But without a replacement for the iron heart, it is only a matter of time before …'

'I meet my maker?' He took a breath, grateful that he could do so. It was no small privilege.

'How can you be so calm?' She flicked a tear away.

'Don't weep, Galena.' He wanted to reach up, tuck the liquorice lock that had broken free behind her lovely ear. He wanted to cup her cheek in his hand and kiss her rosebud lips. He wanted … a future. With her.

'Galena, I've known for a long time that every moment I've had on this earth has been stolen back from death. I should have died at birth with my sister, a dozen times in childhood, at twelve when Father first gave me this heart. Every second since has been a precious gift, and I am at peace with that. When the end comes, I will go in the knowledge that I have been blessed more than any other man.'

Once, his words had been the truth, but now … ah, now they were a lie, as black as her lovely hair. He would give anything to remain at her side forever.

She wrapped her fingers around his and the warmth of her body flowed into him. Raising their interlocked fingers, she laid a small kiss on the back of his hand. In her eyes, he read respect. Perhaps she thought him noble for his high sentiments, but her smile made him regret every one. For now, at least, he had something he could not bear to lose.

Three yards away, his father stirred and shifted position. He would wake soon. Beauden had one more question.

'How long before he must operate again?'

'If the corrosion continues at the same level? Perhaps two months. If it worsens, closer to one.'

One month to replace his faulty heart with one not yet built. One that was still only a series of diagrams. One month to live life to the full—if he could.

He turned to gaze at the galaxies in her eyes. He had a month and he would not waste it.

'Let me go and wake your father.' She began to withdraw her fingers from his, but he tightened his grip.

'In a moment.'

He did not have far to reach to draw her head down to his for a light kiss on her petal-pink mouth. As he tasted the sweetness of her lips and the honey of her breath, he caught his first glimpse of heaven.

***

Galena pushed back the dusty-pink counterpane and slipped from beneath the soft linen sheets. She took time to bathe in the bronze hip tub wreathed in copper pipes. Cleanliness was important when dealing with wounds, so Galena revelled in the luxury of the delicately scented bar of rose soap against her skin.

Her clothing from the previous day had been freshened and pressed. The pink velvet and leather corset was one of six that she owned and by far the prettiest. She coiled her hair and pinned it into place, then checked her reflection in the mirror set into a large brass cog that hung as a wall decoration.

Galena ran a finger over her lips and her spine tingled in recollection. Beauden's kiss last night had been completely unexpected. And yet ... not unwelcome. Not by any means.

She left the bedroom and found her way to the conservatory where she and the doctor would break their fast. The first to arrive, she went to stand in the vast bay window.

She trailed a hand over the potted strelitzia, the flowers' vivid heads raised to the sun, reminding her of the titian glory of Beauden's hair. Looking out on the brilliant summer morning, she saw the light in his eyes when he smiled at her, the cool breeze caressing her skin like the silken touch of his fingers at the nape of her—

'Good morning, Galena. I trust you slept well.'

She started at the doctor's voice; a housebreaker would not have jumped so high.

'Good morning, sir. How fares Beauden today?'

'Well enough. I gave him a second dose of laudanum around midnight and Jimmy says he passed an easy night.'

Dr Somerton appeared less strained than she had previously seen him. He was tired, a little rumpled and lines still bracketed his mouth, but his smile was relaxed.

'I am so glad.'

'Once we've eaten, you can see him. But after that, I'd like to go over the designs for the new heart.'

'Of course, sir.'

'I looked at your drawings last night while I was monitoring Beauden's condition. For someone who has only seen my designs once, you have done remarkable work.'

'Thank you, sir.'

'I think, with some of the elements of your drawing added to mine, we might well have a solution to our problem.' His eyes twinkled.

'Really, sir?'

He offered his arm and led her into the little parlour where several silver dishes sat on a mahogany sideboard.

'Indeed, Galena. When the dean wrote to me about your use of swine flesh, I went over your report and realised what I had been missing. There are a few problems still to address, but I think we have an end in sight.'

Galena blushed with pleasure—no doubt her cheeks were as pink as her silk ruffles. She had received such a hostile reaction to her use of swine's flesh in her experiment and had felt utterly despised for her temerity in challenging medical convention. Now, she was light-headed with relief and joy.

Dr Somerton seated her at the table, then took a plate from the sideboard, filled it and placed it before her, having laded it with sliced ham, scrambled eggs thick with onion, and mushrooms sautéed in butter. He took up another plate and piled it twice as high.

'Coffee, my dear?'

She looked at her breakfast, eyes wide. 'Yes, thank you.'

'Jimmy collected your heart-lung machine from the university and has cleaned it up. He discarded the original swine tissue you had used, it had deteriorated, and he's mended the fittings that were damaged. I'm sure you will find it sound. Jimmy does good work.'

After breakfast, they descended the stairs to the basement to find the bed's rotations were decreasing in speed. Still asleep, Beauden turned his head fitfully.

'How is everything, Jimmy?'

'All well, sir.' Jimmy appeared limp and haggard. 'Now that you are here, sir, I'll go up and get Master Beauden some breakfast.'

'You will do no such thing. Ask Mrs Perkins to send some food down, please, and get yourself off to bed.'

Jimmy touched a hand to his forelock and stumped out as Dr Somerton cast a careful eye over Beauden. He crossed to the cabinet containing medical supplies, leaving Galena standing beside the bed.

Beauden opened his eyes and gave her a sleepy smile.

Galena reached out a hand, lightly touching the back of it to his cheek. The recollection of last night's kiss came back to her in a flurry of fondness and sharp delight, and she acknowledged what now drove her. Her motivations weren't only drawn from affection for Beauden; it was more than that. And it was no longer only about the thrill of scientific discovery. The purpose of her life was to make Beauden Somerton well. Beside that goal, her theories didn't matter, nor did the challenge of great science.

She looked into his eyes, turned her hand over and let it cup his cheek. The heel of her hand brushed over his lips and his kiss tingled on her skin. Galena knew what now motivated her; she had fallen in love.

***

As he woke, Beauden saw an angel. God willing, it was a sight he would see every morning.

He smiled at the thought.

'Morning.' His voice cracked, and he ran a sandpaper tongue over dry lips. 'Is it possible to get a sip of water?'

'Of course.' She filled the spouted cup beside his bed and offered it to him. 'How are you feeling?'

He winced. 'I'm not dead.'

'I had noticed. Are you in any pain?'

He was, but he shrugged it off. 'I've felt worse.'

His father took the place opposite and picked up his wrist. 'Good morning, my son. You are doing well. Your pulse is steady. Now, how much pain are you in?'

He had no chance of getting past his father. 'If you must know, sir, I have all the fires of Hell burning in my chest.'

He lifted a hand, but Galena caught it before he could make contact with his chest. He was surprised at the firmness of her grip.

'Easy there, my boy. Galena has sewn a fine seam down your chest. Don't disturb her handiwork.'

'I beg your pardon, Galena.' Beauden's words were formal, but he stroked his fingers over hers.

Her eyes were bright as a November bonfire and a tiny smile played in the corner of her mouth. He wanted to kiss it. The memory of the previous night had not left him; not her response, not his own ardour. But the revelation would keep.

He turned to his father. 'So, sir, how do I fare?'

His father bent his silver head and lifted the edge of the dressing on Beauden's chest. 'The wound looks good with no suggestion of inflammation. Your complexion has improved—you've colour in your cheeks at last, though some of that is due to the extra oxygen. The blue in your lips is minimal, thank God.'

'Then, may I dress?'

His father hesitated. 'Very well. I will assist you.'

'You are not satisfied with Jimmy's care, Father? Or perhaps you are thinking of changing careers?'

His father raised an eyebrow and grunted. 'You must be feeling better if you are playing the saucy knave.'

Galena chuckled softly behind her hand.

With his father's assistance, Beauden managed to shift into a sitting position, but the effort sucked him dry. He might dress, but he would probably sleep again afterwards.

'Slowly, my boy. You will strain yourself. Don't overdo it.'

'Galena'—Beauden met her eyes—'could I trouble you to get a shirt and my shell? They are in the armoire yonder.'

She slipped garments from his closet and brought them over.

'Thank you. My father and I can manage now.'

She assessed him with a lingering glance. 'I would like to assist.'

She readied the fine cotton shift-like undershirt. 'Shall I slip it over your head?'

'We can manage.' He would not have her dress him like a child.

'On the contrary, Dr Somerton can either assist you to sit or help you to dress, but not both. So, would you like my aid?'

A long pause ensued while their eyes met and did battle on the field of honour. Eventually, his pride conceded defeat. 'Yes, please.'

She tugged the shift down and slipped both arms around him to draw the reinforced corset into place. The sensation of her arms around him was worth every iota of awkwardness. Fortunately, she did not appear to mind that he was a pitiful specimen.

She helped him into a soft shirt next, but then Beauden insisted on privacy while his father helped him on with a pair of loose trousers. By the time he was fully dressed, he was exhausted.

107

'I am going to rest here, if you don't mind.'

His father patted his hand. 'Excellent suggestion. Mrs Perkins will be here shortly with your breakfast. I am going to go over the plans for the new heart with Galena. She has some ideas that I believe will help, with one or two modifications.'

Galena came back into the room carrying a bowl. 'Mrs Perkins sent this down.'

Beauden grimaced. Porridge, however suitable for invalids, was not his favoured breakfast. But he was rather hungry.

Galena put the bowl down and came to his side. 'May I help you?'

'If you could put it in front of me, I would appreciate it.'

'Of course.' She set the tray over his lap, put a spoon ready to his hand and took half a step back.

He had not intended to allow Galena to assist him, but he wanted her near, and if that meant porridge for breakfast, so be it.

He lifted the spoon and dipped it into the oatmeal. Already it weighed as much as his arm, but he refused to ask for assistance. At least the stuff was liberally laced with cream and brown sugar. Almost palatable.

When he glanced up, Beauden saw his father watching the exchange. The old man was no fool. His expression, one of intense concentration, made him appear as if he were dealing with a complex problem. Beauden knew that expression well. For most of his young life, he had assumed his father always looked thus.

Beauden managed a dozen spoonfuls before he called a halt.

Galena bent to lift the tray out of the way, but first, she reached up and gently pushed back a wave of his hair. He revelled at her touch. He wanted to kiss her pretty pout and smooth away her anxious look. But they had no privacy. Instead, he settled for threading his fingers through hers and laid his lips on the back of her hand.

'Thank you, Galena.'

The glance she gave from beneath her lowered lashes and the husk in her voice spoke to him.

'You're welcome. Sleep now. Get better.'

Chapter 10

When Beauden closed his eyes, Galena pulled herself away and went over to where Dr Somerton stood at the wide bench against the wall, rolls of blueprints spilling over it. Her book, with its coloured-ink diagram, lay open on top. The doctor scribbled on a large sketch covered in ink, pencil and coffee stains.

'Mmm.' He frowned and scribbled out a note, adding an asterisk and an arrow to the illustration, the pencil flying. 'No, no. Here instead to support the tissue.'

'I believe Beauden is asleep, Doctor.'

He did not look up. 'Ah, good.'

He scribbled another note. 'Look here at the atria. We must change the shape of the contour. Unfortunately, because of the pendulum system I had to employ in the iron heart, I could not replicate the natural curves.'

She stared at the diagram but still saw smiling copper eyes. Shaking her head, she forced herself to concentrate. 'I did not anticipate that such a small issue could cause such a complication.'

'In any normal heart, it would not, but since ours is more metal than flesh, we have to make up for the natural mechanisms that are unavailable to us. I discovered that with the first prototype.'

Doubt congealed in the pit of her stomach. What if her inexperience led her to make a mistake? There was no margin for error here. Beauden could die at her hands.

'Sir, you have all the knowledge and experience I lack. I'm only a student.' Despite her determination to maintain iron control over her emotions, her voice quavered. 'How can my ideas be of any use to you?'

Dr Somerton grinned. 'Not at all. Have more faith in yourself. Your work has given me an idea.'

He waved a hand over the original blueprint for the gold heart. 'I had intended to make the new heart as I made the old, but out of gold instead so as not to poison Beauden. But then, I realised gold has no magnetic value—I could not use the magnetic field bed to keep the pendulum operating while he sleeps. Such a heart would extend his life, but only for a matter of hours.'

'Ah.' Such a thought had not occurred to her.

'Yet, if I simply made another iron heart, I would have to replace it every eight to ten years. But I am not a young man. I doubted that I would be capable of operating ten years from now. And you see, I have been proved right already.'

'So, you needed an alternative to iron that is also magnetic?'

She did not wish to respond to the sadness in the doctor's last words, and she could not imagine how her work—which said not a word of magnetism—had sparked a revelation.

'Correct, and yet, no. I still intend to use pure gold, or at least eighteen carat gold—pure but hard. So, I need to find a different way to power the heart.'

He turned and looked to where the bed sat on its turntable, slowly revolving. Beauden looked like an angel painted by Michelangelo.

'He is trapped here. He lives, yet he is not fully alive. I want to free him to travel, perhaps to marry. To live as a young man should.'

Galena nodded. 'And have you found it, sir? A new power source?'

'No, my dear. You have.'

The room spun, and she gripped the bench for support. Her skin prickled at his words. She had found it?

'Your experiments with swine flesh.'

He tapped the bright ink diagram she had drawn the previous day. 'You have seen the similarities between it and human tissue. If we line the gold heart with the inner muscles of a swine's heart, then we can use suinae valves between the different chambers of the heart and the heart's own power source.'

'Sir?'

'The atrioventricular and sinoatrial nodes, of course. The gold will merely act as a protective covering and provide structure. I approve your design of the gold filigree cage to replace the missing ribs—it's functional and an elegant solution to the problem.'

Despite her grip on the bench, she sagged a little.

Dr Somerton put a comforting arm around her. 'Sit down, my dear. Come, surely you are not surprised. You were working on the use of swine tissue in medicine—with what purpose except to save a human life?'

She shook her head, dazed. 'I was conducting research, sir. I had an idea and a way to make it work. I did not think ... I had not met you, nor Beauden. I never imagined that my work would be a matter of life and death. I never intended to play God.'

'You are not playing God, my dear.' Dr Somerton pulled over a stool and sat facing her. 'You are playing Abraham.'

'Sir?'

'If you recall the story, God intended to destroy the cities of the plain, but Abraham pleaded with the Almighty to spare their lives. That is what doctors do, Galena. We stand between the patient and God and ask for the skill to spare the patient's life. Sometimes, we win. But always—*always*—we strive and bargain and look for options, any possible option, that will offer another chance.'

Relief ran through her. Not all medical men were afraid to step outside accepted medical practice. Nor should she be. Dr Somerton's words confirmed what she instinctively felt but did not have the experience to put into words.

'Do you really believe that, sir?'

'I do, absolutely. When we as doctors assist a woman with a difficult birth, heal an infected wound or medicine a lethal fever, we are chasing away the Angel of Death. This situation is no different. If we, as the most intelligent of all God's creatures, do not use our knowledge and wisdom to preserve human life, then there is no hope for us and God would do well to wipe us from the face of the earth.'

'But many believe that the soul—'

'Lives in the heart, I know.' His face twisted with a hint of regret. 'But who are we, as mere men and women, to say where the soul resides? Perhaps it doesn't reside anywhere, but just is. In any case, does my son look like a man with no soul?'

Galena looked at Beauden as he lay in peaceful repose and tears welled in her eyes. Beauden had depths of compassion that she had not encountered in any other man; he portrayed a benevolence and humility borne of suffering. His soul was as wide and bright as the noonday sky. And she could have a part in saving his life—a life that had quickly become as precious to her as her own.

She felt Dr Somerton watching her keenly, but she shook her head and looked down at her lap.

When he took one of her trembling hands in his, Galena met his gaze and saw warmth and affection.

'I pride myself, Galena, on being a man with an eye for detail.' He dipped his head forward, giving her a narrow look. 'But it seems that the greatest malady of my son's heart has escaped me until this moment. And not only Beauden's, I think.'

So, he had noticed her admiration for Beauden.

'Sir, I hope I've not displeased you?'

'I can read your face, my dear, like a book from the Minerva Press. No, I'm not upset. And you've done nothing wrong. For some, love is elusive. For others, when they meet someone, it's as though the stars align. I can understand why you would care for

Beauden. He is a wonderful young man. Not that I'm at all biased.'

'I was worried you might not wish for the connection. My family are not distinguished, and Beauden's health is your main concern.'

'My dear, for a woman as intelligent and independent as you, you think far too little of your worth. I could think of no one better suited to be his help-meet. But'—he shook his head—'I fear we have little time to perfect this work. You may well end up with a broken heart of your own.'

She pressed her hands to her stomach to keep the butterflies from breaking free. 'It will work, sir. You are not alone. I will help you to the utmost of my ability. Together, we will save him.'

Dr Somerton smiled broadly and laid his hand lightly on her shoulder. 'I know you will, my dear, and you have my thanks. And, if you and he wish it, I would be blessed to have you as a daughter.'

Galena's eyes widened.

Was there room in her life for love and medicine? Her dream to become a doctor had once seemed an impossible quest, and she had resigned to one day set aside her natural desires for home and family. But was it possible to have both? She wanted to believe. She just didn't dare.

***

Beauden lifted his face to the sun; it was a beautiful day to be out.

He was still recovering, and the closest he had come to being outside this past week was sitting in the wide window of the conservatory and gazing out at the rainswept garden. Yet, despite his boredom during the last few days—the close confinement, constant drizzle and dragging pain—Beauden was grateful to have another, albeit tenuous, lease on life.

Two days after the operation, once they had both recovered from the exigencies of the situation, Galena had gone back to university. Jimmy took her and collected her after lectures; Beauden's father had insisted. When she wasn't attending classes, she studied with his father at the big desk in the conservatory and Beauden would watch from his easy chair, quietly marvelling at her intense thirst for knowledge.

She and his father often disappeared downstairs for hours to work on the plans for the heart, yet she contrived to spend as much of her free time with him as possible. They played chess and dragged out his mother's old game of Speculation. Occasionally, she would sing while he played the piano, and he discovered her appalling taste for gothic fiction. She was currently reading Walpole's horrid novel, so instead, he read her *Ivanhoe*. Sometimes, if they were alone, they would sit hand in hand and say nothing of any consequence.

His father and Galena talked of the future with confidence, but for Beauden, hope was as fragile as she was elusive. He breathed every breath as though it were his last, soaked in every moment in Galena's presence, and thanked God every day that she had come into his life. He savoured every mouthful of food, every minute beside the warm fire, every moment spent in the haven of his household. He didn't fear death—they had been close companions for too long—but he winced at the coming separation from all he loved.

This morning, with the sky a vivid blue and the air sweet, he would be with Galena. This would be his heaven on earth.

'Thank you for coming.'

Galena smiled at him, one hand on her parasol, the other holding her India-muslin skirts. 'You didn't have to wait for me, you know. I'm quite certain that you are anxious to go to your workshop. Jimmy could have come back for me.'

He handed her into the unicarriage. 'Certainly not. In any case, Father has asked me to take a letter to the dean. And I would very much like to see where you study.'

'That would be agreeable.'

This morning, his father had suggested Beauden accompany Galena and deliver the letter to the dean in person. After that, he might spend an hour or two, not more, in his workshop. Will had been to the house twice, so Beauden knew that work continued on apace without him, but that was irrelevant. He itched to get back there.

'Perhaps, when you have attended your lecture this morning, you might accompany me to the workshop?'

'I'd love to.'

As they were passing Victoria Park—the place they had walked scarcely more than a week ago—Galena looked out the window, then smiled back at him excitedly, her eyes as bright as a summer's day.

'Look, Beauden! A matter of months and you will be playing cricket in the park. Won't it be wonderful?'

Her hope and enthusiasm were alluring. Beauden longed to give in and grab hold of the false promise that she and his father clung to so tightly. Instead, he swallowed his sadness and linked his fingers with hers. He had spent fifteen years aware of Death peering over his shoulder and not even their solemn promise that this would work was enough to banish such gloomy company.

'And who shall I play with, Galena? I have but few friends, and those I do work for me.'

Her smile lit up her face. 'Well, we shall arrange a day of picnicking and fun, frivolity and cricket for everyone.'

'And pay them?' His voice was full of mock horror.

'Of course!'

'Good heavens, woman, this is Scotland! You cannot go around saying things like that. I'm sure it is against the law.'

'I think Mr Dickens wrote a book about you, Mr Scrooge.'

'Vixen!'

'Penny-pincher!'

His gaze drifted to her rosy lips as the unicarriage slowed. He'd dared another kiss last night and was on the verge to steal another. He leaned forward, the soft scent of jasmine enveloping him. A burning hunger flared in Beauden; now more than ever he knew what he wanted.

Steam hissed as Jimmy applied the brake, then he opened the door and let down the stairs. Beauden went down first and then turned to assist Galena. She placed her dainty hand in his—the hand that had saved his life.

Beauden nodded to Jimmy and escorted Galena towards the great doors of the university. As she held her skirts clear of the mud, heads turned, and Beauden heard whispers of conversation and felt the odd heated gaze.

'I must visit the dean, but I will meet you here after your lecture.'

She slid her arm from his, her eyes lingering on his lips before she turned and walked away. He watched her disappear into the press of humanity—a diamond lost among beach pebbles.

He had lost the chance to kiss her and felt a fierce desire to claw it back. She was so perfect that she might have been sculpted just for him. And yet, she was everything he could not have. While he was walking death, a monster in the eyes of many, this vibrant beauty would transform the world with her intellect and inner fire. He had nothing to look forward to but the grave. He would not shackle her to a corpse or douse the brilliance of her fire.

But the admiration that burned in her chocolate gaze was impossible to ignore. Against his better judgement and most unwillingly, Beauden allowed himself to plant a tiny seed of hope in his iron heart. Perhaps, just perhaps, this wonderful woman could care for such as he.

Chapter 11

An hour later, as Beauden made his way back to the grand forecourt, he heard a volley of shouts—one male voice raised over a solid wall of murmuring, like the hum of a hundred beehives at midsummer. As he rounded the corner and emerged into the open square, he saw the mob—four or five dozen people enthralled by a speaker positioned on a low step. He shook his fists and stabbed an aggressive finger into their midst.

As he grew closer, Beauden realised that the ranting fiend was none other than the man from the park, Forsythe, and his vitriol was not directed at the crowd. At the focus of his rage, stood a small dark-haired woman and a man who protected her with outstretched arms.

Galena and Jimmy! Aghast, Beauden sped up.

He shouldered his way through the crowd and it parted like the Red Sea. A sheen of stark terror shone on Jimmy's forehead, and Galena was white to the lips. Not from fear, though, that much was certain.

Beauden stood beside Jimmy, shoulder to shoulder, and he could feel Galena pressed against his back, seething. Slowly, over the space of a minute or two, the man and the crowd quieted.

'It appears that Miss Tindale is not only a bluestocking, but a dishonourable one at that. She consorts with the raff and scaff of the streets and spends her nights under a gentleman's roof.'

The crowd let out a collective gasp and a roiling murmur followed. Off to Beauden's right, two anxious young men tried to push through the crowd, their eyes fixed on Forsythe. Beauden fixed his gaze on the aggressor and said nothing. The crowd, deprived of action, slowly quieted once more. After a minute, and without moving a muscle, Beauden judged the time was right.

'Jimmy, please escort Miss Tindale to the unicarriage. I'll be along in a moment, just as soon as I've had a word with this gentleman.'

Forsythe sneered. 'Yes, indeed, Miss Tindale. Your protector wants a word with me. Maybe he's going to point his blade at me again, although I expect he wouldn't dare in front of so many witnesses.'

One of the peacemakers broke free of the crowd. 'Come along, Forsythe, for God's sake! You know how the dean feels about this.'

Beauden saw an opportunity. 'I certainly know how the dean feels. Dean Hopwood is an old friend of my father and is happy to have Miss Tindale safe under our roof since someone saw fit to threaten her.'

The young man who had tried to calm Merrick earlier now laid a hand on his arm, though Forsythe shook him off.

'And who are you, sir?' Forsythe snarled.

'My name is Beauden Somerton. My father is Dr Augustus

Somerton.'

That got a reaction; no doubt every medical student knew his father's name. It was, after all, inscribed on the honour board in the university's great hall.

The sandy-headed peacemaker turned his gaze on Beauden. 'I had assumed Dr Somerton was deceased?'

'He will be very surprised to hear that.' Beauden lightened his voice to help ease the tension. 'He was most certainly alive this morning when he filched a slice of bacon from my plate.'

The mood of the crowd shifted. Beauden knew they could see no impropriety if the dean was in favour of this, or if the legendary Augustus Somerton was involved. Still, they did not move away.

Beauden stood his ground; though he could feel Galena's indignation at his back. Hell hath no fury like a woman maligned in public.

The young man reached out a hand. 'Mr Somerton, I am Douglas Warwick. No hard feelings, I hope?'

Beauden shook Warwick's hand. 'None at all, sir, assuming that this gentleman'—he paused significantly—'having made his accusation in public, will also offer his apology in public.'

The crowd turned as one.

Forsythe was pinned like a butterfly under a hundred sharp stares. Already red with choler, his face now took on a plum hue.

'It will be a cold day in Hell before I apologise to that hussy!'

'Then it seems you are destined for a frosty hereafter.'

Forsythe slowly and deliberately stepped down from his vantage point, his gaze fixed on Beauden, challenging him. He smirked, then turned casually as if to leave.

Beauden would not have it. 'Forsythe!'

Forsythe stopped, his back still to Beauden—and Galena.

'You've forgotten your apology.'

'Go to hell!'

Beauden lunged forward, but Forsythe pivoted and slammed his fist into Beauden's jaw.

Utterly unprepared, Beauden flew backwards, colliding with Jimmy. His glasses went flying, ending up four feet away in the dust. His head spun. Not surgery nor the stuttering decomposition of his heart hurt so much.

Dazed, he gave no objection when someone lifted him by the lapels of his jacket. Galena's scream echoed in his ears and the crowd once again buzzed like an angry swarm.

Beauden shook his head, blinking to clear his vision. Warwick, wide-eyed, slowly swam into view, but it was Forsythe that held Beauden, a look of primitive glee animating his face.

'My God! You're a freak!'

Beauden wrenched himself free and stumbled back, his spine jolting as he hit the ground again. He put his palms to the ground behind him to steady himself and turned his eyes to his assailant.

'Look at him!' Forsythe turned to the crowd. 'No human can have eyes like that!'

Fear was subsumed; a wave of pure rage surged through Beauden. His blood boiled and he clenched his hands into hammers. His reluctance to be seen, his habit of hiding away, shattered. He knew he was too weak to fight, too fragile. But that was irrelevant. He had to protect Galena.

Beauden ignored the stares and shocked whispers of the men around him. He scanned the crowd for Galena, desperate to know that she was unharmed. Jimmy had one arm around her, but not for comfort. He was holding back a fury.

Merrick Forsythe, his ugly smile as smug as the Devil himself, reached towards Beauden and grasped him again by his coat. Beauden would not be caught off guard this time. Forsythe believed him to be a freak. Let him think so.

Forsythe set his feet square as he held onto Beauden, bracing himself to take the extra weight. In that second, Beauden grabbed at Merrick's own coat with his right hand and sunk a punch with his left deep into the side of Merrick's jaw.

As his fist slammed into Forsythe's face, Beauden rolled left, taking the bigger man down with him. Beauden leapt to his feet and took up the traditional boxing stance—Jimmy had taught him how when he was a lad—as his weakness demanded guile, rather than strength. He blocked out the clamouring ranks of spectators. It was just him and the man who had behaved dishonourably to the woman he loved.

Forsythe stood slowly and spat blood at Beauden's feet.

'You're not a man!' His voice radiated disgust. 'You're a monster!'

'And you're a coward who would harass an innocent woman!'

Merrick wiped his bloody mouth with the back of his hand. 'Pah! A decent woman would know her place—and it isn't here!'

'That's not your decision. The dean approved her presence and that of the other ladies.' Beauden took a deep breath, then turned to confront the crowd. 'Gentlemen! Out of the fifty or so men here, is there not one who would defend a lady from such a bully?'

Fifty pairs of eyes examined the dirt of the forecourt.

Douglas Warwick's did not. 'I will.'

The tension in Beauden's shoulders eased with relief. 'Thank you. Mr Warwick, will you escort Miss Tindale and my man to my carriage?'

'No, sir, I will accompany you all.' He gestured politely. 'After you.'

Beauden hesitated and then acquiesced and nodded. He didn't want to go meekly back to the carriage, but in an all-out brawl he was unlikely to succeed.

'This is not over!' Merrick Forsythe stood, fist raised, at the centre of the now silent crowd.

'It is unless you are more than ordinarily stupid, Mr Forsythe.'

Without another word, he took Galena's arm and escorted her through the silent forecourt. They passed through the massive doors and made their way towards the unicarriage parked against the curb.

Beauden felt the ache in his hand and a pain in his chest, both throbbing and sharp. One look at Galena's face told him not to mention it. She was chalky white, but the hectic flags at the top of her cheekbones suggested her malady was not fear.

She walked briskly, and as they reached the carriage, Jimmy let down the step and then hopped up into the cab.

Beauden turned to Warwick and reached out a hand.

'I want to thank you, Mr Warwick.'

Warwick shook his head. 'You owe me no thanks, Mr Somerton. I have been Merrick's friend for three years, but it was not the act of a friend to let him behave as he did today.'

'Will he threaten us again?' Galena's voice was lethally sharp.

'I wish I could say no.'

Beauden looked from one to the other. 'I will send Jimmy with Miss Tindale, but he cannot attend lectures.'

Warwick recoiled slightly when Beauden's gaze met his, but he appeared to recover quickly, meeting Beauden's eyes once more.

'I will remain with Miss Tindale during lectures.' He smiled at Galena. 'If she will have me.'

Her reply was coolly polite, thought she smiled briefly at Warwick. 'I thank you, sir. Now, if you will excuse us, Mr Warwick.'

A minute later, Jimmy threw the vehicle into gear and they moved off, gaining speed as steam poured through the drive chamber.

Beauden nursed his swollen knuckles. He resisted the urge to fight, to turn the carriage around and go back. The desire to beat the living tar out of Merrick Forsythe burned in him. So this is what men did? While it was unfortunate that he had been obliged to strike that fool, he did not regret standing up for the woman he loved. He had always understood the need to defend a loved one—in a purely abstract sense—but now he grasped it as a visceral truth.

Galena sat silently beside him. Tears ran slowly down her cheeks and she stared blankly at the curtained window.

He reached out and gently wiped a teardrop from her cheek.

'Galena, my love, please don't cry. You are quite safe now.'

She turned an incredulous look on him and laughed a strangled sob. 'You think I was afraid for myself?'

'You were afraid for me?'

'What were you thinking!' The words burst out of her like a river in full spate.

His heart broke. 'Galena, I was defending you, your honour. It is something a man must do.'

'I was fine! I'm perfectly capable of handling that buffoon myself!' Her words were fierce, though her voice wobbled precariously.

'I beg to differ.' He spoke more abrasively than he had intended.

She looked up with hot eyes. 'You could have been hurt. Or worse.'

'It would have been worse if I'd put my own safety before yours. You are everything to me.'

He could not bear to watch her sob. 'Come here, Galena.'

He crossed the two feet between them and reached around her, enfolding her to his chest. Upon feeling a sudden shard of pain, he winced and gasped.

Surprised by his sharp intake of breath, Galena pulled out of his arms and inspected at his chest. Her eyes widened in panic, and before he grasped her intention, she gripped the neckline of his shirt and ripped it.

'Oh, dear God!'

She grasped the speaking cup hanging from the wall. 'Jimmy, we must go straight home! Mr Somerton has been injured!'

The unicarriage sped up and slew into a turn, throwing Galena against Beauden. She steadied him, gripping his shoulders, and closely examined his chest.

Beauden looked down. His rigid linen corset was rich with blood.

'You are hurt—and for what? To prove you are as manly as that brazen fool?'

'I don't have pain, so it can't be serious. It's probably only a torn stitch.'

She bit her lip. 'You don't understand.'

'Oh, but I do.' He reached out and touched her hair, tracing the sweeping strands as they rose into her chignon.

'I appreciate your concern for me, but I am no coward, Galena. Protecting you is a privilege I covet. How do I make you understand? You heard everything Forsythe said—he called me a freak.

He called you immoral! I could not let him get away with it. I might have an iron heart, but I am not so cold as to allow any man or person to harm the …'

Galena looked up from his chest to meet his gaze, her eyes pleading for him to finish his sentence. 'Harm what?'

Beauden seized his courage with both hands. To admit his feelings, to pursue her, was to court grief. But he owed her the truth.

'The woman I love.'

Chapter 12

Beauden's words smote Galena like a *coup de coeur*, leaving her dizzy. She had secretly imagined, wondered, dreamed. Never had she expected him to say those words out loud. Or, if she had imagined them, it was in a fantasy of candlelight, with sweet caresses and a bended knee. Not this declaration in the cold light of day, born of anger and danger.

A thrill prickled over her skin. He loved her.

Delight and fear joined battle in her heart. What if he did not survive the procedure? She and Dr Somerton had to replace his heart, they were not simply pulling a tooth. Beauden's life, his soul and her sanity, were all at stake. If they did not succeed, what would the future hold for her—the man she loved dead, her dream of medicine in tatters and the threat of the hangman's rope over it all?

They sped through the narrow gateway into the Somerton's courtyard and Jimmy pulled up with a squeal of anchor pads. Impatient at the bronzed door, Dr Somerton stood with his brother.

Mr Somerton wrenched open the door to the unicarriage and pulled down the step. The doctor was ghastly pale, Galena saw at once, but he gave a sigh of relief when Beauden descended unaided.

'Thank goodness!' He ran both hands and eyes expertly over Beauden.

'Jimmy sent me a mirror message. Really, Beauden, what were you thinking? Is this not why I make a point of having Jimmy with you at all times?'

'He was present and did what needed to be done. He protected Galena until I got there.'

Beauden stepped away from Dr Somerton, and it seemed as if he were putting the distance of maturity between them.

'But understand this—I don't care if I stand at the brink of death; if some bastard threatens my woman, I will deal with him. Not you, not Jimmy, not God himself. It is my responsibility and my right.'

Galena stood mute, her limbs frozen, her heart pounding. Beauden's very public claim sent shock rippling through her.

He held out a hand, helped her down from the carriage and drew her lightly to his side. Galena went willingly and Beauden stood tall and straight, as if he were daring his kin to challenge him.

Galena had assumed her bluestocking ways would see her a spinster. To win the admiration of such a good man left her stunned. And she could not help but notice the gleam in Dr Somerton's eye, or the way his spine straightened.

He waved them both in. 'That may well be, but I'd prefer it if we did not invite the reaper in just yet. We still have a heart to build.'

'Galena.' Mr Somerton stepped out of his brother's shadow and held out his hand to her. 'Thank you for bringing him back so promptly.'

'It was my pleasure, sir.'

'Perhaps once you have assisted my brother, you would tell me about the villain who accosted you. I would like to have a word with him.'

She flushed and took his arm as Beauden walked alongside his father. 'There is no need, sir. I don't believe he will trouble me again.'

He nodded. 'As you wish, of course.'

But his dark eyes were troubled.

Fifteen minutes later, Galena tied the last stitch and held the forceps at an angle so Jimmy could snip the gut string that closed the wound.

'You are profoundly lucky, Beauden. The damage here was minimal thanks to the corset. It stopped the skin and muscle from moving too much. If it were not ...'

She lost her train of thought as their eyes met. He was a boy struck by Cupid's arrow, copper eyes gleaming like a mirror, and her own feelings shone in their reflection. The curve of his lips caused her heart to tumble right out of her breast and into his waiting hands.

It was no wonder she loved him—he'd laid his life on the line for her today, just as he faced death every day with calm valour. But was that the only reason? She admired his appearance but wasn't dazzled by his beauty. He was slightly built and his features, though sculpted by a master craftsman, were not those of a traditionally handsome youth. Even when he was restored to health and his natural colouring returned, he would be attractive but not breathtaking. She admired his mind and his achievements; in spite of his many disadvantages, he had fashioned a career helping others.

Maybe it was all of these things. Or none. Maybe it was simply the spark that had attracted men and women to one another since the dawn of time. Whatever it was, she would be a fool if she did not acknowledge it, if she let this opportunity for love escape her. Galena Tindale was many things, but she was not a fool.

Right now, though, she needed to focus.

Wrenching her eyes from his, she dressed the stitched wound. Her fingers played over his smooth chest and she strove for professional decorum.

Beauden looked at Jimmy, whose broad back was turned towards them, then pulled her hand to his lips and placed a smouldering kiss on her knuckles.

She snatched her hand away as Jimmy turned and heat flashed in her face. Beauden gave her a lethal smile, and she stepped back, allowing Jimmy to help Beauden into one of his fine undershirts before strapping a clean reinforced corset into place.

Dr Somerton crossed the room to stand at the bedside.

'Has Uncle Jacob brought the gold you were expecting, sir?'

Galena noticed the weariness in Beauden's voice. She laid her hand over his and spoke softly. 'You need to rest. Sleep now and remain at home for the rest of the day.'

He shifted, sitting straighter. 'There is a great deal to do still.'

Dr Somerton put his hand on Beauden's shoulder. 'You heard the doctor's order, my boy. Rest now. Tomorrow will be early enough to take the model to Will.'

From his expression, Beauden was inclined to disagree.

Galena stepped in hastily. 'Indeed. I have an idea for the lattice at the front of the chest and I need time to make a model. If I do that today, I can ask Will's opinion tomorrow.'

'Then, after I've rested'—Beauden cast a fulminating glance up at his father—'perhaps you will permit me to assist you, Galena.' His words were formal, though his glance was anything but.

'Excellent.' Dr Somerton stepped up to the bed, fixed the strap around his son and pulled the lever.

The bed slipped into motion and slowly accelerated.

Dr Somerton turned to Galena. 'I am about to depart for a piggery on the Queensferry Road. The farmer is happy to sell me a fresh swine heart to use for practice. Galena, if you would, please tell Mrs Perkins I shall return before dinner.'

'Of course, sir.' Galena nodded respectfully as she realised the doctor's intentions. By having her give instructions to the house-keeper, he would be changing her status from guest to lady of the house. 'And what of Mr Somerton?'

'Jacob has a meeting with an old associate, but he will certainly be here.' He picked up his stick. 'Jimmy, if you could assist me? I have an ice chest I need taken out to the carriage. Rest well, my son.

Galena, I look forward to seeing what you have achieved this evening.'

Both men plodded up the stair and the door shut behind them. Beauden and Galena were alone.

Chapter 13

When Beauden opened his eyes, he found Galena observing him. Apart from the rhythmic churning of the cogs and the soft swoosh of the large metal arms embracing the bed, all that could be heard was their breathing.

Beauden watched his love watching him and considered. He had spoken of his feelings for her this morning but had not declared his love to her. The difference was small yet significant, and a lady's heart was not to be trifled with.

Beauden swallowed hard. He was not comfortable speaking words of love. Not since his mother died had he mentioned love to a woman, but the words wanted to be out, threatening to choke him in their eagerness to be heard. He found it difficult to breath, and his corroded heart throbbed within his chest, aching like an open wound.

'Galena, will you do something for me?'

It seemed as though her words were slow in coming.

'Anything.' She stood only inches from the bed. 'What do you need?'

He could not talk to her like this, like a captive bound on a sacrificial altar. He needed to sit with her, take her hand.

'Be careful not to get too close to the bed, but could you turn it off and undo my straps?'

'But—'

'Please, Galena. I will rest later.'

Beauden could sense her desire and her reluctance, her feelings in conflict with the medical imperative.

'I need to look you in the eye and talk to you about what happened this morning.'

He struggled to still the desperation in his voice, but he would suffocate if he did not speak.

She gauged the interval between the passage of the arms, then reached in and pressed the lever. The rotations began to slow and the bed ground to a halt. The cogs yawned and groaned as she lowered the bed flat.

Freed, Beauden sat up. 'Will you sit beside me?'

Galena picked up her muslin skirts and sat close, so they were almost touching at the hip. He felt overwhelmed by her sudden proximity, and his apology and explanation no longer seemed so crucial. He drowned in her chocolate gaze, the last vestiges of coherent thought or syllable scattering like hens faced with a fox, and common sense followed shortly on their heels.

He lifted his hands and touched her shoulder, her chin, her jaw.

'Galena.'

The word was an homage—half purr, half prayer. He leaned

forward and met her luscious pink lips with his. They met as ice and fire do, with a sizzle he had not expected.

She closed her eyes, her head tilting just a fraction, allowing him access. The heat in her pulled him in—deeper, hungrier, needier. She gave a soft sigh against his lips, and the sweetness of it nearly broke him.

Galena slid one hand up his arm and the gap between them vanished. He deepened the kiss and resisted her delectable bosom pressed against his chest. Instead, he slid a hand to her lovely neck and cradled her head. She caressed the line of his jaw, her other hand sliding along his thigh and higher, finding his waist.

Her lips were a meadow in high summer and he was the bee, dizzy with plunder as he tasted the sweetness of her honey. The skin at her nape was the smoothest satin, her hair like silk. He wound an errant curl around his finger and luxuriated in its tender embrace.

His lips left hers and slid, via her jaw, to the soft hollow below her ear.

Galena groaned and tugged his shirt free, sliding her hands beneath it, moving them across the restrictive corset to the top of the tight linen sheath. She caressed his skin, tracing a light pattern over his flesh, and under the skin, his blood fizzed.

He felt dizzy with the sensation and, as he met her lips with his, an urgent intemperate desire surged through him. An illicit thrill—one he'd known after waking from a sinful dream—overtook him. For a second, the desire he felt disappeared in a wave of shame. He dropped the hand that had been loving her so gently into his lap, to hide the evidence of his lust.

'I'm sorry. I should stop.'

She opened her eyes, her gaze searching his face. Then, she looked down and lifted his hand from his lap, lacing her fingers through it.

He averted his eyes and willed his body to be more discreet. It refused.

She kissed him again, and this time, she led. He would follow her anywhere, and he looked into her eyes. He'd never known chocolate could burn. They were a bonfire of need and hunger that matched his own.

'Don't stop.' She shook her head, just enough to brush her lips over his like a caress. 'I'm honoured that you feel this way about me.'

'I never dreamed a woman like you existed, darling Galena.'

'You are not like any man I've ever met, my dear one.'

'No, I am not. And though I love you desperately, you deserve a man who is whole.'

Desire her as he might, he could offer her nothing. She deserved more than a week, a month, and then heartache. Better to stop this now.

A fierce light shone in her eyes.

'Your body is whole, my darling, and so is your heart. You are more, so much more, than any man I have ever met, Beauden Somerton.'

And she pulled him into a deep current of passion until they were both swept away.

**

The gentleman sat in his shadowed corner, watching Forsythe cross the tavern floor towards him. Pride was there in his eyes, pompous assurance in the set of his shoulders. Academically brilliant, he took the rightness of his ideas for granted.

The gentleman smiled. The trick was not to convince such men to follow your plan, but to let them devise it for themselves. Then they would fight for it to the death.

Forsythe pulled up a chair, reversed it, straddled it. Aggression rolled off him like rain off an oilcloth.

'Thank you for coming.' The gentleman kept his voice low and mild.

'You expected me to come to heel at a peremptory message? I know nothing more than your name and that we share an enemy.'

'Isn't that enough?' The word held subtle contempt. 'I appreciate your trust.'

'Trust?' Forsythe quietly snarled the word, ignoring the barmaid who placed drinks on the table and then disappeared hastily. 'How can I trust a man who would betray so willingly?'

'Perhaps you could hear what I have to say before you talk so glibly of betrayal. What I have to suggest will benefit you, but I suggest it only because I must.'

'So you say.'

'So I say.'

He waited while Merrick picked up his pint and swallowed half of it, then, speaking again, he made sure his words were reasonable, undergirded with compassionate concern.

'You will forgive me my secrecy. I can vindicate you in the eyes of your peers and your university. I know as well as you that the man you fought today is no ordinary man. He has been ... modified. He is no longer fully human. The terrible thing is that it was his own father who changed him into the monster you met today. Augustus Somerton is a man full of hubris, who seeks to change others, to improve on the work of the Creator in such a way that manufactures super beings.'

Merrick Forsythe stared. 'What you say is impossible!'

'So is a man with copper eyes like those you saw today. Or a man with a false heart, a swine heart that will make him far stronger than any ordinary man. Once the technology is perfected, anyone who controls such technology will be able to unleash his unstoppable superhuman tools on the world.'

Forsythe scoffed and swallowed the last of his beer. 'The suinae heart replacement technology will never work.'

'Will it not? Then why has Augustus Somerton taken Miss Tindale into his home? And her research?'

'What do you want? And why do you need me?'

The gentleman raised his hands, palms up—the universal gesture of a man who has nothing to hide. 'I want to stop this travesty. Do you think I want to do this thing?'

He shook his head. 'There is nothing I can do to save Beauden Somerton now. Given what he has become, I should not even try. But I will not let others fall into the same diabolical state if I can help it.'

'And me?'

The gentleman met Forsythe's eyes with his own and spoke with passion, with reluctance, with regret. Better that Forsythe think of himself as the instigator.

'You and your friends are medical students all. You know the human body. You know what is possible, what should be done. When you know what I know, you will be angrier than I, because you will better understand the enormity of the offence.'

'Will we?' Already there was a change in Forsythe's tone. The mockery was less. He wanted to believe.

The gentleman lifted sorrowful eyes. 'You will bear witness to what you saw and expose it to the light for the villainy it is.'

'And Galena Tindale?'

'You know her better than I. Is she working with Somerton of her own free will? Can she be saved?'

The gentleman sipped his whisky and watched Forsythe. It seemed he needed precious little convincing.

Forsythe puffed out his chest. 'She is enthralled by the idea of women doctors. But that kind of responsibility is too much for a female.'

'You think she is in over her head?'

'Of course!'

'She needs a strong man. No doubt Somerton is encouraging her, letting her conduct her abominable research so that he can step in when the time is right.' He set the glass down and laid a sorrowful hand to his brow. 'She is another of his victims, then. It is a shame. If she had any womanly virtue, she would be content with home, hearth and taking soup to the poor. And she would leave medicine and medical ethics to those who are most fitted for it.'

Forsythe nodded. 'Leave Galena to me. I'll see she no longer plays a part in this villainy. And I'll do my part in ridding Edinburgh of this menace.'

'One day, my friend, she will thank you for it.'

Forsythe stood. 'Send me word when you need me. I'll undertake to bring half the university with me. We'll root out this nest of vipers and their perversion of honourable medicine.'

The gentleman stood and offered his hand. 'It is good to have men of decency and honour to count on in times like these. You will hear from me.'

As Forsythe disappeared into the late afternoon crowd, the gentleman smothered a smile. It was indeed good to call on decent and honourable men if you wanted something dark done. A wicked man is only wicked for his own ends. You need a good man to do evil for the greater good.

***

'Are you an artist as well as a healer?'

Beauden paused close behind Galena as she stood at the bench drawing. He dropped the lightest of kisses on the nape of her neck, beneath her inky upswept tresses.

She turned her head and lifted her lips to his. 'I'm afraid not. Did you want to see my etchings?'

'Hussy!'

Her eyes sparkled. 'Sir, I've said nothing untoward. It is your thoughts that are most improper.'

'Hardly a surprise. If you lay the track, my sweet, that is the way the train will go.'

'And generate quite a head of steam.'

Beauden laughed. 'I am utterly shocked at your brazenness, Miss Tindale!'

She fanned her lashes down, her dimples breaking cover for a moment. 'Why should you be shocked, sir? I am a medical student. It is hardly a wonder that I should be interested in how the human body works.'

'I think, madam, that there is no winning this ... discussion. I shall concede now.' He moved an arm to circle her waist. 'What are you working on?'

'The design for the cage that will replace your ribs and protect the new heart.'

He peered over her shoulder at the fine swirls on the page. 'It seems very ornate. I had assumed my new ribs would look like the real thing.'

She shook her head. 'No. Gold is too heavy. If we simply inserted gold-plated ribs, you would topple over.'

'Yes, that might be inconvenient.'

She chuckled and put a hand on his chest, overlaying his iron heart.

'It's not just that. The prothesis has seriously compromised the bone it's been attached to all these years. We will need to remove the damaged sections of your ribcage so that we have viable osseous tissue with which to work. I'm trying to avoid making you susceptible to some form of leukaemia in the future, Beauden. We are not just replacing your heart. We are trying to give you a long, healthy life.'

Silence stretched between them like a taut line.

Galena's lovely face betrayed her subtle tension. Faint frown lines appeared across her gentle brow, her neck and shoulders straining. He could do nothing, however, just as he could do nothing to preserve his own life. He played a passive part in this process, but if love itself could keep him alive, then he was as safe as money in the bank.

It hadn't taken their shared desire earlier or her loving concern for him to come to know, as he knew nothing and no one else, that he loved Galena Tindale and was loved by her in return.

'Galena.' He paused and dug deep for courage. He had to get this right.

'Yes?'

He drew the pencil slowly from her grip and laid it down.

Then, he took both of her hands in his and knelt before her.

Her eyes filled with tears and she pressed her lips together.

'Galena, will you do me the honour of granting me this hand in matrimony?'

He kissed the knuckle of her ring finger and her lips parted, but no words came.

She met his eyes. 'Beauden, this is not about … because we didn't … I'm not ruined, I know that … so there is no need …'

He should have realised. Kissing the backs of her hands, he turned them and pressed lingering kisses on her palms.

'There is every need, Galena! I love you quite desperately, and I hope you love me. I want us to marry as quickly as possible so that we can seize our happiness, whether it be for days or decades. I love you with every fibre of my being. Marry me.'

He measured the pulse in her hands—so rare, so precious. She stood still, her skin pale, as though she were made of the most delicate porcelain. He counted a score of heartbeats before she turned her smiling eyes on him.

'Beauden Somerton, you honour me with this offer and I gladly accept.'

He was on his feet, his lips on hers the instant she finished speaking. But it wasn't enough—in the joy of the moment, he lifted her off her feet and spun her around.

She laughed, her voice pure joy, and pushed at his arms. 'Let me go, you crazy man!'

'Only crazy in love with you, my darling.'

He let her feet touch the floor, and she snuggled into his chest and wound her fingers into his lapel.

'Are you happy, Galena?'

'I am ecstatic. I love you, Beauden. Never doubt it.'

His cheeks stretched, his face splitting with a smile that was no doubt the size of a horseshoe. 'Is there anyone I should speak to?'

She shook her head. 'Papa has been gone for a long time now. My family will simply be happy that I have found love. Besides, they are in York and it is much too far.'

'If you are sure.'

'I am sure.'

She tipped her head and considered, as though she were weighing her words carefully. 'My mother defied convention to marry a physician. She would understand. And my father would be happy. He loved me. His idea of what was best for me and mine did not often coincide, but he would have approved of you.'

'There is one thing—the university may not accept you as a married woman.'

'I know.' She met his eyes. 'That would be a blow. And I will strain every nerve to keep my place. But if it is a choice between you and the university, I choose you. Never doubt.'

'Galena, if you are prepared to marry me knowing what it might mean to your career, then I am more humbled than I can say.'

He pulled the band of gold he had in his breast pocket and slid it onto her finger.

'It belonged to my mother. She would have adored you.'

'Oh, Beauden.' She spoke softly, her voice tinged with the awe women used only for babies and diamonds. 'It's exquisite. Is it rose gold?'

'Yes. And the stone is a pink diamond. It's reasonably rare, but it was mother's favourite.'

He turned it to show the inscription on the side. The letters were tiny.

'Can you read it?'

'*Amare et fideli corde.* Love and faithfulness?'

'*Love and a faithful heart.*'

She ran her thumb over the words. 'I will treasure it.'

He kissed her with gentle reverence. She wore his ring. She was his now. 'Galena Somerton. For as long as we both shall live.'

'For the rest of our lives.'

'Even if it is only—'

She pressed her finger to his lips. 'Forever and a day. I want to raise children and grandchildren and live here in this house with you until we are grey and wrinkled.'

'If you insist. Forever and a day.'

Chapter 14

Beauden placed the tiny block of plaster into Jimmy's hand. The basement workshop was remarkably private now that the rest of the household were upstairs, dressing for dinner.

'We'll fill it tomorrow with the others, but keep it out of sight for now.'

Jimmy looked at the traces of white dust on Beauden's fingers. 'Ye had best clean up before yer lady sees ye, or ye secret will be out.'

Beauden grinned at him. 'I will, don't fret. This is a special night. I've asked Mrs Perkins to pull out all the stops.'

'Don't I know it. Perkins ev'n went down to the cellar for a bottle of ye father's champagne and the good port. It will be a dinner fit for Holyrood House.'

'Excellent. Does my father know?'

'I passed on ye message. He didn't seem surprised.'

No. His father was remarkably prescient; he had seen this coming since that very first day.

'Go on up, Jimmy. There is nothing more to be done tonight.'

Beauden watched his most faithful friend head up the stair.

After sweeping away the chips of wax and plaster dust, Beauden washed the traces of it from his body, then dressed with care. It was not every day a man announced his betrothal.

He was determined to wed as soon as possible, and it was not only that his time was short or that he felt Time's winged chariot hot on his heels. More than anything else, he wanted to luxuriate in the bliss of the married state. To be Galena Tindale's husband was his greatest hope.

Beauden trod lightly up the stairs to the room where Galena slept. The dinner gong sounded, and as he looked down into the hall, her door opened.

She looked utterly radiant. Her evening gown—a deep garnet satin, as rich as merlot gleaming in a glass—was set off her long, sloping shoulders and provided a jewel-like frame for her alabaster décolletage. Her curls were like a raven's wing and had been pinned up in a simple coiffure. A thin bronze chain looped across an intricate corset, and from it hung a shorter, triple-linked chain ending in her Rod of Asclepius. That and his mother's ring were her only ornaments.

'You are exquisite.' He touched his lips to hers, discovering that one such kiss was wholly insufficient.

'You look very dashing, Beauden.' Her voice was as soft as her lips.

She ran her fingers slowly under the broad lapels of his velvet wine-coloured frockcoat and pinned a pink rosebud into the top buttonhole. It perfectly matched the pinstripes and lace of her corset and the shade of her lips. Beauden wanted nothing so much as to remain on the step and kiss her until they were both witless, but they had a celebration to attend.

Beauden and Galena passed through the formal dining room, a noble Palladian chamber, wood-panelled with vivid Chinese silk drapes. The lamps, shaped like bronze dragons, shimmered with iridescent enamel scales; the table, in glorious mahogany, could seat a score.

He took her through into the adjacent drawing room where his father and uncle, both in their formal attire, sat with glasses of sherry in elegant Queen Anne chairs.

Beauden could see his father had perceived the importance of the occasion. Uncle Jacob's smile played around the edges of his mouth, but there was no knowing look in his eyes.

'Nephew, Miss Tindale, good evening.'

'Sherry, Galena?' His father's voice was warm.

'Yes, thank you, sir.'

His father passed out glasses and then lifted his. 'I take it we are celebrating the creation of the moulds for the heart and the ribs. After tomorrow, we will be one vital step closer to our goal.'

It was true, and on any other day, it would have been reason enough for delight, yet Beauden was certain his father suspected more.

'That is a cause for celebration, sir, and I must thank Uncle Jacob for bringing the gold, as well as Galena for helping you prepare the moulds today.'

'It was our pleasure, Beauden.' His uncle touched his glass to

Beauden's father's. 'After all, what else is family for, if not to give aid when needed?'

'Not only to give help in the bad times, Uncle, but I hope, to celebrate with us in the good.'

Beauden took Galena's hand in his and lifted her knuckles to his lips. As he met her eyes, his heart whirled for joy, and she smiled and nodded her encouragement. He had arrived at the moment in which he could put his joy into words.

'Sir, Uncle, I would like to inform you both that Miss Tindale has done me the courtesy of accepting my offer of marriage.'

His father put down the decanter with careful haste. 'My boy, that is wonderful news!'

He enfolded Beauden in a long embrace and then turned to Galena.

'I have longed for a daughter and you are just the young lady I would have chosen. You are brave, bold and beautiful.'

He took Galena's hands and kissed both her cheeks.

Beauden turned to his uncle with a grin. 'Sir, I hope you will join my father in wishing us well.'

Uncle Jacob got to his feet, clapped Beauden on the shoulder and held out his hand.

'But how could I do otherwise, young Beauden? You are truly a very fortunate man, and I could ask for nothing better than a happy future for you both.'

'Thank you, Uncle.'

Beside him, Galena held out a hand to his uncle. 'Thank you, sir. You are very gracious.'

'Not at all.' He ignored Galena's hand and stepped forward. 'But I, too, reserve the right to welcome the bride with a kiss.'

He took Galena by both hands and slowly kissed her cheeks. When he stepped back, her face burned.

Beauden turned to address his father. 'I'd like to let the household know, sir.'

His father waved to the speaking tube, mounted on the wall. 'A splendid idea.'

Beauden lifted the brass mouthpiece and spoke into it, requesting the staff come upstairs before setting down the device.

'So, nephew, when did this happen?'

Beauden's father shook his head at his brother. 'Ah, when the cat's away, Jacob. You and I were both out this afternoon.'

Beauden offered his father a thin, wry, smile. 'You are correct as usual, sir.'

'Will you make a formal announcement in the newspapers, nephew? Or will you simply wait to call the banns? A wedding takes some little time to plan.'

Beauden smiled and squeezed Galena's hand.

'Sir, we do not anticipate a long engagement. I have admired Miss Tindale since the day I met her, and I do not see the purpose of coyness. We none of us know our fates and mine is more precarious than most. I hope to make Miss Tindale my wife with all possible speed.'

His uncle furrowed his brows. 'Surely you will invite Miss Tindale's family to share this day with her. Galena, you will want your mother with you, will you not?'

But his uncle's question was not destined to be answered. The drawing room door opened to reveal Mr and Mrs Perkins, Jimmy, three maids and a scowling boot boy.

Beauden stood before them, hoping his smile spoke for itself, and swept his eyes over them. Mrs Perkins had been his nurse from his cradle, Jimmy his right arm. Most of the staff had been with them since his boyhood and were as much his family as his father and uncle.

'Good evening. You will rejoice with me, I am sure, in the news that Miss Tindale will shortly become Mrs Somerton.'

Not a whisper of surprise showed on any face except for Alan the boot boy. Beauden knew him to be of an age where he was still convinced the whole race of women were devised to plague him.

Mrs Perkins lifted the corner of her apron to her eye.

Perkins beamed and stepped forward. 'I'm sure I speak for all the staff, sir, when I say that we wish you happy.'

'Thank you. I hope you will celebrate my good fortune.'

Beauden reached into his pocket, pulled out a handful of sovereigns and pressed one into each palm. All the women dropped Beauden a curtsey, and he shook hands with Alan and Perkins.

When Jimmy stretched out his hand, Beauden shook his head and pulled him into a swift embrace instead. Jimmy, older than Beauden by a decade, dour and rough, was the closest Beauden had to a brother.

The staff returned downstairs, and as Beauden escorted his fiancée across the hall to the dining room and the feast that awaited them, he thought he caught an abstracted frown on his uncle's face. It was gone, though, before he could do more than imagine it.

Beauden wasn't surprised. He had always sensed his uncle watched over him from afar, like a guardian angel. Certainly, his uncle had done everything he could to support his father's research, but he was not a medical man, and so he was forced to watch events play out, helpless to act. Beauden knew how that felt. But when his uncle came to realise just how much Beauden loved Galena, how vital she was to his happiness, he would cease fretting. Uncle Jacob would soon love Galena as much as his father did. He was certain.

***

It was well into the evening, and Merrick Forsythe sat in the single chair beside his tiny hearth in his lodgings, leafing through his precious copy of *Anatomy, Surgical and Descriptive*. The brand new textbook for medical students, published in America by Henry Grey, was the most up-to-date treatise ever made and had been acquired with considerable difficulty.

Merrick swirled a fingerful of blended whisky, his one indulgence, and contemplated his predicament.

He considered himself the most fortunate of men. With a generous godfather who had sent him to Scotland to study, procuring him this book among other luxuries, he had the respect if not the liking of his peers. Or he had.

Today the dean had summoned him. Merrick's career was in his own hands, apparently. He hadn't been threatened or chastised, not as such. But mention had been made that the university strictly forbade fighting on its grounds.

But what was a man to do? Nothing here, nothing he had ever read, suggested that the organs of lesser species could be used to perform medicine. He would be the first to acknowledge that the frontiers of medicine grew wider every day. Ever since he had read Mantell's work on animalcules, he had been fascinated by the thought that miasma was the product of tiny creatures in the human body attacking it from within. How then could any rational person suggest using the flesh of an animal to replace human tissue? The idea was preposterous, obscene, diabolical.

A muted flash from his mirror messenger distracted him, and he lifted the fine oak lid to read the text on the silvered glass within. He had seen the elegant hand before, but the words were a shock that shuddered right through him. He stared at them, alternately nauseated, grieved and enraged at the information seeping from within the Somerton enclave.

That stupid tart!

Merrick reached for the decanter, poured a large slug into his glass, then swallowed half with barely a tremor.

As he had not expected events to move so briskly, he had not yet discussed this with his peers. For some reason, they were avoiding him. It might be due to the dean's disfavour or a sneaking sympathy for the freakish young Somerton. Merrick's actions there had done him no good and won him no friends, so now, when he needed to win over the hearts and minds of his fellows, he faced an even greater battle.

His words alone would never convince them now. What he needed was a demonstration of some kind, something they could not ignore. If only they could see with their own eyes the evil that had been perpetrated in their very midst.

And it was not only Galena Tindale and the other female students—the monstrous regiment of women bent on corrupting the noble profession of medicine—but the man every student at the university admired. Augustus Somerton was known to be a brilliant lecturer and researcher whose work on compound fractures was now standard medical doctrine. However, he had disappeared into private research, and who could know what other perverted experiments he had conducted since.

Merrick swallowed the rest of the whisky in his glass and poured some more. The time for action was not a fortnight hence as he had both hoped and feared it might be. The time was now. Tomorrow, or the day after, work would begin in earnest to place a swine's heart into a human body and change for all time what it meant to be human.

Merrick could not allow it to happen.

And Galena Tindale …

He had hoped she could be brought to see the wrongness of

what she was doing, but tonight's message made it clear she had sold herself, body and soul, to the enemy.

And for what? A place at the side of Dr Frankenstein? A monster for a husband?

Merrick tipped the whisky in his glass down his throat to blot out the pain. Galena was so beautiful, shone so bright. But, he reminded himself, so had Lucifer. An hour before his fall, he had been the brightest star in heaven.

Merrick did not relish what had to be done, but he wouldn't shirk from his duty either. The whisky had put a fire in his belly and veins.

He set down the medical book; it would not help him now. Scrolling a fresh charge into his messenger, he wrote his response. His hand shook from the force of his emotion.

He looked at the single word, scrawled in black wax on the glass, and closed his eyes. Grief made him dizzy, but not too dizzy to close the cover and send the message. The deed done, he set down the device and poured another dram into his glass for courage.

Chapter 15

Galena smoothed her hands over her favourite gown, a print of pink roses on bamboo lattice over a creamy background. She added a high boned leather corset, deep brown to match the bamboo, and structured enough to support her tool belt. In a moment of sensibility, she attached the triple chain of her Rod of Asclepius to it, looping it at her waist.

Today she was going to the workshop with Beauden. Jimmy had taken the moulds to the workshop last night, along with the sections of the gold heart and the filigree mesh she had carved from wax to form the breastplate. They had been encased in plaster and wooden frames for extra security. By the time she and Beauden arrived, the first part of the process—losing the wax from the casts—would already be complete. Cain had been tasked with melting out the wax and pouring the gold for each of the casts.

Once the gold had been cast from the moulds, Galena would be responsible for overseeing the fit. The sections of the heart must fit together more precisely than the pieces of a child's jigsaw puzzle if Beauden were to survive. If any part needed to be scrapped and remade or adjusted, it would be her call.

It would have been so much easier if Dr Somerton had

elected to come with them, but he wanted to practise the suinae tissue procedure and had acquired a pig's heart for the process.

Galena slid the precious pink diamond onto her finger and pressed her hands over the lump of cold stone in her belly. She was excited and nervous and ... afraid?

Icy foreboding hung over her like a rain cloud. Though the feeling made no sense, for Beauden's family and household could not have been more welcoming.

From the landing outside her bedroom, Galena saw that Mr Somerton stood looking up at the stained-glass image of Myra Somerton, holding her baby daughter and Beauden's human heart.

Galena's foot tapped on the step and he turned, his distant expression quickly replaced by a welcoming smile.

'Good morning, Galena. You look radiant.'

'Good morning, sir, and thank you.'

'Ha!' He gave a warm chuckle. 'No need for formality. You should call me Uncle as Beauden does, for we will be related in just a few weeks, I imagine.'

Galena nodded. Nevertheless, there was a suspicious brightness to his eyes and the set of his shoulders that spoke of a man in pain. His demeanour did not match the buoyancy of his voice.

'I hope there is nothing the matter, sir?'

He shook his head, but she felt the sensation of him drawing away from her, hedging his truths with half-truths.

'No. But I couldn't help thinking of Myra again this morning. She would have loved you dearly, and it is a tragedy she will not have the opportunity.'

'Indeed, sir. You knew Mrs Somerton well? Beauden looks rather like her.'

'Yes, I knew her. Her brother was a dear friend of mine, so we were acquainted long before she fell madly in love with Augustus.'

The jarring note in his tone was at odds with his smile, so Galena swallowed the question she had been about to ask.

'Are you going down to breakfast, sir? Uncle?'

He grinned. 'No, I have several calls to make this morning. Farewell, my dear. I shall see you this evening.'

Galena inclined her head courteously and turned for the breakfast parlour, but she saw it was several long seconds before Beauden's uncle stepped out.

'Good morning, Galena.' Beauden rose as she entered the breakfast parlour, pulled out the chair beside his and kissed her cheek. 'Did you sleep well, my dear?'

'Quite well.'

She noticed the greasepaint on his cheek and circled his wrist with her fingers, the doctor in her automatically taking over. 'And you, Beauden? How are you feeling?'

His pulse was smooth, his skin cool to the touch. Her own heart skipped a beat.

He turned his hand, lifting her fingers to his, kissing her knuckles one after the other before seating her.

'My skin's sallow tone has returned.' He gave a casual shrug as he poured her coffee. 'But, I assure you, I feel perfectly well. I am quite robust enough to see you to the forge today. In fact, I'm looking forward to it.'

Galena smiled and tried to ignore the sick clamour under her ribs.

***

Galena listened to Beauden's conversation as they trotted towards their destination, but the rubberised hooves clopped vigorously over the cobbles in a race with her heart and distracted her.

Had she and Dr Somerton achieved a perfect fit for the moulds? If there was a fault, would she see it in time? The thrill of scientific discovery and the joy of medical advancement paled as she saw the shadow of the reaper inching over the man she loved.

'Darling?' Beauden's voice rippled over her unwelcome thoughts. 'Where are you this morning?'

She placed her mitten-covered fingers to her lips. 'I am sorry, Beauden. The new heart has claimed all my attention.'

He kissed her cheek and smiled. 'Don't think for a moment that I don't appreciate it. In fact, I have a surprise for you later, to show you how much you mean to me.'

Galena looked at her affianced husband, his face alight with joy, but she was beset with worries. 'Thank you.'

He took her face between his hands. 'I hope you like it.'

He wore his leather-rimmed shaded glasses, so she could not

see his eyes, but the timbre of his voice told her all she needed to know.

'I will love it.'

She curled into him, resting her head on his chest. Three inches below her ear, the soft *click, click, click* of the pendulum echoed from its iron moorings deep inside Beauden. It echoed the lamentation within her soul.

Lacing her fingers through Beauden's, she closed her eyes and let her deepest desires ascend as a prayer.

Don't let this be for naught. Please help us save him. Please.

She refused to imagine a world without Beauden. He was so good, so decent, honourable and precious; and she had only just found him. If she lost him now, her life would be as hollow as a husk. Her soul would shatter.

They drew to a steaming, squealing stop outside the workshop doors, and Will came out to greet them. Beauden handed her out and passed Jimmy the tightly wrapped plaster casts. It was all too real. She wanted to climb back into the unicarriage and have Jimmy take her away, defer this to another day. But they were running out of time.

'Ready, sweetheart?'

Galena glanced at his beloved face—sharp angles, disguised complexion, shadowed eyes—and put her hand in his.

'Absolutely. Shall we?'

***

Of course he wasn't mad! Or drunk!

Merrick stared at his peers, his mind reeling. They had been there, just as he had. They had seen the devil, standing there with his unnatural eyes. He told them what he now knew—that Beauden Somerton was some kind of undead fiend without a living heart in his breast. Why in Hell's own name were they refusing to aid him?

Douglas Warwick alone came closer and put his hand on Merrick's shoulder.

'Merrick, it's clear you've had too little sleep and too much whisky. Perhaps—'

Merrick slapped away the hands of the man he'd once called friend, the man who, of all the others, was his equal. His stomach seethed with angry bile.

'You damned fool, Warwick!' He upended the table, sending half-full glasses cascading to the ground. Beer frothed at his ankles. 'You are all damned fools, every one of you!'

'Enough!' Warwick stepped forward. 'You've been drinking deep and every word you have uttered could come out of a horrid novel. As for that man being undead, how did he best you, then?'

The group rippled with angry laughter and someone growled about spilled beer.

Merrick felt the mood of the group turn against him. These were the men he had naively believed would help him rid the city of Dr Somerton and his monstrous son. With Galena Tindale and her unholy research in the doctor's hands, one monster could become a score—a thousand! It might be damnably clever, but it was evil.

With his friends lost, content to wallow in their ignorance and let disaster strike, he had no choice but to leave.

'You will see! I'm no fool—no drunk. There is a monster in Edinburgh that lurks in plain sight. He may wear an elegant coat, but he is a monster.'

He slammed his hand into the doorframe. 'He has already seduced a weak and vain woman into doing his bidding. Wise and honourable as you think yourselves to be, you let him roam free! Well, I will not.'

'For goodness sake, Merrick, you are imagining it! Somerton is a doctor and a scientist—'

'And a blasphemer who would cheat nature!'

Merrick turned on Warwick like a drowning man, his hands clutching at his shoulders. 'Douglas, you were my friend! Come with me now and help me rid this city of the evil walking its streets. I beg you.'

Warwick's face was calm—too calm. Merrick watched in vain for a like anger to kindle in him.

'Merrick, the only evil I see comes from the man who wants us to attack a fellow scientist and learned professor on the basis of a wild and unsubstantiated story. Enough vitriol, my friend. Get some rest.'

Merrick's heart burned and a red veil of rage descended over him. He shoved Warwick into the crowd and fled the bar, bursting out into the midday sunshine.

The Judas' words echoed after him. 'Merrick, listen to reason. You are not yourself …'

If these over-educated idiots could not see the truth when it stood before them in all its horrid unnatural glory, then he would find men willing to aid him elsewhere. He would avenge his name—he was not drunk, or mad. He knew what these fools did not—and he could prove it. With a few men willing to help him, he would prove it.

***

Beauden stood at Galena's shoulder as Cain tipped the last of the wax from the moulds. A thin stream flowed out, catching and flaring as it struck the hot coals.

They had poured Beauden's small tester mould first, followed by the thin filigree breastplate and the individual sections of the heart. There were three—the gently-curved back and the more rounded left and right front pieces. From the rear panel, two thin tubes rose almost an inch, like the sides of a letter *V*. The front halves each had a curving tube with an aperture as wide as a pinkie finger. Now hollow since the wax had been poured out, each awaited the gold filling.

Will clamped the plaster moulds carefully in place on the bench, padding them with soft leather to ensure they did not crack. At the forge, Cain was stripped to the waist and kept his eye on the fist-sized graphite crucible full of gold as the temperature of the coals rose beyond cherry red.

'Are you sure this will work?' Wringing her hands, Galena watched on.

Beauden rested his hand on her shoulder as Cain gripped the crucible with heavy, heat-resistant tongs and turned to the moulds. He poured the larger pieces first—the back of the heart, then the two smaller pieces for the front. The lattice came next; though the mould was the widest, the hollow within was only an eighth of an inch thick.

The gold was a vivid stream, enthralling to watch.

Galena caught her breath.

'Beautiful, isn't it?' Beauden couldn't keep the awe from his voice. 'I love to watch when Cain pours copper or bronze for prosthetic limbs.'

Finally, using the last ounce of gold in the crucible, Cain poured Beauden's small tester mould. It would cool the quickest and would be ready to break open in just over an hour.

Beauden released the breath he had been holding. 'Well done, Cain. And very little residue.'

The big man shrugged. 'It were a pleasure. Glorious to work with, bain't it, sir?'

Galena tapped her lip. 'Cain, the other small items, the clamps and such—will they pose a problem?'

Cain wiped the sweat from his brow and shook his head. 'No, missus. Fine gold wire is easy. I always carry a little for fine parts in limbs, for it don't rust away like them other metals.'

'Thank you, Cain. Galena and I will see you after luncheon.'

The giant winked. 'Reet, Master Beauden. I'll be off to the tap and quench my thirst.'

Galena watched Cain lumber off. 'He won't tell anyone what we're making, will he?'

Will gave her a bright look, and Beauden laughed.

'Don't worry, Galena. Cain isn't much of a conversationalist.'

Will nodded. 'The barmaid at the alehouse knows his order only because he gets the same thing every day.'

'Come and eat lunch, my dear, while we wait for the gold to cool.'

Sighing, she looked towards the bench where the plaster sat strapped upright. 'I do so hate waiting.'

'Believe me, I am just as impatient as you. Sadly, there is nothing to do but have a glass of wine. Mrs Perkins has put together a splendid picnic, and I dare say Father will be along in a little while. I thought he might like to be here for the great unveiling.'

'Oh, he will. Ought we not wait for him?'

Beauden took her hand. 'Oh, I think not. Perhaps we will save him a slice of dessert?' He smiled and led her to the table.

Chapter 16

Merrick did not give a curse for the staring eyes and pointing fingers of the curious householders of Leith as he led his mob towards the house of Dr Somerton.

Servants would be home. And who knew, the monster himself might be within. But all Merrick needed to do was obtain the plans and diagrams, to show the world the truth of the perversion being conducted here.

The courtyard was deserted, desolate. Nothing but grim stone and dead plants. A fitting home for one devoid of life.

Merrick raised his cudgel and beat on the door.

Boom. Boom.

A curtain flickered. Someone was inside. But it did not matter—Merrick had come prepared. He turned to the great unwashed who followed him. They didn't understand his end goal, but they would gladly break down a door, ransack a house and then melt back into the slums from whence they came.

Merrick gestured at the half-dozen strong men behind him. 'Bring up the log.'

A minute later, the huge door splintered open. The surface

might be covered in bronze panels, but the mechanism of the lock was the weak point.

The mob fanned into the house, most men eager to seize what they could, but those to whom he had promised guineas looked to him for direction.

'Come with me.'

***

Beauden glanced sidelong at Will as he retrieved the smallest plaster mould from the bench and held it in his hand to judge the residual warmth. At the expression on Will's face, Beauden stifled a sigh of relief and downed the last of his wine.

He had asked his father to come to the workshop today, though he was yet to arrive. He seldom forgot an appointment, but perhaps Galena was right and he was too engrossed in his researches. Or perhaps he'd been called to an emergency at the clinic. That happened occasionally.

Even as Beauden had shaped the wax last night, he'd known his time was dwindling. The degeneration of the heart was speeding up, he could feel it. Every painful breath, every aching beat of his corroded heart urged him onward. He had even begun to wonder if they would complete the preparations for the operation in time. He could do nothing to save his life—but there was one thing he could do.

'Thank you, Will.'

'A couple of light taps should do it.' Will handed him the plaster mould and a small hammer, then respectfully withdrew.

Beauden cleared his throat. 'Galena, I brought you here for a special reason, if you are willing.'

Galena opened her eyes wide at his words.

He offered her the hammer, handle first. 'If you would do the honours?'

His actions seemed to confuse her.

'You want me to break open the tester mould?'

'In truth, it is a little more important than that. The gold is cool enough to handle now.'

Galena took the hammer's handle firmly and lay a napkin over the plaster before giving it a few light taps.

On the third tap, the plaster shattered into shards and gold peeped through.

With a quick look at Beauden, Galena picked up the gold between her thumb and forefinger, gently lifted it out of the plaster wreckage and smoothed the dust away.

When she spoke, her voice trembled. 'It's a ring.'

'It's a wedding ring.' Beauden could not keep the thread of passion from his voice. 'Your wedding ring.'

She ran her thumb over the fine, sinuous lines etched into the surface and a play of emotions crossed her face. Glowing, she raised her head, her smile brilliant.

'Oh, Beauden, it's beautiful!'

'I made the wax mould last night. The lines are like the ones you made in the design of my breastplate, and it is made from the same gold—the same gold as my new heart.'

Her eyes brimmed with tears as she looked from the ring to him. A plump drop rolled down her cheek. 'That is beautiful.'

'There is an inscription inside.'

She turned the ring into the light. '*Beloved Rib.*'

'Eve was Adam's wife and made from his rib.'

Galena kissed his cheek. 'This gold will be your ribs … and I will be your wife.'

Watching his bride-to-be gently turning the ring between her fingers, Beauden grasped the nettle.

'Galena, I would like us to be married here. Today. If you want to wait, I understand.' He shrugged, not willing to press her if she were at all reluctant. And yet … 'But I want to spend every hour I can with you.'

She brushed away a tear. 'I would love to marry you here, today. Is it possible?'

He grinned, relieved. 'My dear, this is Scotland. All we need to do is join our hands over the anvil and Cain can make us man and wife.'

Her smile was as bright as the noonday sun.

***

Galena stood with her bridegroom before the anvil at the rear of the

172

workshop. All the staff was there, and young Marian stood at her side. Beauden had the foresight to arrange a posy of blush roses as her bouquet.

Cain stood behind the anvil and looked from one to the other. 'Be pleased to join yer hands, sir and mistress.'

Galena reached across to Beauden and he took her trembling fingers in his cool grasp.

'Scottish law asks only that both man and woman speak their intent to live as husband and wife before witnesses. Do ye both so swear?'

'I do.' Tension squeezed Galena's chest as though her corset had been wrenched tighter all of a sudden. She turned to look at the man who was about to become her husband.

'I do.' Beauden's eyes, not hidden behind his secretive lenses, were frank and open.

Galena caught his smile and was finally able to breathe.

'Then, by the law of Scotland, I declare ye ta be husband and wife together.' Cain lifted his hammer in his huge right hand and brought it crashing down on the anvil. 'Joined till death dae ye part!'

The handful of people present cheered loud enough to raise the rafters.

Galena felt dizzy at the speed of events. She had scarcely finished lunch; now she was—good God—now she was Mrs Beauden Somerton!

'A toast!'

Will handed her a champagne flute, one each to Marian and

Judith, and whisky to the men.

'To the best man of our acquaintance, Beauden Somerton, and his lovely bride. May every conceivable happiness be theirs.'

Galena sipped and smiled at the glee with which Beauden's friends celebrated his marriage. This one swift moment in time taken with little preparation was as ideal as any moment could be.

Now, if she ignored the dragging pain of Beauden's illness, she considered her life perfect, more than she ever could have imagined. She turned the gold ring on her finger. It was a far more intimate connection than that of any other married couple. One day very soon, the same gold—poured in one batch from the same crucible—would be sealed within her husband's chest, keeping him alive. It would. She was determined.

Will and Jimmy came forward, more alike than she had realised. Something in the shape of the nose and jaw gave them away.

Will held out a hand. 'Congratulations, Mr Somerton.'

'Thank you, Will. I'm sure you can keep the place functioning until I am free to come back. My wife will no doubt want me all to herself for a time.'

Jimmy said nothing, his head bent. Beauden laid a hand on his shoulder and the look that passed between them spoke volumes. Galena knew that Jimmy was no servant, for all he accepted a wage.

'I wish ye every happiness, Master Beauden.' He handed Beauden back his cane and mirror messenger.

'Thank you, Jimmy, for everything you have done for me over the years. I owe a debt to you for your unstinting care.' He took

Jimmy's hand and shook it.

Jimmy cleared his throat, presumably to banish the last of his emotion. 'Are ye ready to be off, Master Beauden? I've packed the gold into the carriage and 'tis ready when you are.'

'Yes. I am looking forward to surprising Father and Uncle Jacob. I did suggest that Father come today, so he has no one to blame but himself if he keels over with the shock.'

Jimmy gave a wry grin and went to fire up the carriage.

Beauden and Galena endured one more round of handshakes and kisses before they followed Jimmy out.

'I can't believe your father didn't divine your intentions.'

Beauden laughed. 'Neither can I. I really imagined he would come. He must be more caught up in his researches than I gave him credit for.'

'You should send him a message, my dear.'

Beauden handed her into the unicarriage and entered behind her as Jimmy put up the step. He snuggled onto the seat beside her and laced his fingers through hers.

'Nonsense. We will be home in ten minutes, and we will tell him then. I cannot wait to see his face!'

***

Merrick clattered down the stairs to the monster's dank basement, two strong men at his back. As he threw open the door, a silver-haired man in a white coat looked up. A dissected heart sat on the well-lit bench at the side of the room; the doctor, smeared with blood, stopped drying his hands and put his towel down beside a deep sink.

'So, you are conducting one of your fiendish experiments?'

'Who the hell are you?'

'You are Dr Somerton?'

'And this is my house!'

'I thought you were a great doctor,' Merrick spat, the cudgel held lightly in his right hand. 'Your fame has spread throughout the university. Everyone knows of you. That you are a friend and colleague of the dean. That you spent years lecturing and tutoring students.'

'What of it?'

'A month ago, a week ago, I would have been honoured to be in the same room with you. I had hoped that what I had been told was a lie.'

It seemed the great man had feet of clay.

This room, this laboratory was where he had made his monster, where he planned the perversions he would unleash on the world. A large bed-like table sat in the centre of the room, overarched with large, offset rings, one inside the other. It could have no good purpose.

The old man braced himself as though for an onslaught, snatching up the bloody scalpel from his instrument tray.

'Who the devil are you?'

'The man who will stop you from performing any more diabolical experiments.'

Merrick advanced, and when he reached the doctor's side, he upended the table on which the heart sat. The tray and instruments clattered down, and the dissected tissue hit the ground with a wet slap.

Somerton raised a fist. 'Get out of my house, you damned swine!'

Drifting down from upstairs, shouting and the sounds of furniture being smashed could be heard. Hopefully, the two Merrick had left as guards kept other villains from coming to Somerton's aid.

'Damned? I am not damned. That is you, who would interfere in the working of the human body.'

He brought up his cudgel, thrusting it into the doctor's breastbone. 'Where is your son, the monster you made?'

Somerton recoiled, his staring eyes filled with fear now. Good.

'You stay away from my son, you bastard!'

His fist connected with Merrick's nose. Bone crunched and blood spurted.

'Take this place apart!' Merrick screamed to his acolytes. 'Turn it to kindling—and then we will burn it.'

'No!'

The doctor stood only a foot or so from him, backing away like the cur he was.

Merrick waved his club. 'I'll burn it, and then I will find the monster and the whore. But it won't matter to you!'

He swung the cudgel. It connected with the side of the old man's head in a sickening thud and he fell like a stone. Merrick smashed the club down on the doctor's shoulder.

Somerton held up a pleading hand and Merrick took careful aim, striking it with full force. The doctor screamed as his bones crunched and he cradled the wrecked hand even as Merrick slammed more blows into his knee, his ribs, his head.

Merrick's men made short work of the ringed table in the centre of the room, and they had just overturned a large cabinet when a hellish shriek sounded, like an entire racket of banshees.

The fouler ruffian turned to Merrick. 'It's an alarm!'

Merrick stopped cudgelling the unconscious old monster. 'It doesn't matter. When the constables come, they will arrest Somerton for his villainy.'

'We will nae stay here!'

'Cowards!' Merrick shouted at their departing backs, but it was no good.

He turned his attention to the desk, swiping his weapon across the surface, pushing all the books and instruments to the floor. He had begun assaulting the furniture when he heard footsteps on the stairs and a shrill whistle.

Merrick looked up to see a constable running his way. 'Officer!'

But the officer grabbed Merrick's collar, and so Merrick swung around in anger.

'I've brought him down! I've killed him! Now for the monster.'

A second officer wrenched his wrist behind his back.

'Let me go! I'm trying to rid Edinburgh of a monstrous evil!'

He flung off the constable who staggered back but then rallied. The officer's baton struck behind Merrick's ear.

Chapter 17

Galena gave herself up to Beauden's kisses as he slid an arm around her and tilted her chin. Their kiss started with a sweetness that slowly turned sensual. He unfastened the three buttons at her collar and caressed the exposed skin of her throat.

'Should we be doing this? Your heart …'

'My heart will survive the passion, I promise. But I might not if I don't love you tonight as a husband should.' He kissed her with a hunger that was as fierce as it was gentle.

'Well, we cannot have that.'

'No indeed.' He nibbled on her earlobe and she giggled. 'My life is in your hands, my love.'

Pulling her onto his lap, he nuzzled her neck and slid one hand under her skirt, up her calf, and he toyed with her garter. He caressed the curves at the top of her corset with his lips until she was panting and dizzy.

The carriage turned the corner—then sped up.

Beauden raised his head and frowned. 'That is odd.'

The speed increased further and he heard the jacketed hooves of the unicarriage fairly galloping over the cobbles.

As abruptly as he had sped up, Jimmy slammed the vehicle to a halt.

Galena slid from Beauden's lap and set about righting her clothing as Beauden let down the window with a crash.

'What in blue blazes …?'

He stared at the scene before them and threw the door open. They were parked outside his father's house—and so were two police steam cycles. Through the open gateway, he could see the shattered front door.

For once, Beauden's courtesy failed him. He leapt from the carriage and seized a constable by the shoulder. 'What has happened here? My father …'

'I'm sorry, sir. There has been an incident.'

Beauden ran through the wrecked door and into the hallway, Galena at his heels. The vaulted room with its turquoise and silver was a mess. A table had been turned over and a porcelain vase smashed. A dozen shredded tulips lay in a puddle amongst the coarse shards.

As one, Beauden and Galena ran for the basement stair and, at its foot, a scene of carnage met their eyes. Books and papers covered the floor. Galena's drawing of the heart lay open at their feet, but it was torn and ravaged—all but obliterated.

'Father?' Beauden picked his way through the wreckage.

His father lay on the damaged bed, the rings no longer surrounding it. They lay on the floor instead, under the detritus of rage. The bed was now only a tabletop with the bloodied wreck of a man laying on it.

Beauden's stomach twisted in sick horror at the brutality of the attack, yet he felt relieved, too. If his father were dead, they would not have moved him there. As if in response, his bare chest rose and fell in a shuddering paroxysm of pain.

Beside his father stood a tall man, neatly dressed in a well-cut suit of fine worsted.

'Good afternoon, sir, ma'am.' His tone hinted at an implacable will veneered in thin civility. 'You, sir, would be the victim's son? Mr Beauden Somerton?'

Beauden gave him a sharp nod and a brisk inspection. He was impeccably and stylishly dressed, his jacket buttoned asymetrically, embellished with leather detail and bright bronze buttons. A gentleman of some status then.

The fellow turned to Galena, tugged slightly at his luxuriant moustache and bowed.

'And you, ma'am?'

'Mrs Somerton.'

'Ah.'

Beauden's father made a sound from the bed like a breathless moan, or it may have been a broken laugh.

Galena approached him and, stripping off her gloves, began a light examination.

Beauden addressed the gentleman. 'Are you with the police? Has a doctor been summoned? Who is guilty of this atrocity?'

The mantle of responsibility fell on his shoulders. His father had done so much for him, now he had to repay the debt. The policeman looked large, confident and capable, but it was not his father's blood dripping onto the floor.

'We've arrested a man called Merrick Forsythe.'

'No!' Galena turned, white to the lips, and looked at Beauden in utter anguish.

He met her gaze through his coloured lenses and gave his head a tiny shake. After a second, she turned again to his father, her patient, her back bowed as though Forsythe's name were an additional weight.

'I don't have to ask then if you know this man.'

'No, sir, you do not. He is an acquaintance of my wife. They are both students of the Edinburgh Medical College. But that does not tell me why he committed this monstrosity or who you are.'

'I beg your pardon, Mr Somerton.'

That was a polite fiction, Beauden could tell.

'I am Detective Ian McIntyre of Her Majesty's Inspectorate of Constabulary. As for why the man attacked your father, when my constables arrived, he was shouting about blasphemy and monsters. Your father has managed to tell me that Forsythe arrived here bent on committing mischief and attacked him with insane rage, clearly with murderous intent.'

Beauden drew in a long, slow breath. McIntyre appeared to be no fool, and Beauden would not awaken the man's mind against them.

Before he could speak, Galena was at his side. 'Beauden, Inspector, I beg your pardon, but I would like to get medical aid to Father as soon as possible.' She turned to the inspector. 'Has anyone been summoned?'

McIntyre assessed her in an instant. 'Not as yet, ma'am. When we determined that the doctor was alive, my constables moved him for his comfort.'

She tilted her chin up at an imperious angle. 'Then I should like to send to the university to get some assistance. None of his injuries are life-threatening, but they need attending to.'

'I will have a constable summon an ambulance.'

'There is no need. I have everything I require here.'

Her determined air was accompanied by a mulish cast to the lips and a spark in her rich brown eyes.

'If I need more aid, I will send to the dean of the university. He and Father have been friends for longer than either of our lifetimes. He will know who to send.' She brushed a hand over Beauden's. 'As quickly as possible, my dear, please.'

'Who would you like Jimmy to collect?'

'My friend, Olive Mansell. She is staying at the deanery.'

'Consider it done.' Beauden allowed himself no more than a touch of her fingers before he hurried for the stairs. Anger, hatred, vengeance—all fought for position in his heart. It was a relief to be doing something, even if it was only sending Jimmy on an errand.

The detective followed him up to the courtyard where Jimmy was refilling the reservoir on the unicarriage. No doubt the man desired a private interrogation.

'Jimmy, I need you to go to the university and ask Miss Olive Mansell, a friend of Mrs Somerton, to come back here with you. My father has been hurt and we need her assistance in tending to him.'

Jimmy gave McIntyre a surly glance, looking much like Beauden felt, and tipped his cap. 'Right, sir.'

'Just a minute, Jimmy.' Beauden spun to face the detective. 'Was anyone else hurt besides my father?'

The detective spoke. 'The maid managed to lock herself into an attic room and is quite safe. An elderly man, perhaps the butler, received a nastly blow to the head. He was coming around when my constables found him.'

'Good heavens! Perkins, too.' Beauden considered. 'Jimmy, you better send a message to Will. They might go after my workshop next. Or the clinic.'

Jimmy tipped his hat again, let out the damper, then chugged loudly out of the courtyard under a plume of steam.

Beauden pressed both hands to his temples and sighed slowly. 'If there is nothing else, Detective McIntyre, I should see if I can assist my wife. No doubt you will keep us apprised?'

The detective put out a restraining hand. 'A moment, sir. We don't believe that Forsythe acted alone.'

'I did not imagine he had. The damage is more extensive than I thought one man could possibly achieve.'

McIntyre shook his head. 'You mistake me. I am certain that

more than one man acted here—your butler described the men who atttacked him as street thugs—but I believe another intelligence may have plotted the attack.'

'Holy h—' Beauden stopped mid-oath. 'You are serious! Good God, sir, why would you think that?'

'Forsythe was rambling about someone when we loaded him into the Black Maria, someone he appears to believe and trust, but we have no particulars.' He paused and looked at Beauden shrewdly. 'Tell me, sir, do you or your family have any enemies?

'Of course not. My father sees relatively few patients. He has a charity clinic near the South Bridge and works there on occasion. He is generally busy with his research.'

'And what is he researching? Could this attack have been provoked by intellectual envy?'

'What makes you ask that? Because Forsythe tried to destroy the workshop?'

'And because many of the drawings and blueprints our constable found were badly damaged. They seemed to be medical in nature and yet mechanical.'

McIntyre's line of questioning was logical, yet it made Beauden uneasy. It would not take much questioning for the detective to get information about Galena's research from Forsythe. Better a version of the truth to set against Merrick Forsythe's crazed tales.

'The truth is that my father's research is predominently on the heart due to my illness. A weakness of the heart muscle killed my twin sister and almost killed me. Only my father's skill has allowed me to live this long. Father had any number of drawings reflecting aspects of the workings of the heart—but they are merely drawings. The bed Forsythe destroyed was a large rotating magnet that eased the pressure on my heart's faulty valves. My wife's research, also on the heart, is what enabled me to make her acquaintance.'

McIntyre looked at Beauden intently. 'I see. And does your condition require you to wear coloured lenses, even indoors?'

Beauden nodded. 'The medication I take makes it difficult for me to be in the light. Plants like foxglove are used for heart medicine and can affect the pupil of the eye.'

It wasn't quite a lie.

'And the greasepaint, sir?' The detective kept his voice diffident.

'The heart condition has given me a slightly blue cast to my skin.' Beauden took the handkerchief from his pocket and carefully wiped his lips. 'Are you familiar with the term cyanosis?'

McIntyre gave a single nod. 'Thank you for your candour, Mr Somerton. Forsythe was raving about destroying a monster with a dead heart.'

Beauden felt a chill run down his spine, but he smiled grimly. 'I hope you can see, Detective, that I am no ghoul.'

McIntyre tipped his hat. 'I shall return tomorrow and see if Dr Somerton can tell us more about the attack. Thank you for your time.'

Beauden waited only a moment before passing through the shattered door.

***

'How is he?'

Galena's husband of one hour hurried down the stairs. She had given her father-in-law a small dose of laudanum and had started to wash and dress his lesser wounds. She could do little about his cracked rib until Olive arrived, and as for his hand …

Beauden reached her side and looked down at his father. She could imagine what was going through his mind—feelings of guilt for bringing Forsythe's insane fury down on them, wishing that he had been present, desperately hoping that all would be well.

'I'll do.' Her new father's voice was barely a whisper. And no wonder, every movement, every wound must be painful.

'Congratulations, son … daughter.' He turned his head infinitesimally, straining to see them both, then winced.

'Don't move, sir.' She set her hand upon his arm in warning.

'No … I won't.'

'Damn Merrick Forsythe!' Beauden's voice was icy with rage. 'If I get my hands on him, I'll—'

'Easy, my boy. The police have him. Besides'—he drew breath and strength—'better that he not have the opportunity to face you. I fear he knows the truth.'

His face was grey and grim; he had aged a score of years since the morning.

Galena bent over him. 'Sleep, Father. Let us look after you.'

He squinted through one eye. The other had swollen shut.

'Do your best to save the hand, my dear.' The doctor held his voice steady, but Galena heard a surging tide of emotion under it.

'I will do my utmost, sir.'

He slowly closed his eyes. When his breathing steadied and the ratchet of his pain visibly eased, Galena buried her face in the shoulder of her husband's jacket and wept.

Beauden stroked the hair from her face and shushed her gently.

'Will you be able to save his hand?'

She had been dreading the question because she just didn't know. But Beauden deserved the best answer she could give him, even if it was one neither of them wanted.

'It depends on too many variables. Can we set the broken bones effectively? Is there significant damage to the nerves and tendons? I won't really know until the swelling subsides.' She shook her head. 'I wish there was a way to look within the human body.'

'Galena, his hands are his life. Should we ask the dean to recommend someone?'

She bit her lip. 'Olive and I will straighten and strap the hand, then we will wait to see what can be achieved.'

She met her husband's shadowed copper eyes. 'I cannot promise that he will make a full recovery, but even if he does, it will not be soon enough to operate on you.'

Galena reached up and pulled his head to hers, laying her cheek against his so he would not see her tears fall. It was their wedding day and a death sentence was the last thing either of them wanted.

'Shush, my love. It will be all right.' He kissed her and held her tightly. 'You will see.'

Chapter 18

'Right, that should hold it for now.'

Galena breathed a sigh of relief as she locked eyes with Douglas Warwick across her father-in-law's body. She had been horrified when he entered at Olive's side, but now she was glad of his skill.

'How confident are you about the tendons?'

Douglas gave a weary shrug. 'Moderately confident. We won't be able to tell for a while. He may need a second surgery if they threaten to fuse on the middle phalange.'

He dabbed the sweat from his brow with the back of his cuff. 'Galena, your work on the tendons was superb. Your needlework is as fine as any I've seen.'

She was too tired to blush. 'My mother always was proud of my embroidery.'

'You would be wasted embellishing pillows. You will be an excellent surgeon.' He held out a hand as he would to any of his male peers.

She glanced down at his hand, then gratefully accepted it and the respect it demonstrated.

'As will you. I'm so glad you were able to repair the palmar muscle—it was a triumph. And Olive—thank you! It was such a relief to know you were administering the anaesthetic. You never missed a beat!'

'Thank you, Galena.' Olive Mansell looked up from the old wooden chair she had sunk into. 'It was fortunate that Douglas had come to the deanery.'

Galena noted the way Olive's eyes rested on Douglas. While Olive had mentioned several times in the past that she envied his acumen and surgical skill, it was apparent that it was not the extent of her admiration.

'I was happy I could help, but I almost wish I had been with Merrick instead. Who knows, I might have been able to prevent the need for any of this.' Douglas's skin was parchment pale with weariness and anger, his freckles standing out clearly.

'We'll never know, but I doubt it.' Beauden crossed the room towards them. He'd refused to go upstairs, but had stayed out of their way during surgery. 'Only an army could have prevented Merrick from harming anyone in his crazed state.'

'You don't know that.' Douglas was still slightly on edge.

Beauden put his hand over Galena's and she shook her head. 'The detective disagrees. He said Merrick was in a blind rage, beyond all reason. If you were here, Douglas, you would have been struck down as Father was.'

Beauden leaned past her and offered Douglas his hand. 'I appreciate everything you and Miss Mansell have done here. You three must be exhausted.'

Galena slipped off her bloodied apron and assisted Olive. She lifted her eyes to her husband's, though she could not see them behind the tinted lenses. And although the greasepaint hid many of the stresses he was surely facing, his posture betrayed him.

'He will rest easier now, Beauden. Tomorrow, once the swelling subsides, we will immobilise the fingers so they can heal properly.'

'Then you are confident ...?'

She shook her head wearily. It had been an exhausting day, full of wildly fluctuating emotions. 'Only time will tell. I don't think he will lose the hand, but whether he will ever regain full movement, I cannot say. What do you think, Douglas?'

'Aye, it will be a while before we know anything, but I am hopeful.'

Beauden straightened. 'Thank you again. We will let you know how he goes on. Would you care for a light meal, then Jimmy will take you home at your convenience.'

Olive smiled as Galena slipped an arm through hers, but Douglas didn't move.

'A bite to eat would be most agreeable, and Miss Mansell should return to the deanery, but if I might be so forward, I should like to remain here tonight and keep an eye on the doctor. Galena should rest. It has been a taxing day for her, and it is your wedding day after all—or rather, your wedding night.'

Galena bowed her head as her throat and face burst into embarrassed flame.

'I would appreciate that. Thank you, Warwick.' Beauden's voice held sincere gratitude.

Galena blinked back the tears that prickled her eyes.

What a day! Her wedding, Merrick's horrid attack and the surgical operation had taken their toll. Now, God be thanked, it was her wedding night. Her fears about Beauden's operation, her father-in-law's recovery, Merrick Forsythe's hatred—they could wait. Tonight she would love her husband. Tomorrow they would set about finding a way to perform Beauden's surgery so they could have a long and happy life together.

***

Beauden stood in the moonlit forecourt and raised a hand as his unicarriage, carrying Miss Mansell, clopped through the gates and into the night. He was grateful to the young woman and to Warwick. It was the first operation Beauden had been awake for, and he had found it gruesome, fascinating and terrifying in approximately equal parts.

Alone in the darkness, Beauden stood deep in thought. McIntyre had implied that Forsythe had not been the intellect behind the attack, but with his talk about monsters, it seriously narrowed the field of suspects. And then, it begged the question, who had the power to manipulate a credulous Forsythe? It must be a person of power or authority to be able to persuade Forsythe to act for him.

The only person Beauden could think of with both knowledge and standing was the dean. The dean knew of his situation, knew about the need to build a new heart, and about the old one, of course. He had recommended Galena's work to Father, for goodness sake.

And yet, it didn't make sense. The dean had known about Beauden since the beginning, had been Father's sounding board for years. He had urged Olive to come tonight and offered his advice. He would never have attacked Father. Never. They were friends. Besides, what did he have to gain?

A battered, old-fashioned hansom screeched to a halt outside the gate and Beauden's uncle leapt from the vehicle, throwing a pound note at the driver.

'Uncle!'

Uncle Jacob flinched and then hastened towards Beauden, his face grim. 'Beauden! Thank God you are unharmed!'

He clapped a heavy hand to Beauden's shoulder and ran his eyes over him, checking for injury.

'You heard what happened, Uncle?'

'Rumours only. Someone spoke of a doctor's house on the Leith Road that had been attacked by mad hooligans.' He glanced towards the house. 'Good heavens—the door! So it was here? They smashed their way in? Was anyone hurt?'

'Father. He was brutally beaten.'

'Is he …? Will he recover?'

Beauden heard the rage in his uncle's voice, saw his clenched fists.

'He is holding his own. Galena has seen to him.'

'Surely he should be in the hospital. Miss Tindale might be clever, but she is still a student.'

'He did not wish to go, and he came through the surgery well. Now we must wait and hope.'

'Yes.' He gave a reluctant nod and a grimace. 'Yes, of course. But what happened, Beauden? You were not here, were you?'

'No, sir. We returned after the attack, though the police were still here. But we should go in. You will want to see Father. He should be coming out of the anaesthetic shortly.'

Beauden gestured towards the patched front door. An eddy of rage rippled through him, lethally icy. What he wouldn't do to get his hands on the monster who was responsible for all this!

Chapter 19

Douglas had gone upstairs to wash, leaving Galena alone. She tucked in the end of the bandage at her father-in-law's wrist and gently laid his hand at his side. He was no more than semiconscious, still under the effects of the ether, but by no means deeply under.

A hoarse cry sounded from the door. 'Brother!'

Beauden and his uncle came down the last of the basement stairs.

As he crossed the room, Mr Somerton took in the devastation. He reached his brother's side, a deep frown on his face.

'Thank goodness you are here, sir! Please take care not to touch his hand.'

Mr Somerton put his clenched fist to his lips and shook his head slowly. 'I had not imagined … He is so badly injured.'

'He is, but apart from the hand and some broken ribs, he only requires stitches and time. He has no concussion but has deep bruising on his shoulder and hip. He was beaten with a club, the police say.'

'But why?'

Mr Somerton's voice was perplexed, dull even, the undertones of horror no longer present. Galena surmised he must be in shock. If she did not know how much these brothers cared for each other, Mr Somerton's question would seem like mere morbid curiosity.

'Because someone wants to destroy me and my monster.'

'Augustus! Thank God you are alive!' Mr Somerton stretched his hand out, but drew back before he made contact. 'You know who did this?'

'I know who attacked me.' The doctor's voice was a weary thread.

Galena picked up his unbandaged wrist and placed two fingers against it. 'Only a few minutes more, sir. He must rest.'

'Yes, of course.' Mr Somerton's words were unexceptional, but his eyes were like steel.

'Help me, Jacob.' Dr Somerton whispered the words harshly. 'Only a handful of people know the whole truth about Beauden— or how we intend to save him.'

Mr Somerton looked his brother in the eye. 'Has the villain been apprehended?'

Beauden spoke from behind his uncle's shoulder. 'Father's assailant is in custody, but the police are certain he was not working alone.'

Galena watched Jacob and thought he seemed bemused. 'The detective believes that the attacker was working in concert with another.'

Mr Somerton looked up at her with something akin to horror in his face and turned to Beauden. 'Someone close to you then?'

'Someone told that madman where to come and what to look for.' Beauden gestured to the wreckage. 'Few people know where we live. Fewer still know about this workshop.'

Mr Somerton frowned. 'It can only be one of the staff. Heaven knows, your father has never been one to make enemies.'

'It makes no sense. Why would an intimate of this house send a stranger to attack me? To do this, someone must hate me … us … a good deal.'

Dr Somerton closed his eyes, pain written on his face. Whether it was physical or emotional, Galena could not tell and she moved to end the discussion, but his good hand clamped around her wrist and he shook his head slightly.

'I don't know!' Mr Somerton thrust a frustrated hand into his hair. 'What about that medical student who attacked Beauden? He was clearly unhinged.'

Beauden put a hand on his uncle's arm. 'Well, we will know soon enough. He was the attacker, but I can't imagine how he knew where we live. Still, the police will find out.'

'They have him?' Mr Somerton took a deep breath. 'Thank goodness he is no longer a threat!'

'Yes.' Beauden's look of sorrow hardened briefly. 'They have him, and we hope to get some answers as soon as he stops raving about monsters.'

Mr Somerton looked at Beauden and then turned to Dr Somerton. 'I am going to put the fear of God into the police. No one attacks my brother and gets off scot-free. If I can't be of any assistance, I will leave you. Rest, brother, and get better.'

His hand hovered over his brother's and then he drew back, as if with regret, and hurried up the steps.

'You believe that the one who masterminded this is someone close to us, don't you, Father?' Beauden's tone was bleak.

Dr Somerton looked up at Beauden. 'Forsythe was completely demented, but someone had told him of this workshop and of our plans. He knew something of our intention to use metal and swine tissue.'

'You don't believe it was one of the servants, do you?'

The tragedy in her father-in-law's eyes as he met Beauden's broke Galena's heart.

'No, my son.'

Beauden nodded. He glanced towards the now closed door and linked his fingers with Galena's. 'What would you have us do?'

Dr Somerton gave an infinitesimal shake of the head and winced. 'Have Jimmy and the other staff stand guard. And Beauden?'

'Yes, sir?'

'I need you to send a mirror message.'

'To whom, sir? The inspector?'

'No, my boy. To the solicitor, Sherwood. And it is urgent.'

***

200

With a sinking sensation in the pit of his stomach, Beauden waited for a reply from his father's solicitor. The response was not long in coming.

'Well, sir, Sherwood has your instructions. He will draft a new will and take a dirigible at dawn. Now, given your suspicions, do you wish me to contact Inspector McIntyre?'

Say no, Beauden's heart begged him. His father must be badly rattled to act so quickly.

'No. Not until your procedure is complete and we can hide all evidence of it. The world is not yet ready for our medicine. Discovery and delay now might be fatal.'

'We are delayed already, sir, what with the damage here and to your hand.'

Galena touched his arm lightly. 'Beauden, no more tonight. He must rest.'

Beauden closed his eyes and took a moment to compose himself before he opened them again. His father seemed to be in minimal discomfort now, but he was clearly exhausted.

'I'm sorry, sir. We can deal with this in the morning.'

'Just one more thing.' In spite of everything, his father smiled up at him. 'Beauden, Galena, I am so sorry that I missed your special day. I have not had a chance to give you my blessing. I am delighted by this marriage.'

'Thank you, sir.'

Galena bent and kissed his father's cheek. 'Thank you, Father.'

'As your father, I wish you every joy.' He cleared his throat.

'However, as your doctor, Beauden, I must remind you that your heart cannot endure much exertion. I hope you take my meaning.'

Galena's face was on fire, but her voice was quiet, calm. 'I promise you, sir, that we are sensible of his condition. We will take care.'

His father gave a wry smile and closed his eyes. 'I cannot ask for more.'

He must have been utterly shattered for it took only a minute for his breathing to become slow and even.

Beauden caught up Galena's hand and raised it to his lips. Their eyes met and he felt again the elusive joy he'd experienced as they exchanged vows. Finally, he was alone with his wife.

***

Merrick threw the tin mug at the bars of his cell. Cold tea splashed over the floor.

'You will rue the day you locked me in here, fool! I'm trying to save you from the evil hidden in this city!'

Slumping back, Merrick rubbed a hand over his aching head. The arresting constables had been none too gentle with their truncheons, nor had the uniformed lout who'd thrown him into this cell. His scalp had lumps to match the seven hills of Rome; he had a split lip and a wrenched shoulder, but it was the wound in his soul that bothered him the most.

Despite the evidence—the weird bed and fiendish designs—

the police had ignored him when he pointed out the threat. Beaten and handcuffed, he had tried to explain everything to the officer, but the man had looked him up and down as though he was a babbling imbecile.

How had he come to this? He was the shining light among his class and would have his name on a board in Harley Street within ten years, a royal appointment in twenty.

He stumbled further into the tiny cell and sank onto the hard bunk. It stank of misery and urine, the coarse grey blanket rough under his sensitive touch. The rage that had fuelled him waned, the alcohol long since purged from his system. He was mired in a pit of desolation. He knew he wasn't wrong to fear the weird science that Somerton had been practising on his son, the affront to nature that such a man presented, but the authorities would go blindly on, following their short-sighted laws, punishing him for seeing the truth and for his willingness to act.

The duty sergeant tapped on the bars. 'We reached yer oncle. Seems he is no willing ta bail ye oout.'

'He cannot leave me here!' Shock brought a cold sweat to Merrick's brow.

'Nay, he's not about ta do that. Someone will be along ta collect ye in an hour or so.'

The sergeant passed a slip of paper the size of his palm through the bars. It was the print copy of a mirror message. He looked down at his uncle's hasty, imperious handwriting.

Regarding your information about Merrick. Clearly demented.

Please transfer to Beechwood Sanatorium pending permanent arrangements. Terrence Forsythe.

The paper fluttered from Merrick's nerveless fingers. A sanatorium? He wasn't insane.

He pounded on the bars. 'I'm not insane! There is a monster out there. We have to destroy it and the man who made it! I'm not insane!'

He screamed until his voice was hoarse and cracked.

'Forsythe. Be silent.'

Merrick opened his eyes and sighed with relief. 'Thank God, you are here! Did you make them see reason? Will you bail me out? My uncle wants to have me committed.'

The gentleman had dressed in disguise, wearing the humble clothes of an orderly. His voice was the only thing that Merrick recognised; still cultured, sharp and cold as ice.

'You are the one who needs to see reason. You had one task and you failed. An asylum is the best you can hope for now. Augustus Somerton is not dead and he is aware that you know the truth. At least in an asylum you might be safe from him. For a while.'

'I can't go to a sanatorium.'

Surely this could not be happening.

His visitor beckoned. 'There is a way of escape if you are brave enough to take it.'

Chapter 20

As Galena pulled the bedroom curtains and blocked out the moon-less sky, Beauden watched her with a sense of bone-deep joy. It left no room for the grief and weariness he should be feeling. His father was safe, the attacker behind bars and he was alone with his wife. It was their wedding night and given his tenuous hold on life, he wanted to take the chance that benign providence had offered him. They had tonight. Tomorrow was not promised.

Galena's back was to him, her curves accentuated by the corset, her luxuriant hair crowning her delicate alabaster neck. Her beauty drew him like a lodestone.

She spoke calmly, with reflection. 'We will need Douglas's as-sistance in the mor—oh!'

Beauden trailed his lips down her neck, his hands started at her collarbone and slid down her arms, crossing themselves around her waist. He smiled with satisfaction at the breathless surprise in her tone. It was the sound he craved. He pulled her gently against his chest.

'Let's not concern ourselves with tomorrow. Present problems, future doubts—they have no place here tonight, my darling. It's just us, here and now, man and wife.'

He greeted her mouth with his in a gentle, slow, deliberate kiss.

She turned into the kiss, eyes closed.

'I've imagined this night with you.'

Her body trembled. 'I have as well.'

She slid both her hands up his chest to his face, cupping his head and drawing it down. She parted her lips just enough to allow his tongue ingress and his arms banded around her. Desire fizzed through him like champagne; delight at her fervent responses made him dizzy. He deepened the kiss, tipping her back in his eagerness.

'Beauden.'

He moved his lips down her throat, caressing. His eyes were shut, but he could feel the tremor running through her.

'I'm a little worried.'

'Darling, it's natural.'

She shook her head. 'You misunderstand. Love, is this a good idea?'

'The best I've had all day. Besides getting married, of course.'

'But the stress on your heart …'

'Galena, my darling, I understand. But I'm tired of living in fear. All life is tenuous, not only mine, and waiting offers no certainties. I will not let concern for our future rob us of the joy of the present. Now'—he kissed her again—'do you want this?'

'Of course I do. But—'

Raising two fingers, he gently covered her mouth. 'Then you

will have to be very gentle with me.'

Her laugh was also a sob. 'I will, I swear.'

'I'm glad.'

He kissed her and slid his fingers across her belly to tug at the laces of her corset. Unhooked, it fell to the floor. She took a deep breath, then opened her mouth to his. He shuddered with a dizzying rush of desire as she slid the cravat from his throat.

He smiled down at her, one hand under her chin, the other pulling her to him. 'Perhaps we should get out of these constricting clothes and then we will see if we can work out what comes next.'

***

Galena stopped when she got to her chemise. 'Your turn.'

She wanted everything tonight offered, but her natural shyness proved to be a handicap.

Beauden glanced down at her, eyes sombre. 'I'm not beautiful like you.'

He unbuttoned the half dozen brass buttons at the falls of his trousers, his shirt and waistcoat already on the floor at his feet.

'You are to me.'

She adored his physique, strong and spare, and wanted to touch him, to revel in the hardness of his embrace and feel the pleasure of his caresses. She intended to love Beauden tonight with all the passion in her soul.

Slowly, he slipped out of his trousers. She had looked on his bare skin before, but only as a patient. Now, she wanted, needed, to look on him as a lover would. The bottom of his silk undershirt and his linen breeches did not completely hide the evidence of his desire for her. She felt a ripple of anticipation.

She lifted her fingers to meet the hard planes of the corset binding his chest. 'Can we take this off?'

A shadow passed over his face as though he desired and yet feared the consequences. She put her hands on the buckles that held it fast and looked up, her eyes meeting his, and he nodded. He removed his undershirt next. In the dimly lit bedroom, his skin was pale, almost translucent, the recent scar she had made on his chest still raw and puckered.

She stood transfixed for a moment, the evidence of so much suffering and so much calm courage hard to bear.

He lifted one large hand and tried to hide the scar.

'No.' She pulled his hand away.

She knew the risk he took in loving her tonight, and the doctor in her was nervous. But the daring woman she had become applauded him. She would not fail him.

Bending forward, she lightly kissed the ragged skin. 'Never be afraid to share yourself with me as I am not afraid to share myself with you.'

She crossed her hands at her hips, and in one smooth gesture, she pulled the linen chemise up over her head.

The admiration in his gaze as it played over her skin made her heart hammer.

She cupped his lean jaw. 'So, do you have any ideas?'

He traced his fingers from her collarbone over the smooth contour of her breast, stopping just shy of the nipple. His copper eyes met hers, and he raised an eyebrow.

'That is a good one. Do you think you should repeat the experiment?'

His other hand traced a similar path, but he did not stop. Sliding it around her back, he pulled her close.

Tilting her mouth up to receive his, she ran her own hands over the corded tendons in his back and buttocks. He was hard and lean all over it seemed. She slipped her hand between their bodies, over his linen-draped erection, and felt his moan all the way to her toes.

'I have an idea.'

His lips hovered over hers.

'Why don't you get into bed?'

The moment of truth had come. She took his hand and drew him towards the bed they had piled high with pillows to prevent Beauden from lying flat. He pushed down his linen drawers, pulled back the silk counterpane and slid beneath the cotton sheets, then lay against the mounded pillows.

Galena walked around the bed and got in on the other side but, instead of lying down, sat thoughtful, legs tucked beneath her, one hand on his shoulder.

'I think this is the part where I am supposed to close my eyes and think of England. But, in the circumstances, would you mind if I take a more active role?'

His fingers traced her collarbone, touched her cheek. 'God forbid that I should ever want you to be passive or unenthusiastic, darling. If you wish to try your hand at the reins, I'm willing.'

She smiled and leaned forward, one arm stretched across his body, offering a kiss. 'Good.'

Galena moved to face him and, leaning forward, positioned herself astride his thighs, chest to chest, lip to lip. He locked his arms around her, while she ran her hands over his throat, his shoulders, his chest. The kiss built in intensity until mutual breathlessness forced them apart.

Beauden slid his hands up her body and took the weight of her breasts, caressing them with his thumbs. 'May I kiss you here?'

It was one thing to sit astride his legs, the tip of his erection visible between their bodies, but it was quite another to give voice to her immodest desires. She nodded, keeping her eyes downcast.

He bent forward and she arched her back to give him better access. His lips pressed a trail of kisses against her right breast before enclosing her nipple. The subtle suction of his mouth on her caused a pang of lust to hit her sharply, low in her belly. After a few moments, he moved his attentions to her left breast and the pang became a dull ache.

His hands left her breasts and meandered over her body while his lips made love to her lips, jaw, throat. And then, he slid one hand down to where their bodies met and inserted a finger into the curls there. She sucked in a breath at the sudden thrill of pleasure and raised her body slightly to permit him admission.

He cradled her head close and kissed her deeply, his tongue mimicking his actions below. She reached between them, using one hand for balance and the other to position his erection beneath her for the final act of this sensual drama. As they made contact, Beauden arched his neck and moaned into their kiss. Slowly, incrementally, she lowered herself.

Galena kept her weight off him and when the stretching became more noticeable, she retreated until the tightness eased. She did it again and again, each time sinking a little more. Beauden continued to kiss her, his body growing tense.

After several minutes, he slid both hands down her back and held her still. He flexed his spine, pressing upwards, and she gasped. He did it again and again, his rhythm increasing.

Pressing her lips to her husband's, Galena held onto his shoulder. As she surrendered her body and her control, the tension low in her core snapped, bathing her in a bright, white light. Beauden tilted his head back and let out a guttural groan. His movements hitched, then slowed, and he rocked gently before stopping entirely.

Galena leaned against Beauden's skin and revelled in the moment. This was hers alone. This was what she had wanted. Others might see her husband's bare flesh and perform surgery or other acts of personal service, but this exquisite communion was hers.

After taking a few moments to gather her breath, Galena moved slightly. Beauden still had his eyes closed, and she stretched up to kiss him, but he didn't move. His colour hadn't changed; alarming enough, but not ashen. She leaned in, a frisson of panic running up her spine. His chest did not appear to be moving. Galena's heart plummeted.

Quickly, she slid off his body. He took a deep breath and his eyes opened.

Her terror subsided, but it left her shaken.

Beauden met her eyes, stroking her cheek with the back of his fingers. 'Oh, love, I'm sorry! I hurt you.'

She bent against his chest and a tear plopped onto his skin. 'You didn't move. You weren't breathing. I thought I had killed you.'

His body stilled and his hand came down on her shoulder, holding her to him. 'It was just the little death, I think. It is natural after lovemaking.'

She brushed the hair from his forehead and rested her head on his shoulder, her brow against his cheek. Love was truly a double-edged sword with moments of both soaring passion and keening anguish. She could not bear to lose him. Not now. Not ever.

'I was terrified.'

He pushed her hair over her shoulder. 'All is well, love, and I'm glad. I would hate not to be able to love you like that again.'

'You want to do that again?'

He smiled. 'Most fervently. Though perhaps not straight away.' He kissed her cheek. 'I think, Doctor, that I should prescribe a bath and some sleep. Today was exhausting.'

Galena lay down at his side, his arm curled around her, his lips resting against her temple.

'I love you, sweetheart.'

She snuggled closer. 'I love you too, my darling.'

They lay in each other arms, nested in pillows, until sleep took them.

Chapter 21

'I realise that what we are about to tell you may seem wrong or strange.'

Galena sucked her lower lip between her teeth and watched Douglas's face. She had requested this meeting and had persuaded Dr Somerton to allow her to explain the reality of their situation. They needed Douglas's help—without him, Beauden's surgery would be impossible.

She laid her hand on Beauden's arm. 'But please understand that we are putting all our lives in your hands.'

Douglas sat in the high-backed chair from the writing table in the basement workroom. Beauden and Dr Somerton sat side by side in comfortable chairs carried down from the sitting room. The last of the wreckage had finally been cleared from the room, leaving it looking particularly sparse.

'Galena, I am willing to help you if I can. I feel somewhat responsible after all.'

She sighed, but she did not, could not, fully relax. Douglas might well change his mind when he understood what they were asking of him.

When she and Beauden had woken, she could tell by the colour of his skin that his condition had deteriorated overnight. Even with Beauden propped up on pillows, the pendulum had slowed. Not only were his lips cyanosed, but the ash-blue cast to his skin had increased and his ankles and fingers were puffy. His heart relied on the magnetic pull of the bed, and with that sabotaged, the iron poisoning had worsened rapidly. Jimmy and Will had taken the damaged parts of the bed to Beauden's workshop to make the necessary repairs and had sworn to have it back by nightfall. She hoped it would be soon enough.

'You can see by looking at Beauden that he is very ill. If he were your patient, what would your diagnosis be?'

Douglas looked from her to Beauden and then rose. He took up Beauden's slim wrist from the arm of the chair and felt for a pulse, looked into his eyes, minutely observed the colour of his skin.

'That level of cyanosis is consistent with a lack of oxygen in the blood, with poisoning, a host of possibilities. But you don't need my advice. You know what is making him ill.'

'Yes, we know what is making him ill—and what needs to be done to save him.'

Douglas returned to his chair and paused, waiting silently.

Galena had come to the difficult part. Beauden's uniqueness had turned Merrick Forsythe into a raving maniac bent on destroying a blasphemous creation.

She drew a slow breath and clenched her fists.

'For the last fifteen years, Beauden has carried an iron heart within his chest, which performs all the functions of an ordinary heart made of flesh.'

His gaze darted between Beauden and Galena. 'That's impossible!'

'If you agree to perform surgery on my heart in a day or two, you will see that it is not.' Beauden's voice was weary and he shifted uncomfortably in his chair.

'Then what Merrick said was true?' His tone was one of blank incomprehension.

'No!' She looked at her husband. 'And yes. Merrick claimed Beauden was a monster, but you have seen for yourself that he is nothing of the kind. He only has a metal heart in the same way that some men have a metal or wooden leg.'

'If Beauden has had this iron heart for fifteen years, why is it now causing problems?'

'Because iron decays.' Dr Somerton leaned forward, his free hand clutching the arm of the chair tightly. 'You will appreciate that when I put the iron heart into Beauden, he was a boy of twelve. I had no choice, he had only days left to live. I had a prototype and nothing to lose. But obviously, the iron heart had flaws I had not considered.'

'I see.'

'Indeed, for almost a decade, the iron heart has served him well. He has experienced limitations, of course, but he felt well and grew strong. Then the cyanosis started. The iron has been rusting inside his body, leaching into his system. The thing that has kept him alive is now killing him.'

'So, do you intend to replace the heart with another made of iron?'

'Originally, that had been my idea, but even if I am still alive in another decade, I will be in no condition to perform risky surgery. Even before this'—he lifted his splinted and bandaged hand—'my arthritis had begun to trouble me. Beauden needs a heart that will not rust or decay.'

Douglas swung round to Galena, understanding quickening in his eyes. 'Your research into swine hearts—you hope to use suinae tissue, like in your presentation! Were you working with Dr Somerton even then?'

'No.' She glanced down at Beauden and smiled. 'It was a happy accident that my research was exactly what Dr Somerton needed.'

'Is that what you intend to do? Replace Beauden's corrupted heart with a swine heart? Will it work?'

She shook her head. 'No, that's not exactly what we are planning to do. Here, let me show you.'

She pulled an open notebook from the bench beside her and held it out.

'After Dr Somerton told me of his plan to make a golden heart, I sketched out this idea.'

Douglas took the book from her, studying the diagrams, flipping the pages. His eyes grew wide as a unicarriage wheel.

'It is terrifying. Logical, of course. I can see the merit in it, and yet, at the same time, it is inconceivable.' He looked up frowning. 'But if it doesn't work, your husband is dead.'

Beauden watched Douglas closely. 'Mr Warwick, I've known that since I was a child. I've had a sword hanging over me my whole life. As it stands, I have only days or weeks to live. If the attempt is not made, I die anyway.'

Douglas straightened, closing the book and tapping the cover contemplatively. He looked directly at Galena. 'What do you require of me?'

Galena turned to her father-in-law who gave her a reassuring smile.

'We have the gold framework for the heart, Mr Warwick.' Dr Somerton spoke calmly. 'I have practised the technique required to merge the suinae tissue with the metal components, but now I cannot complete the procedure, nor can I assist Galena with the surgery. You can—the question is, will you?'

Douglas looked as if he might pass out. Just when Galena thought he might flee into the street or denounce them all for immoral experimentation, he raised his head.

'Your plan is, without doubt, blasphemous and astonishing.'

Galena's heart crashed to her toes.

'And it's brilliant! I'll do it.'

Galena's heart leapt. Euphoria fizzed in her blood. They had a chance. She knew that so much might still go wrong, but her hopes could not be restrained.

Beauden had a tiny, weary smile on his lips. Dr Somerton sent a glance heavenward and muttered a word of thanks. Galena beamed and caught up Douglas's hand.

'Thank you! Oh, thank you.'

'No, thank you. I daresay, many scientific or medical discoveries were considered evil or blasphemous when they were first discovered. When Vesalius contradicted Galen, his work was considered heresy, and yet, Harvey proved the circulation of blood. Dissection of corpses was considered blasphemy once, so you and I Galena, are already guilty. I would be a fool to ignore my chance to make medical history and save a life—potentially, many lives.'

Douglas's eyes sparkled like the Crown Jewels; his smile, the broadest Galena had ever seen, spread across his face.

'You realise the risks that come with being complicit in such a procedure?' She uttered the words softly.

'Yes, just as I know there is a risk when I treat any patient.'

'As long as you are sure.'

'Oh, I'm sure.' He paused, stood taller. 'Thank you for the opportunity. And, I have a confession.'

'Oh?'

'I never discounted your research, Galena, though I'm ashamed I didn't defend you on the day of your presentation. The problem was my ego. It seemed incomprehensible that a pretty girl had made such an amazing leap of logic. And because I felt inadequate, I allowed Forsythe to bully you, to drive you out of your own presentation. I can only offer you my deepest apologies and my assistance.' He held out his hand.

219

Galena flicked away a tear. 'Thank you, Douglas.' She clasped his hand in hers.

'I'll keep everything you've said in confidence, of course, but I think it would be wise to have more assistance than just my humble self.'

'I agree.'

Galena didn't even need to think about it. It had taken three of them to operate on Dr Somerton's hand. But even if Dr Somerton administered the anaesthesia, Beauden's heart surgery would be a difficult task for only Galena and Douglas.

'I am sure Olive will help, and I dare not ask anyone else.'

He beamed. 'Excellent choice.'

***

Beauden spent the remainder of the day trying to rest while his father, Galena and her friends sat clustered around the desk in the conservatory. They had a great deal of theory to master in a very short time.

Perkins, up and about again after his blow to the head, kept everyone supplied with sandwiches and cold lemonade, but Beauden ate little. Though he said nothing, the taste of metal in his mouth made food unpalatable. Instead, he spent his time sitting in a comfortable high-backed chair with instructions to rest as much as possible.

The previous night had been paradise and then purgatory. He

had watched Galena sleep, but, obliged to sleep propped high on pillows, he had passed a restless night. He felt exhausted, though he denied it.

Jimmy and Will arrived at teatime with the refabricated magnetic arms of his bed and headed for the basement to reattach them. Beauden went to see their progress and found that his limbs tingled with even the slightest exertion, and his fingers on the balustrade felt stiff and fat. He watched the brothers' good-natured banter; he would miss that.

It was not often that he lost hope, but he felt a niggle, somewhere in the vicinity of where his rib cage should be. He was not sanguine about his prospects. It seemed, in the marathon between Medicine and Death, that Death was pulling ahead at last. He felt sick, he ached and was beset by a weariness that made him want to lie down forever. Only the memory of Galena's love—the sweetness of her smile, the way she looked at him, the passion she had revealed last night—made him regret the inevitable end.

When it was almost time for dinner, Galena and Olive went upstairs, and Beauden joined the other men on the chesterfields in the conservatory. Perkins poured whisky, but Beauden sipped his with little appreciation.

His gut churned and his trembling hand shook the glass before it reached his mouth. He lifted a finger to chase the stray drops. His lips felt cold and the skin on the inside of his wrist looked grey.

He slipped the last of his tablets into his mouth and waited. It was no use—even after two minutes he felt no alleviation of his symptoms, and he'd consumed the recommended maximum dose hours ago.

'I am glad you could be our guest again tonight, Warwick.'

Beauden's father had spoken sincerely. Despite his injuries, the lively meeting of medical minds had proved a beneficial stimulant for his father. It had meant Beauden could disguise his weariness and worry with ease.

'It has been a privilege, sir, and I know Olive feels the same.'

After answering a call at the door, Perkins came into the room and stood beside Beauden's father.

'Sir, the inspector has returned. He says he regrets disturbing you so late, but that the matter is urgent.'

Beauden stood and gestured to his lips, devoid of greasepaint. 'I will leave you. Tell the inspector, if he asks, that Galena and I are on our honeymoon.'

Warwick rose, glass in hand. 'I will come with you, Beauden, if I may. I do not wish to intrude on your private concerns.'

They passed into the dining room and pulled the door to. Beauden held up his hand in the time-honoured gesture for silence and perched against the sideboard, his ear turned towards the conservatory door.

'The inspector, sir.' Beauden heard the floorboards creak as Perkins left the room and closed the door.

'Inspector, what can I do for you?'

'Doctor, I regret interrupting your evening. I take it you are somewhat recovered?'

222

'A little. But these things take time.'

'Of course.' A longish pause ensued. 'I understand that your brother, Mr Jacob Somerton, has been a resident of this house recently.'

'Yes indeed.' Beauden's father kept his voice cool. 'I had hoped he would be back for dinner.'

'We have recently become aware that Mr Somerton was seen in the company of Merrick Forsythe on two occasions in recent days. You will appreciate that we tend to take a dim view of coincidences.'

There was another pause in the conversation and Beauden's heart sank.

'Tell me, sir, might your brother harbour any animosity towards you or your household?'

'You suspect my brother of being behind the attack?'

Beauden knew his father had considered such a possibility, as little as he wished to admit it. Though the shock in his tone might have been feigned, his grief was all too real.

'Those enquiries are still continuing, sir, but it would help us a great deal to know if your brother has any real or imagined cause for grievance against you.'

'My younger brother is dependent on me, to some extent.'

Beauden pictured his father's ramrod posture, his piercing stare from beneath grey brows.

'He manages our property in England and also some of our business. He keeps rooms in London and also an apartment in

Brussels.'

'I see.'

'Well, I do not. He is my brother. He has never threatened me or wished me ill. Presumably, if he has been meeting with Forsythe as you claim, you will have interviewed him about it. The madman is in your custody, after all. What account does he give?'

'I am afraid Merrick Forsythe cannot assist us further with our enquiries. He was found hanging in his cell in the small hours.'

Warwick gasped. Beauden turned to see him, fists clenched over his mouth, bowed over in anguish.

'Good God, man! You suspect suicide I take it?' His father's words resonated with anger.

'We do, sir, but he did not do the deed on his own. He was hysterical last evening, so all items that he could use to his own hurt were removed from his cell, including his bootlaces. Someone else found a way to give him those he used to kill himself.'

'And you suspect Jacob of this, too?'

The inspector kept his voice low and calm, but there was a thread of steel in it. 'If he was behind the attack here, sir, then he would have a motive for silencing a man who could implicate him. We have ascertained that no one else could have killed Forsythe, and a man answering Mr Somerton's description gained access to our cells claiming to be a driver for the local asylum. Have you seen your brother today, sir?'

Beauden's father replied, his words a sour cocktail of weariness and grief. 'He has not yet returned home for dinner. I can have someone check if his room has been touched, but he brought little with him. He had only planned on being here for a few days.'

The floorboards creaked again, as if the inspector had risen to his feet.

'You have my card. If your brother returns, we would like to speak with him urgently. Are your son and his wife at home?'

Say no, Father. Beauden clenched his fists, his mind spinning.

'No, they are on their honeymoon. Why?' His father's words were bitter and tired. 'Do you suspect them, too?'

'I am only concerned that if Mr Jacob Somerton was behind the attack, he could well try again. Perhaps, you could let your household know to be cautious?'

Beauden's father acknowledged the warning with an air of abstraction and frustrated worry. 'We will take every precaution. Inspector, is there someone you can recommend to watch this house or to make enquiries on our behalf? We cannot do so at present.'

'There are several retired constables who might suit.'

'Then, if you would be so kind as to send someone? Thank you for your information and assistance, Inspector.'

Beauden heard a few polite murmurs and then the door shut. He waited a moment before he re-entered the room, Warwick following slowly after him.

His father glanced up from the sofa, dazed. He picked up his whisky glass, swallowed the contents and set it down with a shake of his head.

'I wanted to be wrong.'

'So, it is true then. Even the police suspect Uncle Jacob.' Just yesterday, Beauden would have trusted his uncle to Hell and back.

'I didn't want to believe it.' His father's voice was thick with grief. 'Until that madman came in spouting his theories, I would have denied any chance of Jacob's disloyalty. But for a man who didn't know we existed until a week ago, Forsythe knew too much. Even still, while my mind says it is credible for Jacob to be guilty, I don't think my heart ever will. Forgive me Beauden, for a moment I wondered who else might have a motive and only one other person came to mind. I am glad it was not she.'

Beauden set a gentle hand on his father's shoulder. 'I'm sorry, Father.'

He knew just how torn his father must have been. But though Galena knew their secrets, she had chosen to make their world, their trials, her own.

He nodded to Warwick who stood at a distance, giving them privacy. 'You have my condolences also, Warwick. Forsythe was your friend.'

Beauden walked stiffly to the decanter and poured another dram into each glass.

'Thank you.' Warwick accepted the drink and the condolence with a grim nod.

Beauden's father held his glass absently, his gaze fixed on nothing in particular. 'I should have suspected Jacob earlier, but if he was still suffering from old grievances, he hid it well. I could have sworn he loved you like a son, Beauden.'

'Envy for money? Uncle Jacob lives very well.'

His father shook his head. 'No, although it might well be that. Jacob lives the life of a rich man, but the wealth is not his. He has little enough that is his own and he may well imagine that this house, this life, should be his.'

'Why, sir? You are the elder son. He could never have expected to inherit.'

'Perhaps he did not at first, but he was angry when I married your mother. They were much of an age, Jacob and Myra, and she was from an affluent Edinburgh family. If he had married her, your grandfather's wealth would have been his. Still, with your health so precarious, no doubt he did imagine he would inherit.'

Beauden sank into his chair. His stomach ached fiercely and the whisky did little to dull the pain.

Warwick looked up, eyes glittering with tears. 'A desire for wealth is not a justification to ruin lives. If he has manipulated my friend for his own gain and assisted him to take his own life, I cannot simply ignore that.'

'We do not intend to ignore it, Douglas, but we don't know if it is true. I desperately hope that it isn't … that he had no part in this.'

'And if it is true?'

'Then Jacob—or whoever the villain is—is guilty of inciting violence and aiding or abetting a suicide. In either case, he risks the noose. Or transportation.'

The dinner gong sounded, and a door opened upstairs.

Beauden turned uneasy eyes on his father. 'We must tell Galena of this.'

His father put his glass down and nodded decisively. 'Indeed. Jacob has entered and left this house at will. She has the right to know why that has changed. In any case, would you leave your wife unaware of the danger he poses?'

'No, sir. No, I would not.'

Chapter 22

Galena jolted awake, suddenly aware of a presence in her room, and she sat up, terrified. The figure, with its pale gown and long tresses silvered by moonlight, was like that of a ghost. Galena opened her mouth, about to scream.

'Mrs Somerton, wake up ma'am! Master Beauden is in a bad way!'

Galena scrambled out of bed and thrust her arms into her wrapper. 'Mrs Perkins! What happened?'

The older woman wrung her hands. 'He is vomiting blood, ma'am! Jimmy said to wake you and the doctor.'

Galena bolted from the room, ran the length of the passageway and down the stairs. As she rounded the newel post, she could hear Beauden's harsh moans and dreadful retching coming from the basement workshop.

She smelt the blood before she saw it. Jimmy had flung towels on the floor by the head of Beauden's bed, but they were soaked with fresh bloody bile. Beauden lay on his bed, curled on his side with his arms clutched to his belly. He shuddered violently, his sickly blue-grey colour the worst she had ever seen.

Knowing she had only seconds to make a decision, Galena ignored the screaming need to run to her husband and instead threw open the medicine cabinet and snatched up a bottle of opium tincture. Drawing a tiny amount into a syringe, she filled the rest with saline and grabbed a sterile cloth.

Dr Somerton ran into the room just as Beauden retched again and moaned.

'Yes, Galena, quickly! We must stop the vomiting.'

With one arm in a sling, he put his good arm across Beauden's sodden chest and held his forearm. 'I can at least hold him while you give the injection. How much did you use?' He nodded at the syringe.

'Less than a sixteenth of an ounce.' Galena found a bulging vein in Beauden's hand, swabbed it with the sterile cloth and pressed the metal plunger.

Dr Somerton nodded. 'It was wise to be cautious.'

'What has happened, Father?'

'The iron poisoning has caused the vomiting, but I fear his heart is also failing.'

Beauden gagged again, but he barely had the strength to hold his head up and only a tiny amount of bile came up. His eyes flickered open.

'This … isn't how I wanted to say goodbye.'

Through her tears, she managed to smile at him. 'Then don't. We will just have to operate more quickly than we had planned, but we will be ready.'

He focused on her. 'I love you, Galena. Our marriage and your love have given me the greatest happiness.'

His eyelids flickered, and she had just enough time to say, 'I love you, too,' before his eyes rolled back in his head.

She panicked, her fingers flying to his wrist. His heart was still pumping

Breathing a trembling sigh, she wrapped her hand around his still one and a sob broke from her lips.

Dr Somerton rested his hand lightly on Beauden's head like a benediction and turned. 'Jimmy. Take twenty pounds from the cash box. Go to the farm and wake up whoever you need to. I need a fresh swine heart with all the blood vessels attached—a healthy beast, no more than three years old would be best. Take ice and a lined basket with you to rest the heart in and bring it straight back.'

Jimmy dashed from the room.

Galena ran her hands over her husband. 'Father, he's lost a lot of blood.'

'I know. We can't do anything about that yet, but we can give him fluids. Can you set up an intravenous solution? We can increase his blood volume that way.'

'Should we use my pulmonator? It will mean he won't be dependent on the failing heart.'

Dr Somerton looked at his son's limp, bloody body, and when he spoke, his voice was solemn. 'Yes. I think we no longer have a choice. We need to take the iron heart out. Now. Once that is done, and with the filter inserted, his body may purge some of the iron.'

'So there is still hope?'

'We will make sure there is.'

***

Dr Somerton had offered Douglas and Olive his hospitality for the night, so it saved fetching them from the university at midnight. Galena hoped, too, that it would mean the difference in saving Beauden's life.

'Olive, what does the pressure valve say?'

'It is even. Everything is in place.'

'Good.'

Galena had switched from friend and wife to doctor, leader of the most ground-breaking surgery possibly ever undertaken.

Dr Somerton sat at Beauden's head, his good hand operating the anaesthesia valve. Olive stood at Galena's side, Douglas opposite, and all wore white robes and masks.

Galena took a deep breath and picked up the scalpel. With a steady hand, she cut through the skin of Beauden's chest, parallel to the now healed wound she had made during the previous surgery.

Douglas folded back the flaps of skin.

'I don't think I really believed you, Galena, until this moment.'

The moment of truth.

Gently, Galena reached into her husband's flayed chest and curled her gloved hand under the iron heart. Douglas reached his hands in around hers, detaching the heart from the vessels that had enabled it to sustain Beauden's life for fifteen years.

'Ready?' She glanced at Douglas and he removed his hands.

'Yes.'

She took a slow breath and carefully lifted the rotting mechanism free of Beauden's body. Laying it on the waste tray, she peered into the cavity. A particle of rust, dislodged from the heart, remained behind.

'Saline, please.'

Olive placed a black rubber bulb in Galena's hand.

Galena gently cleansed the cavity, making sure the rust fragment was gone. She took up a second bulb to extract the saline rinse.

'Gauze.'

She dabbed the cavity lightly, looking for damaged tissue. When she lifted her head, Olive wiped her brow.

'We are fortunate, sir.' She glanced briefly at Dr Somerton. 'There does not appear to be any damage to the tissues.'

Her words eased the stress on his face. Galena knew his hand caused him a great deal of discomfort, but it would be nothing compared to the torments playing out in his mind.

'Thank heaven for that.'

Minutes crawled by as Galena and Douglas removed the last of the iron-corrupted bone.

***

Jacob Somerton swallowed the last of his ale. It was not his drink of choice, but he could not spare the coin for whisky.

He thumbed over the silver in his pocket. He still had enough for a week or so—his habit of keeping an ample store of sovereigns had paid off.

He pulled his cloth cap lower. He had not been able to return to his room in his brother's house, or even to the White Hart. The police had been there, too, curse them. But they were looking for a gentleman, so he had spent two shillings in a seedy garment shop on a heavy workman's coat and garb. Then he had taken a room for a week at a hedge tavern, introducing himself as Jack Somers.

Now he needed two things—access to a decent sum of cash, and a way to get out of Edinburgh without drawing attention. He had gold aplenty in London, but no way to reach it. His dirigible was in the main holding yard, but a constable sat at the gate. Once again, Jacob considered escaping via sea to Holland but quickly dismissed the idea. By the time he paid his way, there would be nothing left. He would be living on his wits.

Already he felt hunted. An hour since, he had walked past his brother's house, noting the constables loitering outside. Even well-disguised, he had felt their eyes on him. Had he gotten to Forsythe too late? What had he said?

Jacob wished he had taken the time to make Forsythe talk, but he had been intent on silencing him. So, instead of learning what the police knew or suspected, he had been content to watch the boy tie knots in the laces and leap into eternity.

The ale left a bitter taste in his mouth and he set it down, half finished. Had he failed? It seemed he had lost all—his good name, his place in London and the wealth attached to it—and for what? Jacob Somerton, businessman and bon vivant, was not meant to live destitute among the raff and scaff of Edinburgh's poor.

He narrowed his eyes, determined. He would find a way to take back all that had been stolen from him, but he had to ensure he could not be blamed for his brother's demise—or the deaths of Beauden and his bride. If he could not be implicated, then eventually, the house and the investments would be his. He simply had to play a longer game and acquire new allies.

Jacob smiled and leaned back into the shadows of the dingy pub and watched the ruffians drinking at the bar. Perhaps there was yet a way to get what he wanted and make it look as though he had nothing to do with it.

Chapter 23

Beauden had been unconscious for the past five hours, Galena's circular respiration device acting as both heart and lungs.

Jimmy had returned with the suinae tissue, and now, Galena passed the heart to Olive to be washed in saline. Then, overseen by Dr Somerton, they began the procedure of removing the vital sections and inserting them into the gold frame.

While she worked, Galena glanced frequently at Douglas as he monitored Beauden lying limp on his bed.

'You look concerned, Douglas.' She wanted to go to Beauden.

'I am, a little. The extra fluids are helping, but I wish it were possible to replace the blood lost.'

Jimmy at once put down the cloth he had been using to wipe the blood from the arms of the bed and rolled up his sleeve.

Dr Somerton joined Douglas. 'Have you ever performed a blood transfer, Mr Warwick?'

'Not myself, sir. I've seen it done once, and I know the theory, of course. But it can be dangerous. Not all blood is safe.'

'No, but Jimmy's is. We had to use it once before when Beauden was just a boy.'

Jimmy pulled the high-backed chair over and settled himself into it. Dr Somerton laid a thick board from the arm of the chair to the edge of the bed and placed both Beauden's and Jimmy's arms on it. Then, under the doctor's instructions, Douglas took a thin glass pipette and sealed a needle in each end. He slid one end into Beauden's arm and, with an apology, the other into Jimmy's. Jimmy winced and grunted. Dr Somerton released the tourniquet around Jimmy's upper arm and the tube turned red. After twenty minutes, Beauden's colour had improved and Douglas ended the procedure.

Galena carried the new gold heart to where Beauden lay, and Douglas folded back the sterile linen to expose the gaping void in his chest.

'Olive, the silk gauze, please.' Galena kept her eyes firmly fixed on the chest cavity. She dared not be distracted by her husband's face lest her fear overwhelm her.

Mutely, Olive presented the tray. On it lay a gauze sack designed by Olive and knitted from pure silk by Mrs Perkins, then boiled. It would help to balance the gold heart's weight and reduce the stress on the delicate swine tissues. With a nod, Galena indicated the heart, and Olive helped slide it into the faux pericardium.

Galena cradled the heart in her hands. The three sections had been pinned together, encasing the majority of the swine tissue. From the upper part jutted the connections, a combination of gold and flesh that would enable Beauden to live a normal life. Its creation had been an act of love and faith; its installation would be one of reckless hope.

The time had come. A tremor ran the length of her arm and, with the care of a mother laying down her sleeping infant, she positioned it in the chest cavity. It fit perfectly.

She let out a pent-up breath and the others did the same.

'Right.' She glanced at her colleagues, smiling softly. 'That's the easy part over.'

'I have the utmost confidence in you.' Dr Somerton looked at them each in turn, unshed tears glistening in his eyes. 'In you all.'

Galena's courage rose. 'Thank you, Father. We will endeavour to be worthy of it.'

***

Galena and Douglas set the last stitch in the great artery, now attached to the golden heart. She breathed a silent prayer that it would hold. Now, they had to restart the heart before they could secure the golden rib cage in place—and to restart the heart they would have to let blood flow through it.

Galena lifted her hands from Beauden's body and her eyes to Dr Somerton.

'It will work, daughter. You have performed every step perfectly.'

His confidence was sincere but not certain. Still, she felt gratified; there was no alternative now.

Slowly, Galena nodded to Olive. 'Close the valve to the pulmonator.'

It seemed an eternity before the bronze valve shut off and the soft sounds ceased. Olive put the leather oxygen mask over Beauden's face.

'Douglas, the dyno-pulse, please.' In the sudden quiet, her voice echoed.

Douglas checked the connection to the house's steam dynamo. 'Stand back.'

He leaned in and carefully placed the smaller of the two paddles on the sinoatrial node and the larger one on the atrioventricular node, just off centre of the heart.

'Perkins, start at three hundred joules and we will work up from there. There will be less chance of damage.'

'Ready, sir.'

Galena bit her lip.

Dr Somerton took a deep breath.

'Stand back, please.' Douglas pressed the bronze button on the smaller paddle, making the connection.

Everyone gasped as the tissue inside the atria contracted, but the current failed to spread into the A-V node.

Galena's heart plummeted, but Douglas took the setback in his stride.

'Six hundred, Perkins. Clear!'

Again the atria contracted. And then … nothing.

With scant regard for her own safety, Galena leaned close to her husband's ear, her tears falling on his cheek.

'Come back to me, Beauden. We have a life to build together, my darling, one that's bright and precious. Come back to me now.'

'Clear!'

She heard the instruction but moved too late. The current flowed through the paddle, through the node and the adjacent heart tissue into her body. Every one of her muscles spasmed. White-hot stars burst in her vision, but as the blinding pain subsided, Galena saw Beauden—a translucent Beauden—standing beside Douglas, calmly looking down at his body. She tried to reach out, tried to call his name, but the electrical current left her frozen. Her consciousness winked out.

***

Galena opened her eyes to a collage of smiling faces. Her head buzzed, and when she tried to move, it felt as if her limbs were melted wax.

'Is she all right?'

Dr Somerton's voice floated across the room, but she felt too dazed to respond.

Jimmy helped her move slowly into a sitting position. She had been laying on the floor? How peculiar!

She closed her eyes and someone wiped a wet cloth across her forehead. Upon opening her eyes again, she saw the blood—on her hands and staining her smock. A spasm of memory shot through her.

'Beauden!' Her shriek came out as a hoarse whisper. She tried to stand, but her body was still alive with the current from the dynamic machine and would not obey her.

Douglas knelt beside her. 'He is fine. I'm not sure if it had anything to do with the current grounding through you or if it was mere chance, but his heart is beating as well as any I have ever heard. The suinae tissue is holding and there are no bleeds or ruptures. I have closed him up, and Olive has removed the breathing machine.'

'Thank God!' Galena pushed down on her hands and staggered to her feet, Douglas and Jimmy steadying her as she tottered towards her husband.

'He's breathing on his own?' She cupped her hand around his pink cheek and looked up at Olive.

'He is.' Olive grinned at her, then curled her fingers around Beauden's wrist and reverently set it down.

'His pulse is normal. His blood pressure is slightly low, but Dr Somerton assures me it will rise along with his breathing once the anaesthetics have worked their way out.'

Galena carefully studied her husband. The colour of his lips changed with every breath he took, a strong red banishing the blue. She peeled back his eyelid and used the tiny copper light to check his pupil dilation. The pupil reacted, but her own eye was drawn to the receding flecks of iron in the sclera and iris.

She shook her head. 'It's a miracle.'

Dr Somerton came to stand opposite her. 'It is indeed.'

He reached across Beauden's still form for her hand and gently squeezed it in his. 'I did not anticipate just how immediate the effect would be. Perhaps putting him on your ingenious machine long before we replaced the heart unknowingly gave us, and him, a stronger chance.'

Galena nodded and, leaning forward, laid a kiss on Beauden's warm sweet lips.

Douglas put a hand on her shoulder. 'Go and rest, Galena. We can finish up here.'

'No.' She looked up at him. 'I want to help.'

While Olive and Douglas cleaned and adjusted her husband's body to ease the pressure points, Galena picked up the lint padding and bound it over the angry stitches with tender hands and words of love.

***

He was in Hell, his body trussed and roasting like a pig on a spit. Groping on the edge of consciousness, Beauden lifted heavy hands to claw at his chest, to rip away the searing heat that consumed him from the inside out.

His hands were held gently, settled firmly by his sides.

'Calm down, love. You are well. There is no need to fret.'

Inexplicably, the voice calmed his mind, though the pain was as fierce as ever. He opened his mouth to beg for water, but his throat cracked with disuse. His tongue flopped like a dead fish on the floor of his mouth.

'Here, this should help.' The angel spoke again, beyond the blur of vision between his leaden eyelids.

Something cool touched his lips and he forced his tongue from his mouth to lick up the last quivering drop of water offered to him.

'More.'

'Soon, love. We don't want to overdo it.' The voice sounded familiar.

He forced his eyes open to see a pale female face wearing a mask pulled low. Beneath it he could see lips like rose petals and wisps of black hair showing under a surgical cap.

'Galena?'

His father's face appeared, and others drifted to and fro. The room grew dim and began to spin.

'The operation is over. It was successful. Your new heart is beating.'

'Good.' One word took all his strength.

'Very good! Now rest. There will be time enough to talk to-morrow.'

She bent closer, her soft pink lips touching his. 'Thank you for coming back to me, husband.'

He wanted to say more, but something was slowly stealing his consciousness. The pain still burned, but it felt as if it were some-where far away. He closed his eyes and the room faded to black.

Chapter 24

When Galena went up to Beauden's room three mornings later, the pink tone of his skin, devoid of greasepaint, struck her anew. His face, previously lined with weariness and despair, now appeared smooth, although it still showed evidence of his pain.

'I have a special treat for you, husband.'

Galena had come through the bedroom door carrying a tray. Jimmy had followed her and now stood in the doorway.

'And will I like this treat?'

She smiled at his quizzical expression, laid the tray on the dressing table and moved to one side of the bed. Jimmy took the other side.

'We are going to let you sit up for breakfast.'

His expression was reward enough, and Galena stifled a laugh.

She and Jimmy eased Beauden up and forward. He winced and the lines around his mouth deepened, but he didn't complain.

'How bad is the pain?'

'I can manage for the moment.'

Jimmy nodded and slipped through the doorway, leaving Galena alone with Beauden for the first time in days. She held the spoon to his lips.

He took the mouthful and swallowed, his eyes fixed on her.

'Porridge is not a favourite of mine.'

'Mrs Perkins insisted that it is the best thing for invalids.'

He raised an eyebrow. 'That must be the most effective motivator for a quick recovery that I have ever heard.'

She chuckled and fed him another greyish dollop. 'She is devoted to you. When you come down for a meal, she will prepare a feast. Eight courses at least.'

Beauden moved his hand, laying it on her plain calico skirt. 'I have missed you, my wife.'

She put down the spoon and kissed him, slowly at first and then with a growing intensity. 'I have missed you more. I was awake!'

'You are so competitive!'

Her laugh lit her from the inside. She felt as if she were glowing like a Chinese paper lantern in the dull morning room.

She fed Beauden another mouthful of porridge. 'I have been rather busy in any case. It has been a hectic few days.'

'What has happened? How is Father?'

She met his eyes and sensed him relax. 'He is well. His arm is healing without any severe complication, and once the muscles have knit, he can exercise them. Will came early this morning to measure his hand for a supportive brace.'

'Then he will regain the use of his arm?'

'He will, but whether he will be able to perform surgery again, I cannot say. Even the dean, who came to visit him yesterday, would not make a definitive statement.'

'The dean was here?'

She tapped his leg. 'He was. He came to see you as well, but you were still sleeping. You never told me he was your godfather.'

'Didn't I?' He smiled and Galena saw the memories in his eyes.

'He and Father were friends at university. I daresay, if Father had not spent his life working on saving me, he would have had a brilliant career.'

'Silly man.' Galena put down the bowl and took her husband's hands. 'Your father would make the same decision in a heartbeat. Don't imagine, Mr Somerton, that he has wasted his life.'

'I didn't say that.'

'No? You implied it.' She leaned towards him. 'Your father has proved that it is possible for a man to live with a mechanical heart. It ranks with the discovery of the smallpox vaccine as one of the most important medical advances ever.'

Beauden kissed her. 'Tell me what else has been happening. Has Uncle Jacob returned?'

She shook her head. 'No, we have not seen him since your father was attacked five nights ago.'

Beauden slumped back, grief and dismay warring on his face. 'And there has been no sign?'

246

'When your father's solicitor, Mr Sherwood, came the day after your surgery, he said your uncle had requested funds as he would be travelling. Of course, your father's instructions were clear. Mr Sherwood made a new will for your father that leaves your uncle only the Brussels flat and a small annuity. He has heard nothing else.'

Beauden rubbed a hand over his face. 'What of the detective? What does he say?'

Her smile was grim. 'I have not seen him, of course—we are supposed to be on our honeymoon—but apparently, the police found two of the ruffians who ransacked the house, but they had spoken only to Merrick. There is no evidence linking your uncle to any crime.'

'Then why isn't he here if he had no part in it all?' His voice splintered like ancient timber.

'He may still be an innocent party, after all?'

'I wish I could believe it.'

***

Jacob stood in the shadows of a tall silver birch. Its branches and foliage twisted and creaked, echoing the throbbing discomfort in his bones. He hated the tavern; its flea-ridden excuse for a mattress, the filthy drapes and disgusting ablutions where one could stand and scrub all day, yet never get clean.

A shudder ran over his body, not from the memory of the rancid squalor he was forced to call home, but from hatred. He should be sipping whisky in the conservatory of his home as head of the Somerton estates, not hiding behind a gnarled tree watching a funeral procession.

God had declared it a day of mourning. There were no chirruping bluebirds sitting between the burgeoning blossoms of the trees. Nor were any blessed with the soft touch of the sun's golden fingers as the clouds blocked any view of her taking her place on her blue-bowled throne. It was chilly and grey, more October than May, and far too gloomy for any to enjoy the beauty of the crisp, late spring air. Jacob really didn't know why he had come.

He found it odd that even though Merrick had died by his own hand, disgraced and condemned, at least a score had chosen to pay their last respects. The only one Jacob recognised was the red-headed fellow who had been at the pub with Forsythe the night Jacob first encountered him. He had a woman on his arm, dressed all in black with a deep bonnet and a short net veil to the chin. It took Jacob several incredulous minutes to realise that the wench was his new niece. He'd not thought she'd attend. How good of her, he thought, bitter bile churning in the hollow pit of his belly. Here he was, penniless, and she had stepped into what should be his.

Jacob had waited for a message from the solicitor after arranging for a transfer of funds. Finally, two days after his last conversation with Augustus, Sherwood had contacted him. His bastard of a brother had cut him off from returning to the estate in England. Once the police were confident that he was not a suspect in the attack, the message said, he would be able to draw on family funds again. The old man's neat copperplate hand on the silvered screen had raised a demon of rage in Jacob's breast.

It was a trick. They wanted to starve him of funds so that he would be forced to go back. It didn't matter that they had no evidence linking him to Forsythe. They would have him cuffed and in a cell in a heartbeat.

Jacob wondered about his nephew's health. Was the fact Galena accompanied a strange man an indication it had taken a turn for the worse? His nephew had been standing with one foot in the grave before all had gone awry. Now, with Augustus's badly damaged hand, there would be no hope for Beauden. Soon, his aching bones told him. With Galena all alone, he could easily manipulate her into convincing the authorities he had not been involved. Still, he had no intention of going back, at least not while his brother and his monster were above ground.

Jacob had begun to make plans, nothing definite as yet. Because whatever he did, he had to be sure that he could not be accused of any crime. If he was untainted in the matter of his brother's death, then the inheritance must come to him. He would have the details of his plan shortly, and then … well, fortune was said to favour the bold, and he was certainly bold enough.

First though, he had to get his hand on some coin.

He pulled his thick black leather coat tighter around his shoulders. Let them think him gone, that he'd fled on the wind, gone to Brussels, to Paris, to Timbuktu. It would give him time to rebuild.

Then, when they least expected it, he would attack. He would vindicate himself, Sherwood be dammed. The solicitor would be the first Jacob would fire once he had his birthright returned.

Before he slipped away, Jacob looked over to the bleak burial ground. His desires were simple—he wanted to get his hands on his lawful inheritance, but first he had to see his brother and his diabolical nephew lowered into the same dank soil where Forsythe now rested.

Chapter 25

Beauden feathered a string of kisses down his wife's throat and between her lovely breasts. God, it felt great to be normal. Galena had returned to their marital bed a week ago after he insisted he was fully healed, and since then, he had taken every opportunity to prove his boast. Now, his body thrilled at her breathless sigh. He kneaded her soft, ripe curves, slid his hands down her satin flanks and gripped her hips. He passed tender lips over her navel and lavished their final attentions on her inner thighs.

He rose up, positioning his body over hers, hands pressing down into the soft linens.

'Mmm.' With a long, slow thrust he entered paradise. The feel of her velvet flesh caressing him, her light kisses playing over his throat, her hands twisting into his hair threatened to overwhelm him.

She arched up into his thrusts, and he slid one hand under her, anchoring her.

'Now. Please.'

'As you wish.' Covering her mouth with his, he drank up her soft cry and followed her into the abyss of ecstasy.

Stretching out beside his wife, Beauden pulled her boneless body into the crook of his arm. Life was bliss. Six weeks ago, he'd not thought to see another day let alone the start of summer. Now he revelled in the soft bed after years spent on the firmly padded table downstairs. But he wasn't tempted to spend his days luxuriating in bed; he felt more alive than he ever remembered feeling. The first week after the operation had been filled with pain and discomfort, but his body had quickly adjusted to the increased supply of oxygenated blood, and it had responded as a desert would to rain.

Galena's bare hip moved against him and he smiled at the sensation of her delicate fingers wrapping around his wrist, stopping over his pulse point.

'Checking on your patient? I'm perfectly well, love.'

'I know, but I can't help it. I'm still nervous.'

'I am fine. My heart is sound and the wound is healed.'

She traced a finger lightly over the raised pink scar and his skin prickled into goose flesh. Her hand slid sideways to explore the outline of his filigree rib cage that showed through his skin.

'You are better than fine. You are wonderful.'

'I'm glad you think so.' He trailed his free hand up and down her waist in leisurely caresses. 'Would you care to go on a wedding trip? We can go to the Lakes for a few weeks and still be home before the beginning of term.'

'That sounds lovely.'

He nuzzled her neck. 'Since I appear to have made a brilliant recovery, astounding even my doctors—'

'Taking all the credit, sir?'

'Perhaps not all … now, ah yes. We could stop for a few days in York. I hear it is worth a visit. Of course, you would have to show me around.'

Her kiss was all the confirmation he needed.

***

As Galena entered the breakfast room with Beauden, Dr Somerton was folding a sheet of creamy vellum. He had become adept at using just the one hand; the other lay in his lap. The bronze plates of the mobility splint kept his individual fingers at the angles required for healing, and he could use the hand at a pinch.

'Good morning, sir.' Beauden offered a polite nod.

'Beauden, it is good to see you looking so well. And Galena, you are looking lovely.'

'Good morning, sir, thank you.' She sat beside her father-in-law. 'Beauden is taking me to the workshop shortly. Would you like me to examine your hand now, or shall we wait until after breakfast?'

'I think we might as well get it over with.'

Galena knew that he hoped a miracle had occurred, some improvement in the night. It was in his tone, in his wistful expression. But the signs were not in his favour.

Dr Somerton put up a hand to stop her attempts to examine him.

'Before you do, my dear, you might like to read this. It is from the dean.'

She was shocked. 'But, sir, that is your personal correspondence.'

Dr Somerton shook his head and held the letter out to her. 'Read it, my dear. Heaven knows there is nothing personal in it.'

She read it, head bowed. A hot flush crawled up her cheeks.

'Galena?' Beauden sounded worried.

She shook her head. 'It is just the board of governors being typically pig-headed. It was bad enough that they had to admit single women to the hallowed halls of the university, but in my married state ...'

'Dean Hopwood has reminded the board that the fathers of each of the female students signed to give their consent to their ward's enrolment.'

'Galena has permission to attend the university.' Beauden shook his head. 'What then is the issue?'

'Since Galena's father is deceased, her brother gave consent. But Galena is no longer under her brother's protection, so the board is claiming his permission no longer stands.'

Beauden looked at the letter. 'What utter folly!'

'I agree, my boy, and so does Hopwood. He has pointed out that you, Beauden, now have authority over Galena's actions. He believes that if you write to the university, giving your consent as Galena's husband, they will not continue to refuse her the right to return.'

Galena folded the letter and laid it down with cool, calm fingers. The solution was simple, and yet it rankled. She had performed life-saving surgery as well as any man. She knew she had Beauden's consent and his blessing to study, but she despised needing it.

Beauden crouched in front of her chair and enfolded her in his arms. She nestled her head against his shoulder.

'Sweetheart, you and I both know you are more than capable, and my consent—or lack thereof—should not matter. But will you permit me to write to them so that you can return to the university? It is what you have always wanted, is it not?'

'It just seems wrong.'

'I do not disagree, daughter.' Dr Somerton reached out and laid his hand lightly on hers. 'But you have a choice. Will you allow them to deny you your dream because the world is not the way you would wish it to be?'

'You have already saved my life, Galena.' Beauden stood and wrapped one arm around her. 'Show them your mettle. Show them what a woman can do.'

Perkins tapped on the door and entered. 'Detective McIntyre is here to see you, sir.'

'Show him in, Perkins.'

After the round of greetings, the detective took a seat beside Dr Somerton.

Galena, with Beauden now seated at her side, felt the scorching intensity of the detective's appraisal. She wondered if she was imagining it—McIntyre seemed particularly interested in Beauden. Of course he would be suspicious. Beauden was a different man to the wraith he had been when he met the detective. Now, his cheeks were ruddy, his lips pink, and his shoulders were back, no longer hunched over with the weight of the iron heart. His eyes, however, were still flecked with tiny amounts of iron, a lasting reminder of the past.

'Mr Somerton, Mrs Somerton. It is a pleasure to see you looking so well. You have been on your honeymoon, I understand.'

'Yes indeed.' Beauden met the detective's eyes calmly, despite the man's scrutiny of his face. 'What can we do for you, Detective?'

Inspector McIntyre spread his hands out flat upon his knees and looked at them. 'Dr Somerton, you might remember, incapacitated as you were, that you asked me to recommend someone who could look into your brother's whereabouts and make enquiries.'

'And you sent me a retired constable. Duncan. He is still making enquiries and—'

'I'm afraid Mrs Duncan contacted us last evening. Her husband has not been seen for three days. Yesterday was a family occasion— he would not have missed it.'

Beauden's eyes flicked up, understanding etched on his features. 'And you believe ill fortune has befallen him?'

'I don't believe fortune had anything to do with it, sir, but yes. May I ask, what information did Duncan last offer you?'

Dr Somerton rose and stumped across the room. The news had bowed him still further.

If Duncan was dead, Dr Somerton would lay the fault at his own door, Galena was sure of it.

He drew a sheaf of papers from a drawer and passed them to the detective. 'Please keep them. I have read them. We only know that a man resembling Jacob was seen near the docks and in the South Bridge district.'

The detective pocketed the papers. 'And you have had no word from Mr Somerton?'

'Not one.'

'Would you have expected to?'

Dr Somerton looked up, haggard. 'My brother is an excessively proud man, Detective. He would expect us to accept him back without explanation. But there are too many unanswered questions for that, and he knows it. He does not want to answer questions, even to assure us of his innocence. If he is innocent, he will feel aggrieved that we ever doubted him. If he is guilty, I cannot say.'

McIntyre stood, his hat in his hand, and looked at Beauden once more. 'Mr Somerton, given the sudden and dramatic improvement in your health, is it possible that your uncle was intent on harming you? Arsenic can be very slow acting.'

Beauden laughed drily. 'No, sir, on that count at least, my uncle is innocent. My heart was failing, as I told you, but my doctors performed a procedure that has helped immeasurably.'

'Then I am glad for you, sir.' He set his hat on his head. 'I will see myself out.'

As the door clicked shut, Galena went to sit by her father-in-law.

'The fault is not yours, sir.'

'My head knows it, but my heart does not agree.' Dr Somerton shook his head. 'In any case, Galena, there is nothing I can do. Now, will you put an old man out of his misery and look at this hand? We will see how good your workmanship is.'

Slowly, Galena unfastened the apparatus from each finger, trepidation in her heart. This was her work, hers and Douglas's. If it didn't mend, she would wonder her whole life long if she had done enough.

Galena removed the splint. The doctor's scars were still livid, but they had knitted well.

'There is no tenderness or ache, sir?'

'No, none. Everything indicates that the broken bones have mended.'

He moved the hand. It appeared weak and limp, and he could curl the fingers only slightly.

'The strength will gradually come back into it. You have not used it for a month.'

It was true, but even the very best surgeon could have done little for the depredations arthritis had already made on her father-in-law's hand. The brutality of Merrick's attack had only sped up the process.

Beauden put his hand on his father's shoulder. 'And I have

some ideas, sir, for something that might be of use to you. I am taking Galena to the workshop today, and I hope to have something tangible to show you in a few days.'

'That is good to know. Thank you.' Dr Somerton looked at his hand once more and flexed the fingers slightly. 'Well, daughter, what do you wish to do about the dean's letter?'

Galena looked up at her husband. 'I will not let my training go for naught because of my pride. Write the letter, Beauden. There will be time to change the world later.'

'A wise choice, my dear.' Dr Somerton patted her hand and stood awkwardly. 'And now, shall we breakfast?'

***

Jacob flung back the ill-fitting door of the den he and his tiny household occupied in the third of the South Bridge Vaults near the Cowgate. Once workshops of small trades, the rooms were now only occupied by less laudable professions.

He tore the coat from his back and threw it at the trull he had established to cook for him and the child. He had acquired her with the brat from the bawd in the next lane. Having burned her face in a kitchen fire, Frannie was worthless as a whore.

'Mister, what's amiss?'

He said nothing, but hurled his hat at her and followed it with his open palm. She cried out at the blow and fell back. He stood in front of the kitchen fire but scarcely felt the heat; the icy rage in his heart had consumed him.

'What's wrong, Mister?'

Still seething, Jacob forced his temper down. He would not damage the child. She was his bread and butter. The imp was to pickpocketing what Charles Babbage was to mathematics—pure unrivalled genius.

'Nothing, Sukie.' He held out a peremptory hand. 'What have you today?'

The child emptied the hidden pockets in her pinafore, their contents tumbling out—two dainty handkerchiefs, a pocket watch and a man's coin purse with a guinea in it.

'There's a good girl. For that, you shall have honey on your bread.'

He turned away from the child's delight, wanting only to be alone with his rage. Here he was, living in a slum and all his grand plans lying in the dust. Today he had succumbed to the lure of his brother's house. Of course, it might still be watched, but it had been more than a month, and the only man who had any inkling of his whereabouts had been … dealt with.

Jacob had stood outside, under the spreading elm, and looked into the Somerton's courtyard. The garden beds that had been gloomy and untended six weeks ago were now filled with bright blooms. He had anticipated mourning wreaths but had been confronted with garlands. Then, when his rage was almost full, the mended door had opened and Beauden stepped out. He wore no glasses and vitality shone from every pore. He looked so like his mother, the image of the woman Jacob had loved. Beauden had looked down at his beaming wife on his arm, then bent and kissed her before the unicarriage swung around the corner.

Jacob had slipped away then, lest his nephew or eagle-eyed Jimmy Ayre catch sight of him. As he had made the fifteen-minute walk home, his brain had reeled. There was no way in Hades that Augustus could have operated; Jacob had seen his broken hand for himself. So who had healed that boy? And what options did Jacob have left?

Chapter 26

Galena scrubbed her hands in mild carbolic solution and turned to her patient. She would much prefer to be studying with Olive and Douglas, but the university board was still considering Beauden's letter that supported her request for readmission. While they deliberated, she could at least use her skills to keep busy. The dean believed the board would eventually bow to the inevitable, but in the meantime, Galena suffered through the interminable process. Glaciers moved rapidly in comparison.

So here she was, assisting Dr Somerton with day to day cases of illness and injury among the poor. His clinic was in a rough area, near the South Bridge just off the Cowgate; not merely poor but squalid and seedy.

Old Ethel sat on the treatment table and peered at her with one rheumy eye. 'Be mighty clammy, bain't it, missus? This wet heat, tis no gud fer man nay beast.'

'It is rather warm in here, isn't it?'

While the small clinic was well-equipped and furnished, the examination room Galena worked in was situated far from the single window. The muggy stillness of the day, and the press of bodies in the outer chamber, accentuated its airlessness.

The crone shook her head. 'Will bring ill tidings, lass. T'was ever so.'

Galena merely smiled and kept bandaging, trying to ignore the sick, dizziness that threatened to overwhelm her. After she had seen this patient, she would snatch a mouthful of water.

Ethel looked at her with a practised eye. 'Ye should sit doon, lass, befer ye fall doon. Ye be no so very far along, be ye.'

Galena winced. She had received a similar comment two days earlier from another venerable dame. She might not be certain of her condition, but it seemed everyone else was.

'The wound is healing well, Mrs Woodstock, and there doesn't seem to be any infection. You have done an excellent job keeping it clean.'

Dr Somerton peered around the corner and came in, the room shrinking with the addition of another body.

'Ah, Ethel. How are you?'

'Weel eno, Doctor.' Ethel simpered and smiled her black-toothed grin, coy as a maiden. 'Yon lass has stitched up the hand gud as new.'

'Good, good.' He looked at her sharply. 'And how is your son getting on? No trouble with his chest?'

'Not a particle o' trouble.' The old lady beamed, then turned to Galena. 'My Donald were attacked by ruffians coming home on Hogmanay, three years since. Stabbed he were, close by the heart. The doctor opened up his chest and sewed him up, right as rain. It were a true miracle.'

263

'That is excellent.'

Ethel looked down, noting Dr Somerton's hand in its bronze-and-leather harness. 'You ken that we heer in the shadow of the bridge hold no truck with those who hurt ye and yer house. Tha' ill-faured divil who was bragging aboot doin ye harm, my Donald knocked his lights out and hauled him doon ta the constable hiself.'

'Thank you, Ethel. And thank Donald for me.'

Ethel gave him another sidelong smile, nodded her thanks to Galena, and bustled out.

Dr Somerton flicked a casual glance over Galena, but then she felt the change in his scrutiny. He looked her over again, the inspection very much a professional one.

'Are you well, my dear?'

'Well enough, sir. Just a little hot. Will you tell me about Donald Woodstock?'

Dr Somerton leaned against the doorframe. 'He had taken a knife to the chest that grazed the superior vena cava, but we got to it in time. It is Donald's and a hundred cases like his over the years that have allowed me to examine the human heart. Some I have been able to save, but all have taught me what I needed to work on Beauden. Hopefully, one day, we will be able to treat the heart as routinely as you treated Ethel's palm.'

'I hope so. And who was the "ill-faured divil" Ethel referred to?'

'Ah, he was one of the men Forsythe paid to come to our home. But when McIntyre questioned him, he learned little more than that.'

'What a shame.'

'It is indeed.' He paused and bent forward, his eyes roving over her face. 'You are still regretting your lost study time, but I am perfectly happy to tutor you at home until Hopwood brings the board around. Besides, you are more than capable of studying the work yourself. You will achieve your dream. Do not doubt.'

'Yes, sir.' Galena could not talk about this now. Not with reawakened suspicion so fresh in her mind. 'Is there something I can help you with?'

'No, Galena. Not at the moment. Only four more patients are in the waiting room, so Henry and I can deal with them. Send a message to Jimmy and have him take you home.'

Once Dr Somerton left, Galena took off her pinafore and rubbed her cervical vertebrae. She was sure Ethel was right. The dizziness, the tenderness, the abrupt cessation of her natural cycle—in any other woman she would be certain of the diagnosis. She felt an awareness, too, that she could not explain medically.

Was this what she wanted?

She laughed—it was a foolish thought. She was either expecting a child now, or she soon would be, given her husband's passionate attentions.

It would make her happy—a child was a blessing—and yet she wanted, passionately wanted, to receive an acknowledgement that she, Galena Somerton, had the right to practise medicine. Not as a pair of hands for her father-in-law. Not under the auspices of any man, but in her own right. However, even if the board accepted Beauden's letter, her return would be short-lived. How could she continue to study when she had the responsibilities of motherhood and the care of a home? Perhaps she could manage it. After all, she had the best guardian angels at her side. She would do her damnedest and the Devil take the hindermost.

As Galena pulled off her smock, another patient was ushered into Dr Somerton's examination room. He could do a great deal now that he had the support of the mechanical brace Beauden and Will had constructed. It was only temporary, though. Even now, Beauden was at the workshop designing a more advanced version, and no doubt there would be a second and a third.

But Dr Somerton would never operate again—Merrick had seen to that—and he was already looking for a practitioner to take over the clinic. Olive had passed on the rumour that the dean planned to offer Dr Somerton a lecturing role. As a doctor, Galena could work here, take up the role that her father-in-law was obliged to lay down. The window of opportunity was small, but she might just reach it.

Galena took a tentative step forward. No dizziness, thank heavens. She would have to tell Beauden tonight. He would be delighted, and medical career or no, she would be delighted to have Beauden's child in her arms.

A disturbance at the front of the clinic caught her attention. The nurse followed a young woman—no, a mere girl to where Galena stood in the doorway to her examination room.

'Miss! Miss, ye canna go back there! Ye must wait ta be called.'

But the girl wouldn't wait. Wafer-thin and short-statured, she might have easily passed for a child. Galena judged her to be about eighteen, though there was something in her eyes that looked ancient.

The girl stretched out her hands; they were calloused and red, nails bitten to the quick. Her nose was red, her eyes brimming with tears, but what stood out was the livid burn scar swallowing up her right cheek and ear.

'Doctor, please! I need ye ta come. 'Tis me lassie.'

Galena gestured a halt to the frustrated nurse. 'It is well, Millie.'

'But she—'

'No matter.' Galena leaned towards the girl. 'Where is your child?'

The girl seized Galena's wrist in an eager claw-like hand and pulled her forward.

Struck by dizziness again, Galena pulled her wrist free and laid a protective hand over her belly as the girl turned an anguished face towards her.

She was a puzzle, for even the poor here were generally neatly clothed and clean. Yet this girl sported a soot-streaked face, dishevelled hair, a tatty gabardine dress under a well-worn, black boned corset. And Galena could see something else, too. Was it fear?

Galena smoothed her hands over her leather corset and

touched the Rod of Asclepius hanging at her waist, avoiding the girl's grasping grip.

'We must hurry! Please ...'

The hair on Galena's arms rose, some primeval sixth sense holding her back, but at the same time, the words of the oath she might one day take echoed through her mind, telling her to ignore her qualms and put the patient first. It was her duty.

Galena seized the black medical bag her father-in-law had given her and smiled at the disgruntled nurse.

'Millie, I must make a house call.'

Galena followed the girl into the street. 'What is your name?'

'Frannie, miss.'

'I will help your child, Frannie. I promise.'

***

Beauden burst into his father's clinic, the room all but empty. Only his father, sitting on the hard wooden form in the waiting area, and the middle-aged nurse were present. Beauden stopped short. Though he had run just a few steps from the carriage, fear squeezed the air from his lungs. His heart thundered, the suinae tissue pounding against its golden armour. He had never thought to feel this way again. There were no little white pills now to alleviate the pain in his chest.

'She hasn't returned yet.' His father's voice was cold and grey.

Beauden gripped his father's shoulder, terror and anger making his gut churn and his words tremble. 'How could you let her go without a proper escort?'

'She would not wait. The woman insisted she must come at once. I don't think Galena even considered her own safety.'

Beauden pressed his fingers to his forehead. 'I dare say she did not.'

His father dragged himself up from his chair. 'I did not see the woman. Galena left while I was seeing a patient. I sent Millie out to find her, but there was no sign.'

He swung his gaze like a lash, his words sharp as scalpels. 'How far did you follow her?'

'Down the lane, sir, and I turned into the Cowgate, but there were no sign. It were only a few minutes after, I swear it.'

'Tell me of the woman, Millie. Had you seen her before?'

His need was urgent, and every minute was perilous.

She gnawed on her lip, considering. 'I dinna think so, Master Beauden. She has nay been in here.'

Beauden pressed his fists to his forehead and strove to stay calm. Galena had darted off into the Edinburgh slums without telling anyone where she was going. When he found her, patient or not, he was going to have a brisk discussion with his wife. And he would find her. He would.

'How long ago now, Father?'

'I waited an hour before I sent you a message. I kept expecting her back.'

Beauden's eyes darted to the ancient clock on the wall, the bronze gears tarnished motley green. His heart sank like a stone in a millpond.

'An hour and a half.' His words were a whispered curse.

Millie snivelled in the corner. 'I would ha' stopped her, sir, but she paid me nay heed. She was exhausted, poor wee thing, no surprise in her condition. Yer father had bade her go home, but she would nay turn away from one in need.'

Beauden closed his eyes, shutting out Millie's anguish and his father's unspoken dread. He wanted to reassure Millie, to tell her that she was not to blame, but the words would not come. A cold black fog rolled over him, fuelled by rage and bitterness. Who was this woman to make such demands on his wife? It was his right to protect Galena; his duty not to let her go haring off with never a thought to her own safety.

His father rose. 'Go home, Millie. You can do no more here tonight.'

The nurse twisted her white apron. 'If I may, sir, I'll bide while ye go oot ta search. It may be that the lass will return here.'

Beauden nodded and drew his father towards the door, seeking privacy.

'I sent Jimmy to collect Will and Cain. They will scour the streets for her. We will search this area.'

His father frowned, his brow like a furrowed field. He looked every one of his sixty years.

'By all means, but it is not the streets that concern me. We cannot burst into every man's house. I fear that we could walk past and never see or sense her.'

'Good God, sir, then what? We must try!'

'I think we should inform the detective, son.'

The blood pumping through Beauden's chest froze solid. 'You think Uncle has had a hand in her disappearance?'

'I don't think it, I fear it. I had hoped he'd vanished, but then Constable Duncan disappeared.' He shook his head. 'My bones are uneasy. That is all.'

'And if he has?' Beauden pulled the messenger from his pocket and rolled on the silver paper.

'Then we need every man we can muster. There is a great deal of wickedness here in the slum, but I have worked here for twenty years and many of the locals respect us. I can give you scores of addresses, people who will help.'

He put a hand on Beauden's arm. 'I fear what Jacob has become. If he has taken her … especially now.'

Beauden paused, stylus at the ready. 'Why, sir?'

'Rather than orchestrating events from behind the scenes, I believe that Jacob may be acting directly against us. He knows that Galena is the chink in our armour, and …'

'Yes?'

'I could be wrong—I almost hope I am—but the signs are all there.'

'For God's sake, sir!' Beauden's voice cracked, his apprehension turning to palpable fear. 'Tell me!'

His father looked away sorrowfully. 'There is a chance that she could be with child.'

The messenger slipped through Beauden's nerveless fingers and clattered to the floor. He swooped on it and picked it up, his hand shaking as he reached out to his father.

'She cannot be. She would have said something.'

'I doubt that she is sure. The pregnancy would be at a very early stage.'

Beauden had been panicked before, now he was shaken to his core.

'We must find her. Now. I can't wait for Jimmy to get back.' He stepped onto the rain-slicked pavement and threw a coin to a loitering urchin. 'Sammy, call me a unicarriage!'

His father followed. 'I will stay here until the others come and we will organise a search.'

'Thank you, though I cannot wait. I have to go. I have to do something.'

His thoughts spun in circles, a windmill going nowhere. Fear. Despair. Anger. They all jostled for space in his heart. He had to find her. The thought of her in Jacob's hands, at his mercy, chilled him to the bone. He prayed silently that they would find her. Quickly.

His wife and his child.

Chapter 27

Jacob took his ease in the only comfortable chair in this damnable den and looked at his prize. This plan, at least, had worked perfectly. Once Frannie had established the pattern of Augustus's visits to his little clinic, all that Jacob had needed was patience.

Galena Tindale—he still thought of her thus—sat on a hard wooden chair, bound hand and foot, then tied tight to the chair for good measure. He had pinioned her arms behind her back and shoved a wad of oily rag into her mouth. He would have preferred to let her beg and whimper, perhaps plead for mercy, but only half an hour ago, he had heard his nephew pass by shouting her name.

She hadn't moved, of course, hadn't managed to let her husband know that she was here. The tip of his blade pressed against her throat had seen to that.

He took a swig of cheap gin and remembered the moment his success had been complete. She had trotted in, stumbling a little in the dimness after being in the bright light outside. He had seen her hand go to her nose and it had offended him. The smell of the place still galled him, but her disgust of the stench was another reason to hate her. She had crossed to the spot by the hearth where he had made Sukie lay down, a pathetic bundle of bones. Her back had been straight, her head held proudly; she carried a medical bag so like his brother's it might have been cut from the same leather. Oblivious of the dirty stone floor, she had got down on one knee beside the child, bronze-and-black-striped skirts foaming around her, the buckles on her brown leather corset glinting in the weak firelight. She had looked like an angel of mercy. But there was no mercy here.

When he had moved from the dark corner to stand beside her and had yanked her to her feet, he had felt her fear—palpable, desirable, overwhelming. She had been stunned for a moment, but then her response had kicked in. She had fought him hard, giving him no choice but to fling her down and tie her up.

'Mr Jacob, I must give her some water. She is fainting.'

He rose and shoved Frannie aside. Galena was indeed deathly pale, her head lolling, her eyes closed. Her hands, secured against the base of her spine, were purple.

He slapped her cheek. Slapped it again, then, with one ear carefully cocked against his nephew's return, pulled the rag from her mouth and threw it down on the hearth.

Sukie, curled up near the warmth, looked up at him in terror and pulled her skirts closer. Her thumb went into her mouth.

'Give her water then, but quickly.'

Frannie complied, but Galena took no more than a mouthful.

'You said you meant her no harm, that you only needed to talk to her.'

'You stupid girl. I lied.'

He turned his gaze to Galena. She was awake now, regarding him with distrust. Revulsion. But not fear. That would soon change.

'I suppose you want to know why I brought you here.'

Her eyes followed him. Her tongue played over dry lips.

'No.' Her voice held a tremor.

He knew what it meant. 'You lie.'

'I don't lie. I'm not like you, Jacob.'

He slapped her again. 'You are going to give me my revenge on my brother and the abomination you call husband.'

Behind him, Frannie sobbed.

Galena shook her head again. 'No.'

'Idiot! I don't intend to ask nicely. If they want you back, they will pay handsomely.'

'So, you are a thief as well as a murderer. You must be very proud of yourself.'

'You stupid slut! Do you want me to kill you?'

He shoved the chair and it tipped. Galena fell with it, thudding onto the hard floor. Her head bounced, missing the hearth by inches.

Jacob lifted his foot to kick at the chair, but Frannie grabbed at his arm, her whine turned to anger.

'Ye said ye would nay hurt her. Ye are a monster, a fiend!'

He pulled Frannie up by her thin red hair and looked into her eyes. She should know better than to turn against him. He had been good to her and now she betrayed him. He put one hand around

275

her throat and then the other.

Her eyes went wide. Blood vessels ruptured in the clear white of her eyes, staining them with the crimson flag of approaching death. She tried to fling herself back, out of his grasp, but he held on. Her hands came up, nails clawing at his face, trying to grip his collar. Her lips moved, but only gurgles escaped.

He heard screaming and realised it came from Galena, from where she sat on the floor, staring up at the dance of death above her.

Knowing that she watched him, that she would see he had the power of life and death over her, that she would know he wouldn't hesitate to wring the life out of her, too, sent a shudder of pleasure through him.

Who knew that squeezing the life out of another could be so cathartic? He'd always had others do it for him, but here, now, there was no one he could convince or manipulate into ending a life for him. He had no option but to dirty his own hands.

As Frannie's hands fell away from his collar, he released a deep breath and a ton of pent up frustration before he let her limp body drop to the floor.

'Now I will take what should have been mine. The money will be mine, the property, and I will have my revenge for all the humiliations I suffered because of my damned brother. He had our father's admiration, a career. Myra chose him. Meanwhile, I was expected to manage it all for him. For him and his son.'

He swung round, a final question interrupting his thoughts.

'How did Augustus operate? He could never have used that hand. Who would perform such an operation and damn their own souls for interfering with nature?'

He reached down and grabbed a hank of Galena's midnight hair, jerking her head back so that she cried out.

'It was you? There is no other possibility.'

He pulled his hand away as if burned, but after a few moments, the rage-blindness cleared. Beauden's clever little bride lay whimpering on the dirt floor, and the pile of rags beside the hearth was empty—the urchin had fled. She would not have gone to the police; she had believed him when he told her that she would hang, but she could easily blab the truth to some busybody.

He had to move on with his plan. There was no more time to gloat.

Jacob pulled his mirror messenger from his pocket. He had just enough silvered transfer paper for one message, but he wouldn't need more than that. With the stylus, he took care to craft his message elegantly and then closed the lid to send it. The light flashed.

Now he just had to move his last piece into place and then ... checkmate.

Chapter 28

Beauden slumped against the wall of his father's clinic. He had returned after searching the streets for over an hour.

'I couldn't find any sign of Galena. Neither could Jimmy.'

His father nodded. 'I've asked McIntyre to meet us at the house.'

Beauden ran a hand down his face and accepted the whisky glass from his father. If only it could deaden the pain.

'Did you search every street?'

'Every street. Every alley. I asked every man, woman and child I saw. No one could tell me a thing.'

Beauden had always calmly accepted the prospect of his own death, but he felt Galena's disappearance like a knife in his gut. If something should happen to her, no golden heart could keep him alive.

His father's mirror messenger chimed and his father snatched it up, flipping it open. His face crumpled, and Beauden's hopes with it.

Wordlessly, his father handed him the ornate device.

Five thousand pounds to Victoria Park. Come alone and she will remain unharmed. You have one hour.

'God damn him to hell! I would never have believed it of him. Never!'

'Mea culpa. I have done this.' Full of anguish, his father bent over, ashen, as though someone had dealt him a blow to the gut.

Even in his moment of desperation over Galena, Beauden could sympathise with his father's pain. The final proof of Jacob's perfidy must be a crushing blow.

'I'm sorry, Father. Truly. I wish it were not so.'

'Did I do this, Beauden? Make him into a monster who would hurt his family for gain?'

'No, sir. You did not. No matter what you or anyone else might have done, it does not excuse kidnapping Galena.' He paused. 'Sir. The demands ...'

'I know. Victoria Park. Five thousand pounds.'

'Has he lost his bloody mind? Do we even have such a sum?' Beauden snapped the lid shut and thrust the tiny case back towards his father.

'Who is to say it is not a trap?'

His father straightened, as though grief would have to wait its turn. He tapped a pensive fingertip on the lid.

'He only says that she will remain unharmed. He says nothing of returning her. But no—we do not have ready access to that kind of money. We have some gold still in the workshop from making the heart. Also, we have ...'

'Mother's jewels?'

'I will gladly trade them for Galena, but we cannot trust Jacob to act honourably.'

'We can trust him to act dishonourably.' Beauden seethed. The threat to Galena now out in the open sent adrenaline roaring through his veins.

'What is his plan, Father? To know that means we have a chance. Otherwise, he will have us dancing to his tune, and … Galena may suffer for it.'

His father opened the door. 'Come on, my boy. We have to meet McIntyre and get the jewels out of the safe. We know Jacob better than anyone else in Edinburgh. Let us see if we cannot outwit him.'

'This is no game of wits, sir.'

'Yes it is, son. It's just one we cannot afford to lose.'

***

Beauden slipped out of the conservatory and down the servants' stair, his feet silent, his heart beating to raise the dead.

Jimmy, Will and Cain sat around the table, each with half a glass of ale in front of them.

'Jimmy, I need you to go and collect as many trustworthy men as you can and be back here in time to take Father to Victoria Park. That is vital. He must not be late. He must seem to be alone.'

'Aye?'

Beauden handed over the key to the gun room. 'Take a rifle, loaded. Once Jacob has the money, I don't trust him not to put a bullet between Father's eyes. We cannot take the risk.'

'So I'm to keep the doctor safe?'

'At all costs. If Jacob thinks he has succeeded, he will either make an attempt to leave the city or lead us to Galena. To make matters worse, McIntyre is trying to convince Father to have a constable nearby.' Beauden ran his hands through his hair. 'Only shoot to save Father's life, Jimmy. Or Galena's.'

'And where will ye be, sir?'

Beauden grimaced. 'That is where Will comes in. We think we know how he will try to leave the city. He will either try the dirigible or make for the docks. I am going to secure the dirigible. Will, Cain, I need you to muster as many men as you can to scour the docks. He will be heading to Amsterdam or Bremerhaven.'

Will nodded as Jimmy spoke. 'And then?'

'If they capture him, send for me at once and see if you can persuade him to tell you where Mrs Somerton is. If there is no sign of him, meet me at the storage yard.'

Beauden turned to leave, but felt a hand on his shoulder.

'Ye canna mean to go there wi'out a weapon. You should have a pistol.'

'It's too dangerous. Firing a pistol in an acre brimming with hydrogen-filled airships would be suicide.'

'At least ha' this, sir.' Will slipped out a beautifully crafted dagger with a bronze-and-leather-wrapped handle. The pommel of tight copper wire ran down to coil around the guard before becoming one with the etched iron blade. It was the work of a master craftsman—half engineer, half artist, all friend.

'Thank you.' Beauden spoke softly as he took Will's prized possession. He stuck the weapon into his belt. 'I hope I can return it to you unused.'

'I hope you shove it through the bastard's craw. Stealin' away such a sweet lady.'

'If there be anythin' we can do, only ask it.' Jimmy met his eyes without any of the usual deference, his face honest, open, craggy.

Beauden's gaze fell to Jimmy's well-worn, ankle-length, thick, black wool-linen coat. His utterly unremarkable, undistinguished black coat.

'Actually, there is one more thing.'

***

Dusk dwindled as Beauden crept towards the grassy acre of private moorings on the outskirts of town. Finding the chain securing the dirigible yard broken, he slipped through the gate, treading warily. Jacob should be meeting with his father about now, making this the perfect time to see if this was his escape route.

Beauden rounded the corner, and just past the first anchor point, his dark lantern picked out a booted foot.

Bending closer, he discovered the uniformed body of the yard master lying in a huddle, the hilt of a dagger protruding from his ribs. A cursory examination was all that was needed. It seemed that Jacob had indeed been here and had become even more vicious than Beauden had expected.

His hand on his weapon, he inched forward. A dozen airships were roped in the yard, the property of various companies and individuals. He knew the Somerton airship; he had once made a day trip to Stirling aboard her.

The twilight made the ships' colours hard to see, but he knew the configuration he was looking for—a Giffard Deluxe, almost a hundred and fifty feet long and cigar-shaped. He found it halfway down the yard with the boarding tower pushed into place.

Ascending cautiously, Beauden tested every step, trading speed for silence. His mind screamed to go faster, adrenaline coursing through him.

Part of him wanted Jacob to be here. Beauden was no longer an invalid and the desire to avenge his father and his wife seared though him. The airship was as silent as the grave, but with the yardmaster dead and a boarding planned, he knew he was in the right spot. Would Galena be here, though, or was he on a fool's errand?

He stepped onto the narrow walkway that ran the length of the carriage on both sides. Only the stern had more than two feet of space or more safety that a narrow wooden handrail. Five feet wide, the stern had been designed for ease of loading and unloading gear and fuel.

Beauden tried the handle of the access port that led into the tiny carriage and cursed. It was locked. He slipped the set of lock picks from his pocket and blessed Will for his forethought.

Little light filtered into the carriage, but Beauden could make out the curtain that hid the washbasin and commode space to starboard and the bunks against the portside wall. Both spaces were empty. The ship's kitchenette was a basin and a square foot of bench, with a cupboard above and one below. At its widest, the carriage was scarcely more than eight feet across and narrowed to six at the stern. To his left, two easy chairs sat beside portholes, and beyond them, a door led into the tiny cockpit that tapered to a point in the bow.

Beauden pricked up his ears at the pop and hiss of the firebox in its sealed room below the floor. The steam turbines on either side of the carriage were spinning slowly, driven by the wisps of escaping steam but not enough to create motion. The design made the vehicle's speeds possible—fifteen knots in a calm sky—but at what risk? A vehicle that was held aloft by volatile gases and yet propelled by steam was a safety nightmare. No wonder the yardmaster was dead. He would have had Jacob arrested if he had lit the engine with a score of hydrogen airships just yards away. His uncle had become reckless.

Beauden stopped, considering the reality of the situation. There was no pilot on board—unless one was tied up in the cockpit. The ship was at anchor, but with her engines running, casting off would take only a matter of seconds—all that was needed was to release the mooring lines and turn the engine valves. Presumably,

Jacob planned to return and make his escape as quickly as possible. Had he brought a manservant aboard to stoke the fire, or had he done so himself?

With a hand on the hilt of Will's dagger and a whispered prayer that it would not be needed, Beauden slipped past the bunks to the door that led into the storage locker in the rear. He knew it held a trundle for a servant.

The door opened with a whine and Beauden cringed.

'Galena!'

She opened her eyes, staring at him as though he were an apparition.

Beauden fell to his knees beside the trundle and turned her gently.

'You're alive. Thank God.'

She winced at his touch and again when she tried to move.

With exquisite care, he slipped the knife between the rope at her wrists and cut her bonds. She moaned around the gag clamped between her teeth, and he carefully sliced the rag and pulled it from her mouth.

Arms free, she whimpered and turned to face him. Appalled by her bruised and abraded flesh, Beauden stuck the knife back into his belt and rubbed her arms. Her face was swollen, her cheekbone bruised. Her lips moved but no words came. He lay her down and fetched a glass from the washbasin, putting an inch of water into it before heading back into the storage room. The door swung shut behind him.

'Here.'

She sipped and swallowed. 'Ah, Beauden, love. Thank God!'

He held her lightly for a moment. They had to get out of here, but she was pale and trembling.

'I'm going to kill that bastard for this.'

Bruise for bruise, whimper for whimper, he would break that heartless devil. A volcano of hate surged through him, but then he looked into her exhausted brown eyes. He had to choose. And he chose Galena. Her need for safety, for any care he could give her, was more important than taking revenge on his demon uncle.

'Perhaps not right now?' Her voice was still hoarse.

'No. Let's get you home first.'

He fixed his eyes, his mind on her and let logic rule. He needed to do that now, the need had never been greater, but neither had it been more difficult.

She moved awkwardly, and a glance showed him another rope under the hem of her dress. He dealt with it quickly.

'Can you stand, darling?'

He held out his arms, supporting her as she rose and clung to the storage nets. Tied for so long, her arms and legs must be screaming with the sudden rush of blood.

'How long have you been here?'

She shook her head. 'Forever. But, I don't know ... perhaps an hour.'

'Can you manage now? We need to get out of here.'

'Yes.' She grimaced with pain.

A flurry of footsteps sounded outside, and they both turned. Someone was running up the steps of the boarding tower. A door thudded.

Galena swayed. 'We're moving?'

'He's dropped the mooring line. Of course, with the storage door closed, Uncle has no idea that I'm aboard.'

'What can we do?'

'We can stop the ship.'

'How? The steam engine?' She looked down at the hatch at their feet. 'Can you stop the propellers?'

He shook his head. 'No. Because of the fire risk, the hatch can't be opened once the dirigible is underway. We'll have to do it from the cockpit.'

'Tell me what to do.'

He put a hand under her chin and looked into her eyes. 'Galena, you're hurt. I will deal with Jacob.'

'Beauden, if you can't stop him, he *will* kill me. And he will have no compunction about killing you, flesh and blood notwithstanding.' She put her fingers to his cheek. 'It will take both of us to stop your uncle.'

***

Blood thundered in Galena's ears as she and Beauden waited for their moment. She spoke softly so as not to be heard over the whirring of the ship.

'We seem to be ascending.'

'Yes, he needs to get to cruising height. Once the spinning turbines have achieved that, Jacob will have to go out and reposition the turbines.'

She knew that much about lighter-than-air craft, but little more. 'And that will be our chance?'

Beauden nodded and pulled her close.

The craft slowed and Galena heard the soft hiss of steam escaping from the engine below.

Fear clutched at her vitals, making her feel sick. She had refused to give in to it before; reacting to Jacob's taunts and threats would have been pointless—one couldn't reason with a madman. She had been afraid when he killed Frannie in front of her and then dragged her to the dirigible yard, but she had listened, helpless, to his fevered ravings, afraid only for herself. Now, he had Beauden in his clutches, and Galena knew that Jacob Somerton wanted nothing more than to kill his nephew.

But Beauden had not lived the last few hours with her. He had not watched a brutal maniac choke the life from an innocent girl. Her belly knotted, thinking that he might still trust his uncle.

'Beware, love.' She squeezed his hand. 'He's not the man you remember. He will stop at nothing.'

Beauden kissed her slowly, his heart on his lips, and he touched one finger to her cheek. Galena kissed him right back. It couldn't end like this. But if it did, she would have this.

They heard the cockpit door open with a thud and then the side door. The wind howled in.

Beauden put a hand on her shoulder, then opened the door softly.

'Run for the cockpit. Lock yourself in, barricade it if you can. Don't stop for anything!'

He stepped through the doorway and into the tiny cabin.

Adrenaline surged through her veins like a herd of wild ponies. She managed a fleeting touch on Beauden's arm, then sprinted towards the cockpit, lifting her skirts with one hand and pressing the other to her belly.

She stumbled. Her ankles ached from the bruising her bonds had left. Reaching out, she grasped the door handle and prayed there was a key.

In the safety of the cockpit, she spun around.

Oh God!

The door had no lock, only a thin latch. It wouldn't hold Jacob for long. If Beauden could not keep him at bay, one heel to the door and the latch would splinter like kindling—and then they would both be dead.

She turned to face the bow of the ship and screamed.

On the other side of the thin glass windows that offered a wide view over the rooftops, stood Jacob Somerton.

His lips curled, his face breaking into a feral smile.

Chapter 29

As Beauden reached out to pull the heavy external door shut, he heard Galena scream. Scant seconds later, his uncle's fist collided with his chin.

'I had a feeling someone might think of the yard, but seeing you here in the flesh is both a gift and a surprise, nephew.'

The wind howled through the door as Jacob reached above the frame and grasped a long pole with a wicked hook at the end; a grappling hook.

Beauden rolled away and pushed up onto his hands as Jacob took his first, tentative swing. By the time he swung again, Beauden was upright, the copper-hilted dagger in his hand. But Jacob had a much longer reach with the pole, and while its wicked tip was not razor sharp, it would do plenty of damage regardless.

'Did my brother succeed, then, in implanting his gold heart in you, boy? Or is this new health and strength the result of a different form of necromancy?'

'I am well, Uncle.' Beauden inched closer to the kitchen cupboard on the starboard side. 'I thought you would be glad.'

'Once, I would have been. But that was before your father

turned you into a monster with his cursed experiments.'

He swung again and the hook glanced over Beauden's waist-coat.

'That knife is worse than useless, boy. No reach and too small to do more than skin a rat.'

Beauden reached into the small wash bowl, pulled out a drinking glass and hurled it at his uncle's head. It missed, smashing on the doorframe instead, but the respite allowed Beauden to get his back to the cockpit door. Jacob would not get to his wife, not while he had breath in his lungs.

'Now, Galena, now! Bring her down!'

The dirigible convulsed, steam coursing audibly from the engine through the copper pipes to the four turbines. Jacob must have recognised the shudder of the vessel as the beginning of descent; he glared at Beauden, his expression growing deathly serious.

Beauden saw the tension in his uncle and anticipated an attack. Quickly, he snatched up a small occasional table that sat beside the armchair on his right and held it out like a shield, managing to parry the next two blows.

Despite his uncle's violence, his ceaseless assault and maniacal strength, Beauden kept his wits about him. His body was finally working with him, not against him, oxygen flowing to his muscles the way it was supposed to. The blood pumping through his body made him feel stronger than ever before, and in spite of the danger, he felt a thrill of adrenaline.

Still, he fixed his eyes on his uncle. His long lessons in defending himself had honed his mind and his body, but his skills were purely defensive. Beauden knew that would not be enough to save him and Galena.

The third blow came towards his legs and Beauden felt the crunch first. It brought him to his knees. Instinctively, he slammed the table down on the pole, pulling it out of Jacob's hand. His mind was full of fury; at Jacob for his crimes towards Galena, and at fate, for seeking his destruction. He thrust the table forward. Jacob grasped it and swung hard. Beauden spun, out of control, away from the cockpit door and into the easy chair on the port side. He lost his grip on the table and Jacob flung it away.

In the next second, his uncle came towards him, hands outstretched, an unholy glint in his eye. Beauden knew better than to be trapped in the chair and he dove to the side, catching Jacob's arm in mid-flight, pulling him down. Both men fell into the open doorway, Jacob below and Beauden on top, reaching for his uncle's throat.

Being down did not dampen his uncle's hatred. 'I'll kill you and your slut. Then I will go back for my damned brother.'

Beauden reared back and held his knife to Jacob's neck, just below his ear. 'Why, Uncle? So much hatred.'

'It should have all been mine.'

Jacob paid no heed to the knife at his throat. He pushed Beauden's elbow slightly and, in a split second, brought his head up, striking Beauden with his forehead before pushing his body off.

***

Galena spun away from the peephole in the cabin door. She had seen her husband fall and her mind screamed at her to go to him. But she resisted. She had been trained to respond coolly in a crisis, to think first, and so she held back. Her physical strength was feeble. Jacob would swat her aside like a gnat, then she and Beauden would both die. But she was in control of the environment.

Galena turned to the controls. Four sliding levers, neatly labelled, regulated the steam going to the turbines. Quickly, she cut three and left only one turning.

She was thrown against the instrumentation panel. Hearing a curse, she turned again to the peephole. Jacob staggered to his feet and held onto the cabin door. Beauden lay on the floor, still groggy from the blow, but Jacob picked him up by the lapels of his long black coat.

'Stabilise the airship or he dies.'

'You plan to kill us anyway, you monster!' she shouted through the door. 'Put him in the chair and step away. Then I will stabilise it.'

Jacob pushed Beauden towards the open doorway, but Beauden, now fully conscious, fought him every step of the way. He put up his hands as if to find something to hold onto, but he missed the edge of the doorway and both men staggered through.

Galena heard no scream, just a series of thuds moving forward along the narrow walkway. Suddenly, they came into view though

293

the wide windows. Jacob had his back to the bow, Beauden to the stern, and they fought, wrestling outside the cabin.

Galena hovered her hands over the instruments, ready to assist Beauden if she could, but the fight seemed evenly matched. Then, Jacob swung his hand towards Beauden and Beauden pulled back. A glitter of reflected light shone and then Galena saw the knife her husband had been carrying in his uncle's hand.

Beauden turned his head and his eyes met hers as the world stood still.

Chapter 30

'To port, love, to port!' Beauden clamped his hands down on the rail as Galena slid the port turbine to full and the starboard to zero.

Jacob was thrown off balance. He staggered towards the gate he had opened earlier when repositioning the turbines, and time slowed as he began to topple. Beauden lunged forward, anchoring himself to the balustrade as he reached for his uncle's hand.

With a snarl, Jacob pulled away, and as Beauden watched him fall, he knew it was a sight that would wake him, screaming, in the months to come.

Jacob plummeted towards the whirling turbine, hands trailing in the air, horrified face staring up at Beauden. His scream lasted scarcely more than a second before his body hit the blades, and Beauden heard a mechanical grinding like he never wanted to hear again. Jacob's body was sucked through the horizontal propeller and spat out, the huge copper-sheathed blades making short work of bone, flesh and clothing.

Jacob's last guttural scream still hung in the air as Beauden hung, gasping against the railing, clutching it for dear life.

His stomach lurched. The turbine was red with gore.

But there was no time to mourn—a puff of smoke and a flash of flame caught his eye. There was a scrap of cloth in the turbine intake, the breast of Jacob's waistcoat, but that was not the problem. Beauden noted with horror that a metal buckle was attached to the cloth—and it was grinding away at the mechanism.

As he clung to the rail, too dazed to panic, Beauden could see the edge of the airship yard below. They were over two hundred feet in the air, but they had travelled no more than that distance laterally.

The airship shifted again, the tiniest amount—Galena was bringing it back to level. A whine filled his ears as the other turbines were gradually eased up.

One hand on the rail, Beauden staggered for the door to the cabin. He crashed into Galena as she stepped onto the landing.

'Beauden!' Her hands were on his arms, his face; one part careful physician, nine parts panicked wife.

He could not delay; they had only seconds before catastrophe. He pulled her inside.

'I'm all right, but there's a fire in the turbine. We must take her out over the water. We can't let her explode over the city.'

Together they ran for the cockpit.

'Can we turn off the turbines?'

Galena's voice held real terror. She had been through so much in the last few hours.

'We can, but it's all or nothing. We can't turn off just one. It's a balance thing.'

'Then turn them off.' She reached for the lever and he snatched it away, held it tightly.

'We can't, love! We won't drop if we do—the gas will keep us afloat, but the prevailing wind will take us right back into the city. We'll be threatening hundreds of lives.'

His words cut through the dread and he watched understanding dawn on her face.

'All right. We can turn the others to take us out over the harbour. It is only half a mile.'

He glimpsed a sand bucket in the corner, and he touched her cheek. 'Then turn us and head as fast as you can for the sea.'

'What are you going to do?' The tremor in her hands was pitiful, but she was straight as a poker.

'I need to slow the flames.' He snatched up the bucket, a plan forming. 'Take us a little way out, then cut the turbines. Can you do that?'

'Yes.'

With a poignant look, he ran from the cockpit and inched his way along the walkway until he reached the spot where Jacob had fallen. Kneeling, he locked one arm and one leg carefully around the rail support and gently tipped the sand into the flame. It flickered under the onslaught, but too much sand blew away before it reached the turbine. Soon, the bucket was empty. Beauden stared in horror as the mechanism burst back into angry orange life.

He swung his attention from the flaming engine to the twinkling lights of Edinburgh below. He couldn't jettison the carriage he was in or the engines. Then he noticed that two starboard turbines were pushing forward, but the loss of the front port engine meant they were not heading straight out. Instead, they were following the coast, heading for Leith.

There was only one thing to do. He moved carefully to the starboard side and looked through the windows.

'Reduce power to half!'

Galena nodded and immediately he felt the drop in power.

He fell to his knees beside the front starboard turbine and flipped the cover over the small wheel that controlled direction. With as much force as he could exert, he dragged the wheel over until the turbine angled down.

They drove forward evenly, but every yard of forward momentum lost them a foot of altitude. Beauden stared out over the lights, coming up fast below. If he calculated correctly, they would have just enough time to make it out over the harbour before the airship plunged into it. If not … there would be an almighty blaze when flame and hydrogen met.

Beauden ran to the cockpit. 'Come Galena! We must be ready to jump.'

They moved out onto the walkway, facing out over a sea of rooftops. The air was thick with smoke; a glance told them that the flames were two feet high and growing steadily.

The wind whipped Galena's black hair over her face. 'What is feeding it?'

'I think the oil reservoirs are damaged.'

She nodded. 'I can see water ahead!'

Thirty yards away, a score of boats lay on the sand. Beyond them, another dozen bobbed at anchor. The dirigible was coming down fast, and the smoke stung his eyes and made him choke.

Making a difficult decision, Beauden tore away the front of his shirt and wrapped the two halves around his hands, then stepped onto the top rung of the chain ladder that hung from the boarding gate. Hanging over forty feet of open air, he held grimly onto the rail that grew hotter with each passing moment.

'Galena, love. Come here and keep your back to me. I will stop you falling.'

He could feel the steel in her spine as she positioned herself in front of him. He stepped down a rung, and she followed. They each took another step, Beauden's arms stretched out, holding the chain tight and securing Galena in front of him. The ladder swayed under their weight and she sobbed.

'Hold tight, love. I have you.'

Roofs were directly below them now, and Beauden could detect the faint smell of the sea. The ladder swayed again, this time slamming Beauden into a gutter. He felt a stab of pain and the sensation of liquid on his calf, rapidly cooling in the night air. He thought he heard Galena cry out in alarm, but the night was suddenly full of the sounds of bells and police whistles.

As they flew over the breaking waves, the flames from the engine turbine ignited the wooden decking. The tongue of flame shot up, licking against the rigid poles that attached the cabin to the hydrogen-filled envelope above.

'One more step down, love.'

They both stood on the lowest rung, flames racing towards them along the decking.

He turned his lips to her ear. 'We have to jump! In three, two, one!'

Beauden closed his eyes, leaned back and let go of the chain ladder.

The fall seemed to take a hundred years and less than a split second. The jolt reverberated through Beauden's body as he hit the water, and then, so close, came a second thud. The water closed over him like the lid of a tomb. He fought the urge to gasp, and instead, thrust his arms out, searching blindly for Galena. His fingers brushed against something and he felt the thrill of success. But it was short-lived.

Chapter 31

Cold. It was so very cold. Galena felt battered, bruised from their fall. She clamped her mouth closed and her lungs burned. She stopped flailing; it was no use. Her sodden petticoats outweighed the air still trapped in her lungs. Above her head, there was a distant thud, like a wine barrel falling onto a cobbled road. A shockwave rippled through the water, and a gout of flame briefly turned murky night into brilliant day.

She turned as best she could in her leaden garb, but she couldn't see Beauden. The pain in her chest intensified and her heart gave a silent scream.

Then, his face loomed before her, hair floating like a nimbus. He cupped her head, pressing his lips to hers. Blessed air flooded her mouth. His hands closed around her waist and he pushed her up, back to light and air and life.

But he was sinking. With the hope he had given her, she reached for him, clawed at the collar of his heavy coat. He looked up at her and smiled. Something clutched at her hair and then her arm. She clung to Beauden, desperate not to lose him. If she lost her grip, he was doomed, she knew it.

Breaking the surface of the water, she gasped in a lungful of life-giving air only to choke on a wave. She was being pulled higher when Beauden surfaced beside her and more arms reached down for him.

Beauden fell into the small fishing boat beside her and retched up a lungful of water. A lined face, all woollen cap and white whiskers, peered at her.

As Galena struggled to breathe, she felt a knife slide under her corset laces and then up through the fabric of her gown. Douglas turned her on her side and slapped her back hard. A small lake flowed out of her mouth and into the bottom of the boat.

As she took her first real lungful of air, Douglas set two fingers to her carotid artery. She took another breath and sat up.

'Beauden?'

Within a second, her husband was at her side, pulling her into his arms. Douglas gave him all of ten seconds before he pulled him back and thrust a mug of liquid fire into her hand. She took a sip and coughed violently. Jimmy dropped a blanket around her and gently guided the cup back to her lips.

'Drink it up, lass. Ye are in sair need. Ye look like a skelpie.'

'Thank you.' Her second sip burned slightly less than the first. 'Love, are you all right?'

'Yes.'

'He will be weel enough when he's ta'en another dram.' Jimmy looked at her keenly. 'He swallowed a good portion of the sea, lass, but God be thanked he brought it up again. Twill do no good pounding on that chest.'

Galena slid into Beauden's arms and Douglas turned away to talk to the ancient sailor, giving her a glimmer of privacy. Jimmy, too, simply laid a hand on Beauden's shoulder and moved away.

'Thank you.' She knew she had not imagined it. 'You tried to save me rather than yourself.'

He stroked her cheek and his copper hazel eyes looked into hers. 'There is no need to thank me. I was saving my own life, for I could not live without you.'

She clung to him. 'I'm sorry. I shouldn't have gone alone.'

'Shh, there's no need.' Beauden held her close and stroked her back.

'I didn't realise it was a trap. Not until I saw him there when I went to tend the child.' She slapped a hand over her mouth. 'Oh God, the child! And he killed Frannie!'

Douglas turned to them, his face sombre. 'That was her name? The young woman he killed?'

A deep shudder ran through Galena. 'Yes. You know about that? He killed her in front of me. Did he kill the child, too? Sukie?'

Jimmy poured another dram of whisky into Beauden's mug. 'The inspector said nothing aboot any bairn being killed. Someone summoned that devil's neighbours and they called the constable. But the villain had fled and ta'en ye with him. We found yer medical bag in that hovel, and the young woman, but nay sign of a child.'

'Beauden, we must find her. I doubt she has any other kin, and she is little more than a babe, five or six at most.'

Beauden held her close. 'We will find her. She cannot have gone far. Jimmy?'

'Aye. I'll send word ta Will.'

'Thank you.' Galena put her hand over Jimmy's, then leaned across and kissed his cheek.

Beauden looked around. 'Where is Will? And is my father all right?'

'The doctor is fine.' Jimmy scowled. 'That villain was at Victoria Park, but your father pressed him for some word on Mrs Somerton's safety, and then one of McIntyre's fool constables scared yer uncle off. We came here, hot foot. Yer father and Will have gone to the dirigible yard.'

The old sailor tied his tiny vessel to a bollard. Jimmy leapt out, then handed Beauden ashore. Beauden's mouth was bracketed with weariness and his shoulders were bowed, but there was a calm glow about him that Galena recognised from their few brief moments of happiness.

Douglas lifted her in his arms and attempted to pass her to Jimmy.

'I will take her.' Beauden reached for her, but Douglas glowered at him, his voice like a drill sergeant.

'You will do no such thing. Both of you are to avoid any exertion. I need to keep an eye on you tonight. There is still the risk of pneumonia or delayed drowning.'

As they waited for Jimmy to bring up the unicarriage, Beauden reached into his pocket. He had a few shillings and a handful of guineas. He put them all into the hands of the astonished sailor.

'Thank you. We owe you our lives.'

***

Beauden smiled as Galena fell asleep minutes after they slid into the unicarriage, her head pillowed on his chest.

Douglas, perched on the rear-facing bench opposite them, sat forward with alarm. Reaching out, he listened to her chest with the small trumpet-shaped device he used. He sighed with relief and shook his head.

'She is asleep. No wonder. She must be exhausted.'

Beauden nodded and kept his voice soft. 'Is there still danger?'

'Some. I do need you to rest.' His eyes met Beauden's. 'You were both very lucky.'

'I am very lucky.'

'You've both been through hell.'

'And I'd go back in a heartbeat if that's what I must do to keep her.'

Douglas smiled a weary smile. 'I am going to close my eyes now. It has been quite a night.'

He was as good as his word.

Beauden bent his head and kissed his sleeping wife on her pale pink lips, on her milky brow. He stroked one hand over her sodden black hair and one finger under her jaw. Then he laid his hand over her belly like a benediction.

'I love you,' he whispered. 'Forever and always, Galena. You are the most incredible woman I've ever met. Thank you for being mine.'

He kissed her lips again, softly, reverently.

In his arms, Galena Somerton smiled in her sleep.

Chapter 32

Galena listened to the disembodied voice floating from her father-in-law's newly purchased gramophone. In honour of the occasion, the strains of an auld Scots ballad floated out, the tale of Helen of Kirkconnell and her tragic lover. A shiver ran up her spine.

The conservatory fire was warm against the chill of this January night. Beyond the enormous glass windows, soft white flakes drifted down from heaven, transforming the world into something pure and wonderful. Christmas had been very quiet, Hogmanay too. Now, after the six months of mourning that society expected, this Burns Night was a special occasion, a true celebration.

Galena abstractedly smoothed her hand over the curves of her belly. They were turning a corner, from one great exploit that had brought her and Beauden love and hope, to a new adventure for them all.

Dr Somerton had invited Douglas and Olive to join them, as well as the dean and several old friends. He was making the effort to reforge some of the social bonds that had been broken during Beauden's long illness. The house staff and Beauden's workshop colleagues had also been invited. Marian stood shyly with Mordechai Samuels. Will and Judith were there too, with the little girl who had been Jacob's last, unwitting pawn. The police had seen the skulking child when they removed Frannie's body, and Jimmy had coaxed her out of hiding. Now little Sukie, or Susan as they called her, lived under Will's roof in his sister's care. The house had not been this full since Jacob's small memorial held two weeks after the events of that terrible night.

Beauden had set his face against honouring his late uncle with a memorial, but his father had been right, Galena thought. Surely a lifetime of fraternal love could not be obliterated in the violence of a few weeks. In time, Beauden had come to remember some of the benevolent aspects of his uncle; the generous jokester, the good-natured companion. Neither he nor Galena would ever forget the terror of that night or the icy kiss of the sea, but they could also remember the man, not just the monster he had become.

Beauden walked towards her from across the room and handed her a glass of punch. She smiled up at him, unbelievably happy. While life had not unfolded exactly as she had planned, she was still studying under Dr Somerton, was married to a courageous and exceptional man, and the dean had suggested there would be a chance for her to study at the university again when she was ready. That might be a year away, but all would work out in the end. If life had taught her anything in the last months, it was that.

In the hum of conversation at the far side of the room, someone called for a toast. Their guests turned and made a beeline for where they sat. Douglas, the forerunner of the larger contingent, handed Beauden a glass of whisky.

'To Beauden and Galena and their precious babe.'

There was a loud chorus as everyone echoed the toast.

Dr Somerton came to stand before them. 'Beauden, Galena, Will and your friends at the workshop have perfected a most ingenious device.'

Will drew up pushing a smart baby carriage. 'It has better suspension.'

He pushed it back and forth several times, the action smooth and seamless.

'And that isn't all.'

He flicked a gold lever and a soft puff of hydraulics caused the canopy to fall back. The bassinet stretched, shuddered and then folded to make a seat.

'Will and Cain need to patent this.' Dr Somerton raised his glass to the two men.

Galena noted proudly that his hand was now completely healed. He would not hold a scalpel again, but, since he had begun lecturing at the university, he had become reconciled to the loss. For all else, the hand worked perfectly.

Galena beamed. 'Will, Cain, that is incredible. The baby will be able to sit up and look out at the world as we do. Thank you so much.'

After several minutes of small talk, Perkins sounded the gong for their lavish, traditional supper. Dr Somerton, with Olive on his arm, led the guests into the dining room.

Beauden looked down at Galena. 'We should go in.'

She nodded, then pushed a hand to her belly, wincing.

'Are you all right, Galena?'

'I am well, love.' She smiled and shrugged. 'Though I think someone is celebrating Burns Night by dancing a jig on my bladder.'

Beauden sat beside her on the love seat and rested his hand her stomach. 'He is active tonight.'

'Or she.'

He grinned. 'Indeed. Do you think the child will be a girl, then?'

She hesitated, reluctant to put such amorphous thoughts into words. 'At first, I thought it might be a boy—then I was sure it was a girl. But now?'

'Perhaps one of each?'

She smiled a secret smile. 'You were a twin. And my mother, too.'

Her husband looked at her, aghast. His cheeks flushed, his eyes brightened and his mouth made a perfect *O*.

From the dining room, laughter and frivolity beckoned. Here, they were all but alone.

'I was thinking of names. Myra for a daughter and Augustus for a son?'

'My darling, twins? Are you sure?'

She smoothed a hand over her gown. 'No, I'm not sure, but ... here.'

She grasped his hand and placed it high on her belly, just below

310

her ribs, and pressed down firmly.

'Do you feel that?'

'It's very firm. Is that a head?'

'I think so. Now ...'

She moved his hand a few inches to the left. 'What about that?'

'Good God!' His shock became delight.

'Are you pleased?'

'Very—but also terrified!'

She drew his lips to hers and let the familiar magic claim her. It always did. It always would.

'I'm not. We've faced danger together. We've faced death together. Nothing can frighten me while I have you.'

She kissed him again and laid her hand against his chest where his golden heart beat softly. 'I love you, Beauden Somerton. For as long as we both shall live.'

Author notes

A note from MC D'alton:

A part of me is inexplicably drawn to the darkness in humanity. Not in some vulgar, inhuman sort of way, but in an inquisitive exploration of 'what if?' The television series *Penny Dreadful* awoke in me a love for classic stories and creatures such as Frankenstein (one of my all-time faves), the original Dracula, Dorian Gray, and werewolves. These characters and monsters of yesteryear are the real deal; the inspiration for many other romantically entangled beasts from Hades that have followed over the years.

Needless to say, when I approached Melanie with my thoughts and ideas to create a loveable monster who was, in fact, more humane than most humans, our story came to life! A man with a soul of gold but a heart of iron, and a woman born in a time when women were deemed fragile, incompetent and weak, who was none of these things and his only hope.

Galena is my heroine in so many ways. She is independent, brilliant, a go-getter, a trendsetter, a mover and a shaker, and in our steampunk world, the inventor and co-inventor of medical science so brilliant it'll blow you away!

Beauden is our monster—a man who should never have lived

past his fifth birthday, made of flesh, blood and wrought iron. Most people of his time would believe him soulless, a child of the Devil and a threat to all things living.

But, as all good romances go, it turns out he is anything but!

And then, we come to the heart of the matter—the beautiful golden heart that needed to replace the rotting, corroded iron beast devouring our hero from within. I had so much fun returning to my anatomy and physiology books. Add the freedom to imagine God's perfect creation and voila! You have magic!

I spent hours imagining, sketching, planning, building (in my head) the heart that would save Beauden Somerton. I read up on a great hero, Dr Chris Barnard, a South African doctor who achieved the unbelievable. His ground-breaking scientific and medical explorations and transplantations, combined with the research and now actual medical procedures of using swine and bovine tissue to replace the sickly diseased parts of the human heart were the foundation for allowing me to build Beauden's golden heart.

The golden heart is shaped similarly to the real flesh and blood pulmonary pump found in humans. It is essentially an exoskeleton for the bits of suinae tissue planted within. Now you may ask, how is this possible?

In reality, it is not, but in the world of steampunk and speculative science it is. A writer is allowed a wee bit o' creative leeway. It's not hard to imagine once you're sucked into our Victorian-age Edinburgh with its dirigibles and mirror messengers, steam-powered unicarriages and dynamic steam-generated electrical power, not to mention the delicate invention of Galena's heart-lung machine. We laid the foundation for the tissue to connect to metal by mentioning Dr Augustus Somerton's experiments and the fact he had implanted an iron heart into his son. We further substantiate this theory by showing you Beauden's workshop and his own inventions, creating limbs for amputees, and a hand that would eventually use his father's medical advancements to connect metal to tissue.

We also laid the foundation for the electrical conduction that takes place within a real heart by showing the reader how the doctor relied on momentum and kinetic energy, and that Beauden was confined to sleeping on a large magnetic bed that eased the strain the iron heart put on his body and also recharged his heart. Other questions arose. How would the corroding iron affect our hero? Carrying such a heavy burden (literally) within his chest would affect his movements, his health, his skin tone—and, of course, the colour of our darling monster's eyes. It was quite a journey.

The heavy iron heart remained within our hero's chest cavity by means of a boned support system built from the ribs removed from Beauden's chest. His chest was then protected by the whale-boned corset he wore, which was designed by his father. This again lay the foundation for the final golden rib cage. A sling held the heart in place inside his chest cavity and a filigree rib cage replaced the removed bones.

We researched differing mixtures of gold and added a certain creative flair to show that Beauden's gold heart would not corrode and was not too heavy. And, of course, who could ignore the old cliché, 'a heart of gold,' which hinted subtly at our hero's true demeanour.

So, there you have it, a short and sweet explanation of how our fantastic steampunk world and all her characters came into being for your reading pleasure!

A note from Melanie Page:

Co-writing a book is an entirely different kettle of fish to bearing the sole creative responsibility. At times, I felt like an anchor, bouncing along the sea floor, being dragged by a racing yacht. We started discussing the idea and fleshing out the concept in September 2017. Soon afterwards, MC drafted the first chapter and we were off. In the first two weeks, we had ten thousand words. My head was spinning, but MC was in full flight. My role was to say WHOA! I said it a lot. Also, why did that character do that, or think that, or say that, or … you get the picture.

First, let's sort the fact from the fiction. Bachvarov? Nope. We made him up. But the other medical history was largely real, like the ancient prosthetic leg and the development of that discipline. Awesome! The Scottish marriage law was real too. Gretna Green became famous as the place where young couples, unable to wed in England, could tie the knot quickly and easily. Though marriage law has changed, marriages are still conducted in the old smithy there.

A mechanical heart? MC made that up too, but then, just the other day, I was sitting in the hospital waiting room and chanced upon an article about a beat-less heart, made from hard plastics and using maglev technology. So, it is real and was invented by a fellow Queenslander. How cool is that?

I particularly liked using real history. For example, in one scene, Merrick sits in his room reading a medical tome—the first edition of *Gray's Anatomy*, which had been published the year before. That made me do a little happy dance.

I loved creating the textures of the Somertons' world, the steampunkery (is that even a word?), the detail of the house and technology. I loved fleshing out the characters with nuanced speech and action, the little details that speak volumes. Beauden presented a challenge: he was weak, shadowed, forced by his long illness to be passive. He was, in so many ways, the opposite of what a hero is expected to be. To make him a hero we searched for the man inside. Beauden was not simply waiting around to see whether his father's invention could save him. He lived a productive life to the best of his ability. Vonnegut says that every character must want something, even if it is only a glass of water. We asked ourselves, apart from not dying, what did Beauden want? Galena was feisty, though all the spunk in the world could not help her win a place in the man's world she inhabited, her intelligence and her compassion could.

We tried to make the villains authentic. Often, villains are caricatures. Merrick and Jacob both believe they are right. This, plus a splash of greed and ego, means that committing wickedness is acceptable—that the ends justify the means. Ultimately, good triumphs and love has its reward.

So, that is how *Iron Heart* came into being—from MC's fevered imagination, through my fingertips, down to the page in front of you. I hope you have enjoyed it.